FIC
YEP

City of Fire

Angrily, Scirye chased after the brown-haired boy who had stopped in front of the shattered case with the throwing stars. "This is no place for you," she ordered, pulling at Leech's arm. "You'll just get in the way."

"Playtime's over," Leech snapped at her, "so take your costume and get lost. Leave this to people who know how to fight."

The boy was holding one of the stars like a spiked baseball.

Scirye gave a snort of disgust. "You don't even know how to use one of those," she snapped, and plucked one from the half dozen in his other hand. "You hold it by the tip." She held up the star between her index finger and thumb as her sister had shown her. She had done well in practice, but she wondered how she would fare in real combat.

Leech's face grew stormy as he snatched it back. He looked as if he were going to argue, but froze when the dragon's laugh echoed around the dome like the rumbling of an avalanche.

The dragon's scar twisted his smile into a menacing leer as he leaned downward. "Do you really think any of you can stop me?"

D0191371

SCS MIDDLE SCHOOL
8888 - 162 Street
Surrey, BC
V4N 3G1

MAY
MAY 0 1 2012

City of Fire

– CITY TRILOGY I –

Laurence Yep

A TOM DOHERTY ASSOCIATES BOOK
NEW YORK

NOTE: If you purchased this book without a cover, you should be aware that this book is stolen property. It was reported as "unsold and destroyed" to the publisher, and neither the author nor the publisher has received any payment for this "stripped book."

This is a work of fiction. All of the characters, organizations, and events portrayed in this novel are either products of the author's imagination or are used fictitiously.

CITY OF FIRE

Copyright © 2009 by Laurence Yep

City of Ice excerpt copyright © 2009 by Laurence Yep

Reader's Guide copyright © 2009 by Tor Books

All rights reserved.

A Starscape Book
Published by Tom Doherty Associates, LLC
175 Fifth Avenue
New York, NY 10010

www.tor-forge.com

ISBN 978-0-7653-5879-0

First Edition: September 2009
First Mass Market Edition: August 2010

Printed in May 2010 in the United States of America by Offset Paperback Manufacturers, Dallas, Pennsylvania.

0 9 8 7 6 5 4 3 2 1

To Ray, who's setting out on his own great adventure

Guide to Pronunciation
of Kushan Names

Klestetstse (Klays-tayts-tsay): More often shortened to Kles (Klays). Scirye's lap griffin, a gift from Princess Maimantstse.

Lady Tabiti (Ta-bee-tee): A legendary Sarmatian warrior chief.

Lady Sudarshane (Soo-dar-sha-nay): Scirye's mother.

Lord Tsirauñe (Tsee-rou-nay): Scirye's father.

Nishke (Neesh-kay): Scirye's older sister.

Prince Etre (Ay-tray): Kushan Consul.

Princess Maimantstse (My-man-tsuh-tsay): Cousin of Scirye's father.

Sakre Menantse (Sa-kray May-nan-tsay): A name for the Kushan Empire, meaning "Blessed of the Moon."

Sakre Yapoy (Sa-kray Ya-poi): Another name for the Kushan Empire, meaning "the Blessed Land."

Scirye (Skeer-yay): Mistress of Kles.

City of Fire

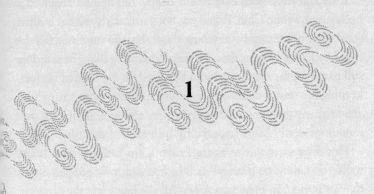

Bayang

Her prey was only ten feet away now.

The boy called Leech had a shock of brown hair but the fold at the corner of his eyes suggested some Asian blood. He was small for his twelve years, but that was probably from lack of proper nourishment since he had grown up on the vicious streets and alleys of San Francisco. He was quick but not particularly strong. Nor did he seem aware of his powers yet. But she knew better than to be deceived. Beneath the childish exterior beat the heart of a cold-blooded killer who had to be stopped before his special abilities could turn him into a monster.

His chubby friend, Koko, presented only a slight difficulty. Oh, Koko looked harmless enough with his pear-shaped body and plump cheeks, but he carried a faint whiff of magic—though not enough to threaten Bayang.

It should have been easy to kill Leech, but he had acquired a bodyguard, Primo Chin. Primo was not particularly tall but built as solid as a boulder, and everything about the man suggested that he could be lethal with his fists and feet. Whether walking or standing still like now, the man was always balanced on the balls of his feet, keeping his center of gravity about his hips, ready to spring into action at any moment. And his eyes were always scanning his surroundings alertly. More importantly, he reeked of wizardry.

Her discreet inquiries about Primo Chin had met with blank walls—no family, no history—as if he had suddenly popped out of thin air into a San Francisco street. All she knew was the obvious: that Primo had plenty of money but never spent it unless it was on her prey.

Bayang concluded that unknown persons had sent Primo to protect Leech. After she was done here, she would have to ferret out their identities and deal with them, too. But that could wait. First things first.

Despite the urgency, Bayang had bided her time. Patience was the reason why she had survived this long and why she had been successful in all of her tasks, even murder.

When Primo began educating the boy in both fighting skills as well as regular school subjects, she had worried a bit. She knew Primo was actually preparing her prey for his true powers by developing his body's agility and balance and his mind's focus and knowledge.

If Primo had begun the actual lessons, Bayang would have had no choice but to attack immediately. Even if it meant her death, her prey could not be allowed to survive.

However, as long as Primo's instruction remained at a basic stage, Bayang had waited, hoping that an opportunity would present itself. When she learned they had bought tickets for the incoming show at the Hearn Museum, she knew that her moment had come. She would make her move within the galleries where the crowd would mask her approach and the man would be distracted by the displays.

She purchased a ticket, too, joining the line on the appointed morning. The museum's massive, windowless, cream-colored walls dwarfed the people eager to see the new exhibit, the Treasures of the Silk Road, that was going to open today. Two-story-length banners hung down the front and the sides with pictures of gold and jewels, and in smaller letters at the bottom proclaimed: "Kushan: The Empire of the Moon."

San Francisco was a city that valued spectacle and style in everything from its architecture to its criminals and even its politicians. And what could be more spectacular or stylish than to see priceless antiques that no one else in America had seen?

The spectators were in a holiday mood because the autumn sun had burned through the morning fog, and sparkled through the water rising from the fountain. Water sprites, looking graceful even in their baggy civil-service uniforms, molded the fountain spray into ever-changing shapes that seemed to dance across the surface of the reflecting pool. A naiad was tidying up some dead leaves at the base of her tree, its branches pruned over many years forming knobs. Seagulls had floated in on the winds from the sea and were drifting lazily in the cool, crisp air.

The fine morning seemed like a good omen for her task. As Bayang felt the sun against her face, she reflected idly that it was not bad for a human city.

She had not asked to be an assassin and even now part of her hated killing. Time and again, she had asked to be transferred to other duties, but her superiors had refused. They told her that this assignment fit her talents the best and, besides, she had developed an unusual tolerance of humans. Most of her people would have been uncomfortable meeting a single hairless ape, let alone rubbing shoulders with them. More importantly, what she did was for the good of their people.

However, after so many centuries plying her trade, the explanations had worn thin and she was weary of her missions. She forced those thoughts aside, telling herself she needed to focus on the task at hand. Her eyes swept the scene again.

On one side of the broad museum steps, a newsreel crew was setting up a large, cumbersome movie camera to record the momentous occasion.

Food sellers had wheeled their carts next to the line of waiting spectators. Already, enticing smells were rising from the pots and grills as frog-shaped imps heated the food. Bamboo trays of dim sum were already steaming and kebabs were sizzling on the grill so that the air was filled with delectable smells.

A vendor in fool's motley was helping his pumpkinlike imp blow up balloons. A mountebank in rented wizard's robes and cap had set up some boxes and was trying to interest a group of young men in a game of "Find the Pixie Beneath the Walnut Shells."

In fact, before the spectators reached the sanctuary of the museum, they were going to have to run a gauntlet of peddlers, entertainers, swindlers, and beggars—very similar, Bayang thought, to the group running City Hall across the plaza, except that the politicians had brass name plates to separate themselves from the rabble by the museum.

She glanced down when she felt a slight tugging. A three-inch imp with purple leathery skin straddled her purse as it attempted to pry open the clasp.

The imp grinned up at her sheepishly and touched his forehead. "Morning, ma'am."

Bayang took pride in her disguises. Any apprentice witch could change her physical appearance, but it took skill to transform what lay beneath the skin. Bayang had become a good enough actor to go on the stage if she wished.

She had assumed the character of an office worker in her sixties, with a back slightly hunched from slaving over a desk most of her life, eyes squinting because she couldn't afford eyeglasses on her meager salary. She appeared to the whole world as a mousy woman who thought herself extremely daring for playing hooky from her job this morning. In short, someone whom most people would ignore.

Suddenly her face wrinkled into a puzzled but kindly expression that was in contrast to her low, menacing words to the imp trying to open her purse. "Go away or I'll feed you to the pigeons. Ones with dull beaks so it will take a long time."

"No need to get nasty," the imp complained as it dropped out of sight among the forest of legs.

When Bayang raised her head, she saw Primo studying her. He couldn't have heard her warning to the imp so, still keeping in character, she spoke loudly and excitedly to her neighbor in line, a middle-aged man, about how good the nearby salamander was at juggling flaming balls, and when the salamander swallowed the balls one after another, she applauded as if she had never seen anything so marvelous in her dull, gray life. When his master held out his belled hat, she dropped a quarter into it as if she considered that a queenly award.

From the corner of her eyes, she saw that Primo was surveying another part of the crowd now, apparently having decided she was harmless.

As the great bronze doors suddenly swung open and the ripple of excitement passed through the humans, she knew that it was almost time to finish her task and once again protect her people.

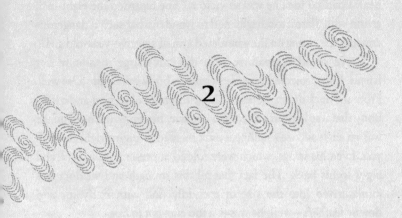

2

Scirye

"Oh, please don't touch my griffin, Madame," Scirye begged in her slightly accented English. "The last person who did that lost a finger."

The lady's gloved hand paused uncertainly in midair. "But he's *so* adorable."

Scirye widened her eyes in what she hoped was an expression of worried innocence.

"Oh, that's just to lure you close," she said. "And before you know it, snip!" She used the fingers of her free hand like a pair of scissors. "Kles's gobbling down your finger just like it was a worm. And there's blood gushing all over. He's been banned from . . . five countries." The girl had been about to say ten, but even she thought that might be too much to be credible.

Scirye hid a secret smile as the lady snatched back her hand. "Oh, dear. I had no idea he was so vicious." She regarded the eight-inch griffin with alarm, too frightened to wonder what such a dangerous creature was doing on the gauntleted arm of a twelve-year-old girl.

Scirye could sympathize with the lady's urge to admire her friend. Kles projected power not only in body but in mind, as well. From the neck down, he was a lion with a muscular chest and a lithe body that was lightning sheathed in tawny fur. From the neck up, he was an eagle whose intelligent eyes seemed to pierce right through you. Even his wings, which were folded at present, gave a graceful taper to his back. The fact that all this strength and wisdom was miniaturized into the size of a cuddly doll with fluffy fur and downy feathers—well, he was just too cute not to hug.

Scirye was enjoying the game she had just invented and was wondering how many other people she could trick, but then Kles had to go and spoil her fun. Though in theory a griffin owed absolute obedience to his mistress or master, sometimes, as he had apologetically informed Scirye on another occasion, even a griffin must answer to a higher authority—namely Scirye's mother, Lady Sudarshane.

So, instead of growling menacingly, he gave a low chirrup that vibrated from deep within his throat—which Scirye regarded as far superior to a cat's purr because it suggested a soft cushion by a warm fire. "Oh, I don't mind . . . ," Kles said to the lady in a deep, silky voice, "as long as it's you, my darling."

The lady hesitated, glancing back and forth between Scirye and Kles as if wondering whom to believe. So while Scirye scowled at his betrayal, Kles fluffed up his fur encouragingly. Such a cuddly creature was impossible to resist. The lady stretched out her hand timidly, ready to pull it back if Kles began to open his small but powerful beak. When Kles chirruped invitingly again, the lady could not resist stroking the fine down of his throat and then the fur of his haunches.

"Oh, what a dear creature," the lady gushed. "But I thought griffins were much bigger," she said. "Is he a baby?"

Despite her duties as the Kushan liaison for the exhibit's opening, Lady Sudarshane had been keeping an eye on Scirye. She glided over now, tall and regal as a queen, determined to prevent whatever havoc her daughter might be trying to create.

Lady Sudarshane had frequently sighed to her offspring that Scirye had too much imagination and too little self-control. She took hold of Scirye's free arm in a warm but firm warning grip.

"Griffins come in all sizes, Mrs. Rudenko," Lady Sudarshane explained in her warm, polished manner. "Klestetstse is full-grown." (Ever the diplomat, she addressed everyone by their formal name but Kles's had presented a problem since it meant "shabby" and was rather demeaning as a word. He had solved her dilemma by informing her that since he had grown into such a magnificent specimen of griffinhood, it amused him to keep his odd name—like nicknaming a huge, hulking giant Tiny.)

"His body might have grown up but not his mind." Scirye sniffed spitefully.

Kles's claws were only the size of sewing needles but just as sharp. So when he pinched her through the gauntlet, she felt like wincing, but fought to keep her face blank, refusing to give him that satisfaction.

Lady Sudarshane ignored her daughter's comment and went on explaining smoothly, "The largest griffins were capable of carrying an armored warrior, and we still ride them for sport. Aerial polo can be quite invigorating. But Klestetstse is a lap griffin, specially bred for hunting, much as a falcon is."

"Only we do it better," Kles said, polishing his claws against his chest.

Kles, Scirye thought, *has all the pride of a full-size griffin squeezed into the body of a parrot.*

Mrs. Rudenko clasped her hands together enthusiastically. "My granddaughter would love a lap griffin of her own. I simply must have one. Money is no object."

Lady Sudarshane put on her most woeful look. "Alas, lap griffins are only for the royal family, who consider them as part of the royal retinue rather than pets. Klestetstse was given to my daughter, Scirye, as a special favor from the Princess Maimantstse."

"That sounds like quite an honor," Mrs. Rudenko said, examining Scirye for the first time. "You must be quite . . . special."

Scirye's ancestors had come from an area where many cultures and people had mingled. As a result, Scirye's skin was a pleasingly light tan but her red hair and green eyes and dusting of freckles suggested that she should be dancing Irish jigs. "And . . . and . . ."— Mrs. Rudenko hunted for a polite bit of praise—"you look so quaint in your costume."

Scirye's outfit was a sore spot and the girl scowled. Before the storm could break, Lady Sudarshane took Mrs. Rudenko's arm. "If you would like to learn more about griffins, Mrs. Rudenko, let me show you the displays in Room C."

As her mother guided Kles's admirer away, Kles snapped his beak at Scirye's fingertip. "Don't slander about the noblest race ever created."

Scirye retaliated with a tap of her finger on his head. "Ow, that hurt, Kles."

They glared at each other a moment, but neither could hold a grudge for long against the other. "Truce?" She grinned.

"Truce," he agreed, and before his mistress could create more mischief, Kles suggested looking around. "I've never seen so many treasures displayed even in the royal palace," Kles murmured. "They were always kept hidden in the vaults."

Wherever they looked, there was the sparkle of gold, carnelian, garnets, turquoise, and lapis lazuli. Individually, the gems in the other rooms had huge price tags, but the stones in this last and largest gallery were beyond price, for they had belonged to the earliest Kushan rulers. Soft light fell through the opaque panes of the skylight overhead, and from lamps with special lenses to highlight the objects beneath them.

At one end of the chamber, the mayor and the Kushan Consul, Prince Etre, were chatting behind a podium, waiting for the radio crew to do a last sound check of the microphones before the live national broadcast.

Scirye slipped by a couple of museum staff wrestling a full-length photo of Emperor Kanishka XII into place. He was dressed in the uniform of a griffin warrior, complete with winged helmet and spurs. The girl and Kles bowed their heads respectfully as they passed.

Then they made their way around the radio engineers huddled over the bulky equipment before the broadcast went on the air, Scirye nearly tripping over the long outer cloak that was part of her costume. Irritably, she dragged the hem up from the floor and then found she was standing in front of a display of ancient drinking cups made by gilding enemy skulls. "Ugh," she said, making a face.

Seeing her revulsion, Kles skipped the history lesson he had been about to give and simply murmured, "It was long ago, and the times were different then."

"They were savages," Scirye declared.

"They were also your ancestors," Kles pointed out.

"Only on paper," Scirye argued. "I left the Kushan Empire when I was four. I'm . . . I'm a citizen of the world. That's what I am," she announced, snatching at a phrase she had overheard somewhere.

Though Kles understood English, he could not read it well so he used it as an excuse now to further his mistress's education. "What does the display card say?"

Scirye read it obligingly in a soft voice. "For over two thousand years, the Kushan Empire in Central Asia has sat between the East and West. The silk in this case is from China, the ivory from Siam, spices from Malaysia, diamonds from Golconda in India, and felt tapestries from the northern steppes."

Kles nodded to the dozens of shining coins laid in rows like offerings before a statue of Kubera, the dwarf god of wealth. "And those come from China, the kingdoms of Alexander the Great's successors, Persia, Rome, Byzantium, and on into modern times."

Scirye, though, cared little about money. "You don't say?" She yawned.

When he saw her lack of interest, Kles immediately dropped his lecture on the Silk Road. He glanced about and said, "I think the next case will be more to your liking."

Scirye perked up when she saw that it contained weapons and Kles adapted his instruction. "You know, ideas as well as trade goods traveled back and forth along the Silk Road. And your ancestors were great synthesizers, taking the best from the East as well as the West." He gestured at a gilded, jeweled matchlock. "Kushan engineers improved Chinese gunpowder and used it in iron barrels cast with Byzantine techniques to create guns that kept the Parthians, Huns, Persians, Arabs, and Turks at bay."

However, Scirye's attention was on weapons she could actually use. Her eyes swept from the matchlock to the rows of small golden spiked wheels next to it. Each was decorated with the dancing image of Oesho, the god of destruction whom the Hindus called Shiva but who also wore the lion pelt and club of the Greek hero, Heracles. Above them on the wall were throwing axes. Though the shafts had been decorated with gold and rubies, the axe blades were old steel—relics of a long dead Kushan king whose descendants had honored his memory by replacing the ordinary shafts with ornamental ones. Time and use had worn away the engraving on the blades but Scirye thought they were scenes of Oesho's battles.

"I wonder how these would throw?" she wondered out loud.

Her sister, Nishke, had instructed her in the use of both stars and axes just last week, for she belonged to the elite guard, the Pippalanta. They were required to be proficient with all weapons from ancient to modern.

Oblivious to the crowd, Scirye practiced with different throwing motions until Kles scolded, "Stop that. You almost knocked off the Archbishop's miter."

Scirye eyed the tall cap and then looked about for something to throw. "I bet he's got a snack stuffed inside that."

"Your mother will be back at any moment," Kles suggested, "so it might be wiser to go on wondering rather than find out."

With a disappointed grunt, Scirye lowered her free arm and moved on.

There were so many dazzling objects in the room that she would have walked right by the ancient, faded carpet that hung within a long case on the wall near the archway.

"Wait," Kles said.

The carpet showed the legendary scene in which Oado, the god of the wind, raced Salene, the god of the moon, and Elios, the god of the sun. All three gods wore Indian robes and Persian slippers but had dressed their hair in Greek style. Darting about the borders of the carpet were griffins and leogryphs, creatures with eagle wings and parrot beaks but the bodies of lions.

Scirye glanced at the placard next to the carpet. "You're just interested in anything that can fly."

"I've only heard about something like this. Flying carpets are extremely rare," Kles said reverently. "They say that the threads are woven from griffin wool. Some of it might even be from a distant ancestor of mine."

Scirye leaned forward to read more of the placard. "I think some fast-talking merchant invented that story. This says that flying carpets are only myths and not based in fact."

Kles pointed a claw at the border with the intricately woven gold thread. "That's because the museum people think that's just a design, but it's a very ancient script." It was the same script in which the griffin's commandments were carved into the rock walls of the eyrie and which every griffin had to learn. "And I suspect you not only have to read that script, but you also have to be of the Old Blood."

Kles would have liked to puzzle out the spell, but his mistress turned to the huge statue of Nanaia who was seated upon her companion lion. The goddess carried out many tasks for her children, which was why the sculptor had shown her with four hands. In her upper right hand, Nanaia held the bowl of water that never emptied because she made the crops possible. Despite that, Scirye was not sure she would want to meet the goddess even when she was feeling benevolent. Divine flames rose from her shoulders and wreathed her head in a halo that suggested she could unleash a terrible power if she became displeased.

"Did you ever see her, Kles?" she teased. "The Consul told me she wanders the palace hallways at night. I think it'd be fun."

"No." Kles shuddered and then bowed his head to mighty Nanaia, loving Nanaia, deadly Nanaia. "And be glad you haven't either."

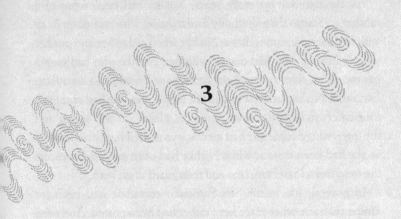

3

Scirye

"Guilty conscience?" teased Nishke. Like Lady Sudar-shane, she, too, had been keeping a watchful eye on her little sister.

Because both sisters had their father's sharp nose and broad chin, they were pretty rather than beautiful like their mother. But those same features lent them an air of strength, which was especially useful to Nishke.

The tall, dark-skinned Nishke looked every inch the Pippal guard in long trousers, and armor of iron plaques that looked like the scales of a dragon. Embossed steel disks, which doubled not only as decoration but as for defense, hung from crisscrossed straps over the armor. The face of Salene, god of the moon, was engraved on each disk. Nishke's rich, black hair was hidden by a helmet decorated with golden griffins.

All through Scirye's early years, Nishke had been more of a mother to Scirye than the Lady Sudarshane, who was often busy with her consular duties. It was Nishke who read to her and put her to bed, Nishke who had played with her, Nishke who had taught her the secret ways a careful girl could have fun within a consulate. Even after Nishke had left to join the Pippalanta, she had sent back long letters to her little sister about the places she was seeing and the interesting people she had met. Scirye missed her sister terribly so she had been ecstatic when Nishke had been assigned to escort the treasures to San Francisco and then guard them here.

In general, life in the San Francisco consulate had been far kinder than any other place her mother had been posted. And even better now that Nishke was here for a long stay.

"Whose conscience," Kles inquired, "my mistress's or mine?"

"Both of you delinquents," Nishke joked.

Scirye liked her sister's laugh. It reminded her of small bells on the harness of a griffin as it flew through the sky. In the privacy of her own room, she had even practiced that laugh.

The Lady Sudarshane came through the archway, having left an enraptured Mrs. Rudenko by the griffin display.

Scirye felt her throat catch as it did sometimes when she saw her mother. Lady Sudarshane had red hair like Scirye's but it was so much fuller and curlier, falling like foaming waves to her shoulders. Her skin was as pale as alabaster, and her eyes, which had Asian folds at the corners, gave her an exotic look.

Scirye's mother made everything she did seem so elegant, while Scirye was always the opposite: clumsy, awkward, ugly. Where Lady Sudarshane seemed to float across the floor, Scirye felt like she stumped along.

Lady Sudarshane's ancient outfit only enhanced her beauty—as if a statue of one of the goddesses had come to life. The collar of her red-and-black robe was decorated with hundreds of tiny gold flowers while rows of gold hearts inlaid with turquoise filled the sleeve cuffs and tear-shaped gold pieces danced around the bottom hem.

Even her odd cap seemed quaint when she wore it, rather than comical. The hat had stuffed horns, one of bright yellow silk and the other of dark violet. All sorts of mystical signs had been embroidered on them to indicate that Lady Sudarshane was a wise woman.

"Really, Scirye," Lady Sudarshane said in Kushana, "we simply can't have you frightening the natives."

"Why, mother," Scirye replied in the same old tongue, "whatever do you mean? I was entertaining Mrs. Rudenko with a little fairy tale."

Lady Sudarshane sighed. "I would prefer it if you bored the natives from now on, dear. And lift your chimiton. It's dragging on the floor again."

Scirye found that the heavy cloak had slipped off her shoulder once more and she hauled it back up. "It's not my fault that it won't stay put. Why can't I wear my normal clothes instead of all this stuff? You're the one who's always trying to convince the reporters that we're a modern, civilized people. Why dress like barbarians?"

"It's not 'barbarian,'" Kles scolded her. "It's a mixture of the best of Greek and Parthian."

"Don't forget Indian," Nishke added.

"Only barbarians can't make up their minds and stick with one style," Scirye groused, indicating her long, red silk tunic with lavender-striped sleeves which was cinched by a bronze belt above her waist with a circular silver buckle with crossed axes beneath the moon. All the Kushan wore the symbol of their empire somewhere on their costumes. Draped over her left shoulder was a cloaklike piece of cloth that was wrapped diagonally around her torso and on which she kept tripping. Silk purple trousers with red chevrons were tucked into antelope-skin boots. She intended to keep the foot gear since they felt as if they had been molded to her calves and feet.

The Lady straightened her daughter's costume. "We need to be colorful enough to grab the front page. If we dress in our regular clothes, we'll wind up on a back page next to announcements for the garden club."

"Then why don't we just rent some clown costumes?" Scirye countered.

Nishke joined her mother in trying to calm her sister. "The costumes are part of setting the right atmosphere," she explained. "If you dress like any girl in San Francisco, how will they know you're a Kushan?"

Scirye felt as if her mother and sister were both ganging up on her. She already knew she would never be as noble as her sister or as exquisite as her mother.

Scirye hunched her shoulders sullenly. "That's easy for you to say when you get to dress like a warrior."

Nishke affectionately adjusted a curl hanging against Scirye's cheek. "I happen to *be* a Pippal."

"And so will I," Scirye mumbled. "Just you wait."

The Lady Sudarshane rolled her eyes at Nishke. "This is all your fault. You set a bad example for your little sister."

Nishke held up both hands as she laughed. "Don't blame me. The sisters say you're the one who set a bad example by quitting the sisterhood to join the consular corps."

The corners of Lady Sudarshane's mouth slipped upward. "Well, if I hadn't, I would never have met your father and then where would you two miscreants be? You're going to turn my hair gray yet."

Actually, Nishke had never caused her parents any major worries. She had always known what she wanted and aimed for her goal by the most direct path—whether it was an aerial polo trophy or an appointment to the Pippalanta. Smart and well-liked, she was being groomed for an officer's commission one day.

Scirye, on the other hand, was a source of constant concern for her parents, for her mother often spoke long-distance with her father, who was His Imperial Highness's very own Griffin Master. He carried out the traditional task of overseeing the imperial pride of riding griffins as well as the welfare of all lap griffins. However, in addition to his ancient responsibilities, he also carried out all the other duties that had become attached to the office through the centuries, including acting as the official liaison treaty negotiator between humans and griffins. Or as he put it, he smoothed out ruffled feathers, fur, hair, and toupees.

On the rare occasions when his obligations permitted, he visited them wherever they were posted. Though it was clear he loved Scirye and she looked forward to being with him, it was always painfully obvious that they did not have much in common. This man, so adept at calming a rampaging griffin, didn't have a clue on what to say to a young girl in general, let alone reason with her about her bad behavior.

Even when Scirye was trying to imitate her sister, she always managed to warp it somehow. Where Nishke was cheerful, Scirye was sarcastic. Where the older girl was determined, the younger one was willful. Where Nishke always steered by some inner compass, Scirye wandered first in one direction and then another.

Lady Sudarshane kissed the cheek of her prodigal daughter. "If you can't even wear a costume for one day, how are you going to handle the strict discipline that the Pippalanta demand?"

Scirye started to sputter in protest like the lid on a boiling tea kettle, but before she could explode, Kles joined in. "Lady Scirye, think of yourself as playing a role today, all right?" the griffin wheedled. "The point is to make the Kushan less mysterious to the Americans, and what better way than to show them what has made us a great nation?"

"Okay, but I don't have to like it. I feel like I'm drowning in silk," Scirye grumbled, accepting her fate with poor grace.

Lady Sudarshane gave Kles a grateful look. He always seemed to know the right thing to say to her daughter.

"Now, now, dear," Lady Sudarshane soothed. "If this was good enough for our ancestors, it's good enough for us. Tradition is meant to be distinctive, not comfortable."

Scirye made an exasperated sound as she felt the cloak sagging from her shoulder again. "Argh! Why won't this thing stay put? I could just bite the next person who says how quaint I look!" She started to pull off the cloak, ready to trample it, but Kles batted a wing against her cheek and she stopped at his cautionary touch.

"Well, if you do"—Nishke winked—"make sure it's not someone important."

Before Scirye could reply to her sister, they were nearly trampled by a large woman as she walked backward across the floor. She was gesturing with both hands for a group of newspeople to follow her.

Over her shoulder, she wore a sash proclaiming that she was a museum docent. From her affected voice and mannerisms, she was a frustrated actress. "And we've saved the best for last."

"I'll say," a photographer said. He held up a big boxy camera. "Smile, honey."

A half-dozen other photographers peeled away from the group to cluster about Nishke.

"Excuse me," Nishke said to her mother and sister and then turned to the photographers. "I have to take up my post first." She marched smartly to the center of the room and took her place by a corner of the case where the body of Lady Tabiti lay in honor upon a dais supported by elephants of lapis lazuli. A Pippal stood at each of the three other corners, as well.

Within the case Lady Tabiti rested in a suit of armor made from plaques of dark, apple green jade sewn together with gold thread. Gold inlays of Nanaia the Peaceful adorned each piece of jade. A mask, carved from a large matching piece of jade into the likeness of a beautiful woman, had been set aside to reveal the head of the owner of the armor.

Her body had been preserved remarkably well by the desert-like climate where she usually lay in her mausoleum, so it was possible to see that her face at one time had matched the mask. Ropes of braided hair still showed some of their original fiery red tint, which might have matched Scirye's.

Camera bulbs popped and flashed, but the photographers seemed more interested in Nishke and the Pippalanta guards than in Lady Tabiti herself.

"We should take our posts, too," Lady Sudarshane said, and led her daughter and Kles to a seat in the roped-off area to the right of the podium.

The cloak slipped down yet again so that Scirye tripped and nearly fell on her face. Scowling, she tugged the obnoxious piece of clothing back in place and then slumped in a chair until her mother tapped her shoulder. "Don't slouch, dear. You look like you have a hump." As her daughter sat up straight, Lady Sudarshane fussed with Scirye's clothing. "Nishke should be teaching you how to sit properly in a chair rather than how to fight."

Scirye shot a guilty look at her mother. "What do you mean?" she asked, fearing the worst.

Her mother pursed her lips in amusement. "I know what you two are really doing when you tell me you're going out shopping," her mother said. "You might at least have the decency to come back with a package or two to keep up the pretense."

Scirye desperately tried to concoct an alibi. "We were window shopping."

Her mother tapped her lightly on the head. "No, you're going to the gym where she's teaching you Tumarg. And I might add that fibbing to your mother is *not* Tumarg."

Tumarg was the Way of Light, the Way that Purifies. It embodied not only the martial arts of the Pippalanta but their code of honor, as well.

Scirye's cloak had fallen off her shoulder once more and she pulled it back up as she shot an accusing look at Kles. "Did you tell my mother?"

When the griffin ruffled both his fur and feathers, he was the picture of indignation. "I am your retainer. I would never tell your secrets."

"Yes, shame on you for doubting Klestetstse's loyalty," her mother scolded mildly. "The accounting office asked me about the receipts from the gym so it was easy to put one and one together and get a pair of rebellious daughters."

"Sorry, Kles," Scirye mumbled contritely.

By then, the museum docent had managed to gather up the photographers again so she could continue her performance. "Behold, the most venerated relic of the Kushan Empire." She waved her hand grandly. "The Jade Lady!"

A reporter shoved his hat back with a whistle. "That crazy outfit must be worth a bundle."

The docent did a half-pirouette as she faced the reporters again. "And deservedly so. Lady Tabiti was a princess from far Sarmatia in the Russian steppes who led her tribe of women warriors down to the Kushan Empire and saved it from a Persian invasion. The grateful Kushans nicknamed their fierce saviors the Pippalanta after a fiery pepper plant and hailed Lady Tabiti as Nanaia reborn. When she died, the Empire of the Moon—as the Kushan Empire is often called—buried her like an empress."

The Lady Sudarshane gave a snort at the exaggeration, and the Pippalanta suddenly seemed to have developed a bad case of the giggles.

"What's wrong?" Scirye whispered. Despite Kles's lessons, Scirye still felt as if Kushan's long history was a dense thicket she would never penetrate.

"Well, she came from Sarmatia, but she never claimed to be of royal blood let alone divine ichor," the Lady Sudarshane murmured. "Our friend, the docent, is . . . um . . . embroidering the story quite a bit."

Unaware of how she was amusing the Kushan, the docent spread her arms wide as if she were going to embrace the dais and the guards. "Of all the masterpieces that the Hearn wanted, the Jade Lady is to be the capstone. We assured the Kushan we would protect the exhibit with every device known to technology and every charm and ward known to magic. But the only way that the Kushan would allow Lady Tabiti to come here was if her own Pippalanta were allowed to watch over this exhibit day and night. Of course, her own tribe was assimilated by the Kushans long ago. Even though the Pippalanta are now a regiment open to any woman who can meet their exacting standards, they have continued to add glory to their name."

A reporter jabbed his pencil at a ring carved from bone stained yellow and brown by the years. A triangular wedge protruded from the side and strange signs ran along the band but they were so worn that they were impossible to read. "Well, that looks pretty chintzy for a lady with all that jade."

"It's an archer's ring. It protects the thumb when the archer draws back the string. You can see where the bow strings have cut grooves into the surface." The docent smiled condescendingly. "And that humble ring once belonged to the Emperor Yü, the legendary ruler of China. Centuries later, a Chinese emperor sent it to the Kushan king in gratitude after an alliance between China and the Kushans destroyed the Huns. And then a descendant of that king presented it to the Jade Lady in honor of her service, and she was entombed with it."

Bored, Scirye started to drum a heel against the floor but felt Kles squeeze her wrist in warning. Over the years, they had developed their own silent code of looks and touches.

Stilling her leg, Scirye drew out a small beaded purse from her sash and removed a piece of hard candy from it. As she slipped it into her mouth, Kles cleared his throat.

"Ahem," he coughed softly. "I'm feeling a bit peckish myself."

"You're awfully spoiled, you know that?" Scirye teased. However, she slipped a small tin from the same purse. A faint chirping came from within and the girl stole a worried glance at her mother. But she was too busy being amused by the docent.

It was a tricky maneuver to pull off with just one hand because her griffin was on the other. But she managed to lift the lid and shove her fingers inside, probing until she caught a cricket. Snatching it out, she closed the lid immediately. As the small insect wriggled, she held it between her pinched fingers.

Kles took it carefully, tilting his head back as he swallowed it whole. Then he cleared his throat meaningfully.

"I don't think I should," she joked. "If you get any heavier, I won't be able to carry you on my arm." But she lifted the lid anyway. This time a green shape darted out. Startled, she dropped the tin, which fell open on the floor. The next moment a dozen crickets were hopping merrily about the gallery.

When Scirye heard Kles's wings snap open, she immediately reached out her free hand to seize him. However, the griffin had already launched himself from her gauntlet. Kles might pride himself on being a scholar and a courtier, but there were times when blind instinct could overwhelm his reason and he reverted to a wild beast.

"Mine!" he screamed.

From the corner of her eye, Lady Sudarshane caught the blur of feather and fur. Immediately she knew who was to blame. "Scirye!"

Scirye jumped to her feet and held up her gauntleted arm. "Come back!" she commanded, and then gave the piercing recall whistle over and over.

Lady Sudarshane gave a sigh and did what she could to repair the damage. Everyone was standing around just gaping. "Catch the crickets," she ordered the consular staff. A dozen of the costumed junior officials immediately fell on all fours and began to crawl about. Though the Pippalanta remained at their posts, the museum guards joined the hunt. Between the chirping of the crickets and the noise people made trying to capture them, the radio crew were going frantic trying to adjust the sound levels.

Then flashbulbs began to pop so that Scirye felt as if they were in the midst of a lightning storm.

"Mine!" the griffin shrieked again and dove, taking delight as photographers ducked and scrambled out of his way.

Scirye whistled until she felt her lips grow numb, but finally Kles heard her and, unable to fight his training, returned to the gauntlet. He stood there, panting and embarrassed. "I don't know what got into me," he said sheepishly.

"Your problem is that you're all stomach," Scirye scolded.

Kles hung his head, ashamed. "Everyone must be furious with me."

The girl felt sorry that she had said anything. The proud griffin usually carried himself as if he were twelve feet tall rather than twelve inches so it was strange to see him acting so humble now. She loved Kles as she did no one else besides her family. He was usually the one to console her, so it was her turn now.

She stroked his feathery head gently. "It'll be all right." She added to herself, *I hope.*

Right at that moment, the Kushan Consul, Prince Etre, strolled over. Even if his ancient costume was a bit gaudy, it seemed to suit him more than modern clothes. He moved without the least bit of self-consciousness in wool trousers of orange, red, and yellow, a tunic that hung to his waist, a gold belt with plaques showing eagles, wolves, and griffins fighting with various animals, and an odd cap that rose in a curling peak and ended in a knob that bobbed with each step. Little silver moons and axes festooned the cap's sides.

For this special occasion, he wore his family's most precious heirloom—a golden sheath with a set of knives. Winding around the edge of the golden sheath was a line of animals, each attacking the one ahead in a dance of death. Protruding from the top of the sheath was the golden hilt of a stiletto decorated with a dancing bear. Hidden behind it were two small throwing daggers that Scirye would never have guessed would be there—if the prince hadn't shown her one day. The sheath hung from the belt but there were also straps tying it tightly to his thigh.

He surveyed the spectacle of his consular staff upon their hands and knees. "Backsides weren't quite the image we wanted to present, are they?" he asked Lady Sudarshane.

Scirye knew she needed to speak up before Prince Etre blamed her mother. While the Kushan diplomatic corps thought of themselves as modern as their American and European counterparts, Prince Etre was a throwback to the early Kushans who had been shaped by the vast steppe lands. When he was happy, he didn't just smile—he sang. And when he was angry, he didn't just frown—he raged like one of the great storms that swept across the plains.

Feeling like she was about to jump in front of a lightning bolt, Scirye gulped, "It's all my fault, Your Highness."

Prince Etre regarded the spindly girl and his lips twitched upward in a smile. When he began to laugh, Scirye breathed a sigh of relief. Outside of her family, Scirye liked Prince Etre the best of all the Kushans she had met. Scirye always knew where she stood with the prince. He didn't say nice things to her face and then make snide comments behind her back.

Though his fingers were thick and blunt, the prince neatly snared a cricket in mid-jump, and held it with legs still wriggling between his thumb and index finger. "I had a lap griffin when I was your age," he reminisced. "They can be a bit . . . demanding."

"I humbly beg your pardon, Your Highness"—Kles swallowed—"but I see nothing wrong with expecting what is due my station as a member of Lady Scirye's retinue."

Scirye grabbed Kles's beak before his pride got them into even more trouble. "Hush, Kles," she whispered in his ear. "Leave this to me."

Bowing her head contritely, Scirye said to the prince, "I'm sorry,

Your Highness. Confine me to my room. Put me on bread and water. Chain me to the wall." Her voice rose to a dramatic crescendo. "You can even take away my books, my records, and," she added slyly, "my ping-pong paddle."

Prince Etre's current passion was ping-pong though the paddle was dwarfed in his huge, calloused hand. His staff had been so worn out by his constant practice matches that they were grateful when Scirye had become his steady partner.

The girl hadn't minded because before the prince had been appointed Consul, he had defended the empire's borders and his adventures were stranger than anything even Scirye could imagine. And the prince seemed only too delighted to have such an attentive listener.

The prince jerked upright, the decorations on his cap jingling. "What? Lose my devoted ping-pong opponent? I think that would punish me more than you." He added drily, "And it would certainly punish the rest of the staff who would have to take your place." The prince might be bluff in his manner, but he was no fool and knew what his staff really thought.

What a dear, Scirye thought to herself. *Maybe I'll let him win a few games.* The prince was an enthusiastic if not very good player, but he always took his losses cheerfully.

"Did your griffin cause accidents like mine?" she asked, hoping to find some defense for the scolding she knew her mother would give her later.

The prince regarded her as kindly as if she were his granddaughter. "Well, my fellow was rather excitable so it could get quite messy sometimes. I think there were always some of my clothes drying on a clothesline every day. Lucky for me"—he smiled—"my father said a griffin was the best way to learn responsibility." He added, "But it took me a while."

Lady Sudarshane closed her eyes as if she had a headache. "Please, Your Highness," she begged. "Don't encourage her."

"Now, now." Prince Etre chuckled. "Where would we be without our furry, feathered friends, eh?"

The cricket suddenly flung itself free from Prince Etre, but Kles twisted his head away from Scirye's restraining hand and darted his beak forward to snag the insect adroitly. "Mine!" he said as he happily crunched it.

"Goal!" Prince Etre cheered. "You can be my Number One whenever we play air polo." The Number One was the main offensive player on a polo team.

Kles clacked his beak to show his pleasure. "I'd be honored, Your Highness."

Prince Etre never did anything by halves, especially when he was enjoying himself. Flinging off his cap, he declared, "This is the most fun I've had since I became Consul." He winked at Lady Sudarshane. "And I was so afraid that I'd be stuck at another stuffy ceremony."

"I'm glad Your Highness is so... um... open-minded," Lady Sudarshane said with her usual delicacy.

"Well, mustn't loaf on the sidelines while the first chukker's still going on." Despite his rheumatism, the prince got on all fours and then, laughing like a small boy, he joined the others scrambling around the room.

Lady Sudarshane rounded on her heel and stared down at her daughter and the griffin. "I don't want either of you moving from this spot. Do you understand me?" she demanded.

Scirye and Kles nodded, uneasily contemplating their future. Prince Etre might have forgiven them but Scirye's mother was another matter.

"And, young lady," Lady Sudarshane warned, "we are going to have a good long talk later. A long, long talk." Then, hitching up her costume, she got down on her knees, and with as much dignity as she could muster, she crawled after the Consul.

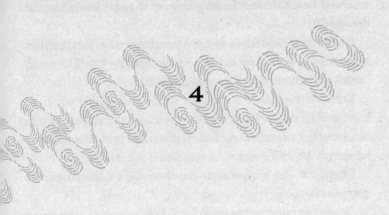

4

Leech

As soon as the museum's doors swung open, Primo and the boys surged into the museum with the rest of the crowd as a film crew recorded their entrance.

In his short, hard life, Leech had never been part of an event as big as this and it was strange to share the same excitement with so many people. In fact, he had never had much in common with anyone except his buddy, Koko.

Light fell through the huge stained-glass panels in the ceiling, coloring the marble tiles of the lobby floor. Leech always enjoyed that initial moment when he first went into the museum. On the outside, the building seemed as massive and strong as a fortress, but inside it was so elegant.

On previous visits, they had always gone to the Chinese gallery first, and Leech slowed, looking forward to going inside but also dreading it.

He was surprised when Primo headed in a different direction, following the signs and banners to the Kushan exhibit instead. "Don't fall behind, boys," the man ordered.

Koko deliberately settled into a stroll as he pulled out a silk handkerchief that he had found or stolen long ago. Always fastidious, he licked a corner of the handkerchief and rubbed at a spot on his shirt. "What's the rush?" he muttered to the smaller boy.

Lately, if Primo wanted to do one thing, then Koko insisted on doing the opposite. It was getting hard to please both.

"It wouldn't hurt to humor Primo," Leech coaxed, deliberately picking up his own pace.

With a skip, Koko caught up with Leech. "Why do you keep doing what he wants? He's not our boss."

"He's our friend," Leech said. "After all, he rescued us from Big Hat and his gang." Six months ago, Koko and Leech had been cornered in an alley when Primo had appeared. Though the odds had been six to one, Primo had been a whirlwind, knocking the gang members to the ground. That act alone would have been enough to earn Leech's undying loyalty because up until then the only one who had been kind to him had been Koko.

However, from the first moment that Leech had seen Primo, the boy felt as if there was an even greater bond between them than friendship. When Leech had tried to talk about that feeling to Koko later in private, his friend had become jealous so Leech had never brought it up again. But it still puzzled him.

"So let's give a thank-you card and go our own way," Koko grumbled.

"And he's teaching us how to fight," Leech said.

"Okay," Koko admitted, starting to drag his feet again, "but we're just using the mug. We're not buddy-buddies. Not like you and me, right?" Koko had made it clear to his friend that he put up with Primo only for the free fighting lessons and food.

Leech hesitated a moment, remembering their first visit to the Chinese Gallery. As soon as he had crossed the threshold, he had felt strangely at home, and yet it was impossible because he had never gone near the museum before this. The farther they went into the gallery, the more the sensation had grown until Leech stopped before a tall, narrow painting of a golden tower—Primo had called it a pagoda. Storm clouds and lightning lit up the surrounding hills as a boy stood before the pagoda's doorway. But it was hard to tell if the boy was taking shelter in the pagoda or about to run away.

Primo had been watching the boy closely. "Are you all right?" Primo had asked when he saw Leech shiver. "You were smiling just a moment ago."

Koko was always protective of his friend so he looked about for a thermostat. "They ought to turn up the heater in this dump."

Leech realized that it wasn't the gallery that was so familiar: it was the scenes in the paintings.

"I've been there," the boy said in a puzzled, frightened voice. "I know I have." The memory, if that's what it was, must have been a horrible one and yet he had not been able to take his eyes away from the picture.

"It's possible," Primo said kindly. "In China, people believe that they're born over and over until they get things right."

That seemed as good an explanation as any for what Leech was feeling about the paintings and especially about Primo. The boy had torn his gaze away from the painting to face Primo. "Is that why I thought I knew you when we first met?"

Primo had glanced from the painting and back to the boy. "Who knows? But maybe we're working out some debt from another life. Perhaps I did something wrong to you in a previous life so I'm trying to make up for it now."

"What was it?" the boy had wondered.

"I hope it was nothing terrible," Primo had said, giving Leech the saddest look the boy had ever seen.

Leech tried to comfort him. "Well, you're being a good friend in this life."

"After you ran away from the orphanage," Koko reminded him, "you would've starved if I hadn't shown you the ropes."

It had taken the rest of the week to assure Koko that Leech was still closer to Koko than anyone else.

Leech was trying his best to keep at Primo's heels as they moved straight like an arrow toward the Kushan exhibit.

At his side, Koko nudged him. "I don't know why I bother with you."

Leech twisted the iron band on his arm the way he always did when he was bothered. The only decoration on the plain surface were two disks. It had been in the same basket in which he had been found at the orphanage. It was the only clue to his past, and the boy had clung to it no matter what, even though he had been teased about wearing such odd jewelry.

"I don't know either," Leech admitted. His first eight years at the orphanage had been pure misery. He had been a target of every bully because he was small for his age and also smarter than the other children. The experience had left him like a beaten puppy, insecure and yet eager to please.

Seeing how uneasy his friend was, Koko relented. "You and me, we're a team now, aren't we? You're the only one I ever trusted with my big secret."

Leech grinned slightly at the memory. "You were so afraid that I'd be shocked. But you know what, buddy? I felt honored. I never had anyone trust me like that."

Koko slid his arm around Leech's shoulders. "So, pals to the end?"

"Of course," Leech assured him. "Anyway, I thought you'd be the one in a rush to see the Kushan exhibit. They say it's full of gold and jewels."

"Now you're talking my lingo." Koko laughed.

The boys caught up with Primo just as he was handing their tickets to the guard at the entrance to the Kushan galleries.

Leech had expected Primo to stop and examine the first room of the Kushan show, but Primo strode on as if late for an appointment. It was Koko who wanted to linger when he saw the glitter of gold and gems in a corner. "Whoa," he said, his mouth making a little *O* of amazement.

Leech caught hold of his friend and started to drag him along. "Come on."

Koko tried to dig in his heels. "We're here to look, aren't we?"

"We'll come back later," Leech promised.

Koko studied the glass covering the case. "I wonder how thick this glass is?"

Leech knew that certain gleam in his friend's eyes and leaned in close. "No, Koko," he said in a fierce, low voice.

"No, what?" Koko whispered back.

"No to stealing anything here," Leech explained in exasperation. "We've quit that," he added, "at least for a while."

"Says you," Koko said defiantly. "A guy's got to stay in practice and they leave all this stuff just lying around." He waved a hand airily at a jeweled crown. "Gold's meant to be spent."

Leech nodded toward the man plowing a way through the crowd ahead of them. "Primo wouldn't like it." He nodded to the two museum guards. One, a beefy human, was dwarfed by his partner, a green troll whose too-small uniform bulged on his huge frame, and whose arms were so long they stretched out of his sleeves and brushed the floor. "And neither would they."

"You're turning into a regular pill. You know that?" Koko complained as he jammed his hands into his pockets.

They sped through room after room, trailing Primo as he searched for something. Finally, they came to the last and largest chamber. Over the doorway was a banner: "Kushan, the Crossroads of the World and of Magic."

Primo adroitly sidestepped around the huge golden statue of a majestic woman riding a lion, and the boys slipped around her as well. Despite the noise in the room, Leech thought he heard a chirping sound. "What's that?"

"Crickets," Primo said. "It must be sound effects." He scratched his head. "But I couldn't say why."

"Goal!" a man cried. He was dressed in a funny costume with a gold-edged sash as he crawled across the floor with something in his cupped fingers. He didn't seem to notice that he had knocked Primo to the side.

A woman, in an antique outfit herself, scurried on her knees after him. "Excuse me." She smiled politely up at Primo as they passed.

The trio watched the man move on, crying "Goal!" in between chuckles. The woman stayed at his heels, apologizing to anyone he might have bumped.

Leech stared at the spectacle surrounding them. Half the room seemed to be in costumes or at least fancy dress, and they were all scrambling about on their knees. "Are all openings like this?"

"Just the fun ones," Primo said, but he seemed just as puzzled as the boys.

The rest of the crowd were spectators like themselves, trying to see the exhibits as they dodged around the crawling hunters.

"Do you think someone lost their keys?" Leech wondered to Koko.

But his friend was standing with his mouth open in ecstasy. The lighting made it seem as if there were dark circles around his eyes, but the eyes themselves shone as brightly as the gold and silver and gems sparkling at them from all sides. "Shut up. I'm in heaven," he murmured.

"Lady Tabiti at last," Primo said. He marched determinedly toward a dais in the center of the room.

"Come on," Leech said, seizing Koko's wrist. He towed his still stupefied friend behind him. "And quit drooling. Someone will slip and fall down."

Primo halted at the dais and, to Leech's surprise, bowed his head with great reverence. And then again twice more.

Curious, Leech sidled up next to him to see the mummy of a woman lying upon her back, completely encased in a suit made out of apple green plaques and sewn together with gold wire.

"What're you doing?" Leech asked Primo.

Primo straightened, his face solemn. "Paying my respects to a beautiful lady."

The boy gazed at the face covered by the jade squares. "How can you tell?"

"The . . . songs and tales all say that's the way she was," Primo said. "And she had a soul to match. When Lady Tabiti was young, her father gave asylum to a noble Kushan family. She and the daughter became best friends and swore to be loyal to one another. Later, when the family was exonerated and returned to the empire, her Kushan friend grew up and married the emperor. By then Lady Tabiti had become the leader of her people. When the Kushan empire was invaded, Lady Tabiti honored her childhood oath. She led her warriors to war and destroyed the invaders. She could have assumed the throne herself, but she chose to serve her friend instead."

Next to them, a pair of tourists seemed more interested in gawking at the Kushan warriors rather than the treasure they protected.

For months the San Francisco newspapers and radio stations had been talking about the real-life "Amazons" as much as about the treasures they were going to guard.

Leech had been expecting muscular giants, so he was disappointed to see that they were just women in funny costumes. Though one of them was tall, the others were of average height. Even some of the human museum guards looked more imposing than them.

The Amazons stood straight as swords, ignoring the chaos all around them as they guarded the dais.

"Have you ever killed anyone?" a fat tourist demanded.

"Not today, sir," the woman said politely in accented English.

"Excuse me," Primo said to the obnoxious man, "but you might want to show some respect."

"It's quite all right, sir." The Amazon flashed him a grateful smile. "You are all Kushan's guests."

Primo nodded approvingly. "Spoken as graciously as she would have wanted."

"How do you kn—," Leech started to ask him when the rumbling began. It sounded like a train was heading straight toward the room. As the floor began to vibrate, cups and other things crashed over in the display cases.

"Earthquake!" someone shouted.

Primo whirled around, searching for the boys. "Stand under a doorway."

The only trouble was that everyone else was rushing for the single exit, as well. The spectators were only one moment away from turning into a panicked mob, and Leech thought they were in more danger of being trampled by the crowd than being crushed in the earthquake.

Primo tried to shield the boys from the stampeding spectators when the floor collapsed near them.

Through the six-foot-wide opening, Leech could see the huge

pipes in the museum's basement. Out of it flew a creature straight out of a nightmare. A flapping wing brushed a tourist teetering on the edge. It hovered overhead as the flailing man fell through the gaping hole.

Another winged horror followed it. And finally a third and fourth.

Their gray, leathery bodies were about six feet long and as slender and supple as serpents. Each of their four legs ended in sharp talons ready to strike, and they flew with four wings, which beat in the same alternating pattern as dragonflies.

Chairs crashed as people jumped to their feet in the roped-off section near the podium. A woman screamed as her husband pulled her away from the hole.

Overhead, the monsters swung their heads back and forth, picking out their first victims.

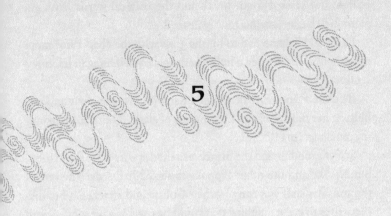

5

Scirye

Lady Sudarshane rose, no longer the diplomat but the warrior she had once been. Her voice rose commandingly over the tumult. "Get the weapons from the cases!"

She set her own example by picking up her chair and striding over to a display of halberds with their spiked, axe-like heads and sharp-pointed spears.

Scirye stared open-mouthed at her mother. In her mind, her mother was a charming, fussy woman who was always telling her what to do, not someone who went about vandalizing museums. In her antique costume, this woman might have stepped out of a painting of an ancient Kushan battle.

Lady Sudarshane swung the chair legs against the window. Dozens of cracks spread outward from the point of impact, but the bulletproof glass did not break and the magical wards held. An alarm bell began jangling loudly instead.

Lady Sudarshane had to hit the glass with the chair three more times before she created a hole but the glass itself hung in fractured sections.

By then, Prince Etre had joined her with his own chair and was helping her finish clearing the window of glass. "Quite an invigorating morning, isn't it?"

Scirye's mother and the prince snatched spears from the exhibit, but Nishke and the other Pippalanta seized halberds. The rest of the consular staff was copying their Consul and attacked other display cases to get at anything that could be used as a weapon. A troll museum guard hadn't bothered with a chair but was hammering one of his stone-like fists against another window while the other guards waited anxiously.

They were the only ones moving. The city dignitaries and the spectators stood gaping just as Scirye was. The monsters were flying in ever widening circles, scanning the people below as if they were no more than a flock of sheep and the monsters were selecting their first victims.

On her wrist, Scirye felt Kles stir. His fur and feathers were bristling as he spread his wings and shrilled his battle cry. Her hair flew every which way as Kles rose with a flap of his wings. He circled a few feet above her head, ready to defend her against monsters nine times his size.

Scirye looked up at him admiringly, knowing that the griffin's heart was bigger than anyone else's in the room—including hers. And that made her love him all the more.

She could not let Kles fight while she stood by like a sack of laundry. If she wanted to be a Pippal, she had to do more than read about them. She had to *act* like them, too.

Scirye had always been a definite sort of girl. When she made up her mind to do something, she did it or she learned how. That was the reason she could speak several languages, could operate the teletype machine in the communications room, could make a soufflé and unstop an embassy sink—admittedly, she had plugged it up in the first place, but that was nit-picking.

The terrified girl forced her numb legs to stumble toward her mother now, away from the frightened spectators. The stumble steadied into a walk and finally into a run.

Lady Sudarshane had skipped the golden, jeweled ceremonial weapons to take a plain spear with a three-pronged blade. It was only when the light reflected off the steel that Scirye saw the patterns that swirled along its length. From her sister, she had learned that the patterns marked the steel creation of a master weapons-maker.

Scirye's eyes searched the case until she saw another one to match her mother's. She was just reaching for it when her mother stopped her. "See our guests to safety," her mother ordered.

"I can fight, too," Scirye said stubbornly. "Nishke's been showing me." The Pippalanta were expected to be as equally proficient with swords, spears, and bows as they were with modern guns.

"We are their hosts," her mother insisted firmly. "And by the rules of hospitality, a host must protect her guests."

"Mistress, we have a duty," Kles reminded her as he kept an eye on the monsters overhead.

"You must help them escape," her mother instructed her.

Tears stung Scirye's eyes, but she knew her mother and the griffin were right.

Pivoting, she ran back toward the dignitaries and spectators who huddled in the center of the room.

"Go," she said, waving her arms at the frightened man in front of her—she thought he might be the mayor. "Get out of here."

"Go, go, go," Kles said, hovering long enough to beat his wings in the direction of the doorway.

As the Pippalanta and museum guards rallied around her mother, Scirye and Kles gathered up the city dignitaries and the other spectators and herded them like sheep from the room.

Mrs. Rudenko fell over a chair and might have been trampled by the people behind her, but Kles darted in, flapping his wings at the oncoming startled faces so that they swept around on either side of him and the woman.

"Don't panic," Scirye shouted. She placed herself at the back of the group, fists ready.

With a screech, a monstrous head darted downward and Scirye crouched. Her limbs were stiff with fright, but it was only a feint. The gray dragonfly, she thought angrily, was only playing with her.

As she straightened to check on her charges, she saw an Asian-looking man using a chair to break into another case. Next to him were two boys. The larger boy was pear-shaped, with hips and legs too big for his slender torso. His black hair had a silvery sheen.

The smaller boy had brown hair with a slender iron ring around each wrist.

"You need to leave, sir," she said to the man.

He smiled grimly at her. "We'll need something that will reach those monsters," he explained as he began helping himself to the throwing stars. Scirye could see the sense of that, so perhaps he did know what he was doing. "But take the boys out of here."

"Right," the bigger boy said with some relief. He was stocky, with most of his weight about his hips.

The brown-haired boy, though, looked stubborn. "We're not going to leave you, Primo. We know how to fight."

"This is no street punk, Leech," Primo said gravely.

"Well, what do you know about fighting dragons?" Leech

demanded. He was fiddling nervously with the iron bracelets on one arm.

"More than I want to," Primo said, and nodded to the other boy. "Get him out of here, Koko."

"Come on," Koko said, grabbed his friend's arm. "We'll just get in Primo's way."

Leech pointed at Scirye. "So will she."

Scirye saw the contempt in his face and it angered her. He was just as bad as her schoolmates in other cities, but thanks to Kles, she didn't put up with that. "I've been trained to fight," she snapped—though she added truthfully to herself, *At least, I've started.* She took a certain satisfaction in shoving him toward the doorway. "You'll just get in the way."

Leech opened his mouth in protest, "I—"

"She's right," Primo said firmly.

His mentor's words hurt, but Leech allowed Koko to pull him toward the doorway. Scirye stayed at their heels while Kles flew protectively overhead.

As they neared the doorway, Scirye saw a mousy woman standing there as if she were watching a movie.

"Didn't you hear me?" Scirye demanded, waving her arm angrily. "Leave!"

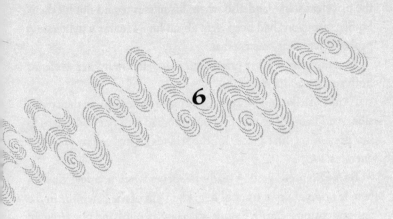

6

Bayang

Bayang had been as surprised as anyone when the floor had caved in, but she had not survived this long without learning to recover quickly from the unexpected—and to take advantage of it.

The cave-in was just the sort of distraction she needed. The dust was still in the air as she began moving purposefully toward her prey.

She paused when the first creature shot out of the hole. When the second and third appeared, she began to retreat toward the doorway where she stayed and watched, even as frightened tourists, dignitaries, and museum guards stumbled past her.

As the menace wheeled in a wide circle high overhead, she noted with interest that Primo had taken his place to the side, where the Kushan and museum guards would not block him when he threw the priceless stars—and also where his misses would not hit them. So her suspicions had been right about him. He was a fighter, and probably a military man at that.

And then she saw her prey coming straight toward her while his bodyguard was distracted.

A quick strike and Bayang could make her escape in the confusion. And then she would find out who had sent the bodyguard to her prey in the first place, for the friends of her enemy were her enemies, too.

Bayang tensed, getting ready to spring when a young Kushan female popped up in front of her. The sight of the hatchling in the antique costume caught Bayang off guard. In one hand, the girl held a spear twice as tall as she was.

"Didn't you hear me? Leave!" the bossy hatchling said, and waved her free hand as if shooing a pigeon from her windowsill.

Bayang came from a proud race. She didn't take kindly to being treated like a scruffy bird, but it was the curse of being too good at disguising herself. The hatchling took her for some mousy old woman who had frozen in fright.

Bayang would have swatted this annoying hatchling away, but she did not want to tip off her quarry as he passed. If she was careful and alert, there would be another opportunity on the way out of the museum.

High above the gallery floor, the monstrous quartet were starting to dart downward and then flying upward again as if they were testing the defenders. The human museum guards struck out at the monsters in vain, and the troll's blows were powerful but so clumsy that they were easy to dodge. Bayang noted with approval, though, that the Amazons and Primo did not waste their energy on the feints. These were no ceremonial guards but veterans hardened in combat.

Bayang felt someone shove her arm and looked down at the costumed Kushan hatchling glowering at her. "Go!"

Bayang was annoyed at having her concentration broken. "Do I look like a cow, little girl?"

It was the hatchling's turn to be indignant. "Little . . . ?" she spluttered with enough irritation to satisfy Bayang.

At that moment, one of the museum guards took out an ancient bow and quiver of arrows. From the way he held them, he was more a danger to himself than to the monsters. When he pulled it back for a test, the brittle wood snapped.

Bayang's prey had been watching the defenders over his shoulder. When he saw the bow snap, he halted. Spinning around on his heel, he sped back into the room.

"We're supposed to go this way," his frustrated friend yelled as he followed. He pointed frantically in the direction of the street.

Bayang's prey looked over his shoulder. "Primo's right. They need weapons that can reach the monsters up there. And," he added as he headed toward the case where more throwing stars still rested in the display case, "they'll need all the help they can get."

With an exasperated sound, Koko followed Bayang's prey to the case.

"Come back here," the hatchling commanded and ran after them.

Bayang considered the possibilities and decided to observe out of sight to see if the monsters would carry out her mission for her.

She was already turning when the gray fliers soared even higher, until their wings were brushing the dome itself, leaving room for a giant emerald creature to emerge from the hole.

About twelve feet long with a wingspan to match, he seemed as massive as a bus. The fire elementals, trembling in their globes, sent the light flickering across his scales and the bands of iron armoring his chest. When he roared, thunder rolled around the circular room and echoed from the ceiling like the trumpet of doom. His fangs were as sharp as daggers and his steel-tipped talons like short swords.

And that was when Bayang knew something even more dangerous was threatening her people than just her original prey; for she knew that dragon. He had haunted her nightmares since she was a hatchling.

Badik was his name and there had been bad blood between her people, the Clan of the Moonglow, and his, the Clan of the Fire Rings, going back to the very First Days. Their conflict had reached its deadliest peak when Badik's people had made a pact with the Kraken, wraithlike horrors from the abyssal canyons where light never penetrated and the water hung foul and still.

Then Badik led the combined army of his people and the Kraken in an invasion—not to conquer Bayang's people, but to exterminate them. The fight had reached the very gates of her people's capital, where the invaders had been destroyed, but only at the cost of much misery, blood, and tears. Unfortunately, Badik had escaped and had eluded his hunters up until now.

The sight of that scarred face filled her with a dread that she thought she had put behind her long ago. She prided herself on her self-control, but suddenly she was a hatchling again, cowering as the battle raged outside in the city.

If Badik was here, then he was a worse threat to her people than her prey, for Badik would be intent on revenge. Whatever scheme Badik was up to, she was sure that it meant devastation for her home. Bayang knew he must be stopped.

But beyond the grander schemes, the fight was now personal. Badik and his army had slaughtered many of Bayang's kin, and there was a blood debt to collect. She hated Badik far more than her original prey and rage boiled up inside her, overcoming any dread she had of the dragon.

On that terrible day when Badik had invaded, she had vowed to punish him for what he had done. Determined never to feel so helpless again, she had set about molding herself into a fighter who always won despite the odds against her, training all her life for just this opportunity.

Off to the side were some metal columns with chains attached, the kind of moveable obstacle that could shut off a doorway or help channel a crowd into a line.

She freed a length of chain about two yards long. Winding a couple of feet around her wrist, she let four feet swing loose beneath her hand.

Bayang would have liked to take her proper form to battle Badik, but she still had her other mission to keep in mind. When Badik was stopped, perhaps there would be a chance to arrange an accident for her prey. After all, sometimes friends fell rather than foes during the excitement of a battle. She could not kill the hatchling in her true form because humans mustn't learn that her people had agents and assassins operating in the human cities; it was important that his death not be traced back to her people. But the hatchling could wait. She had more important accounts to settle.

She straightened up, shoulders no longer hunched, head up and eyes on fire. Twirling the loose length of chain above her, she strode forward to battle Badik just as her family had many years ago.

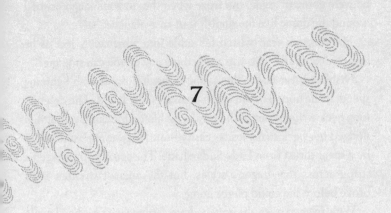

7

Scirye

Angrily, Scirye chased after the brown-haired boy who had stopped in front of the shattered case with the throwing stars. "This is no place for you," she ordered, pulling at Leech's arm. "You'll just get in the way."

"Playtime's over," Leech snapped at her, "so take your costume and get lost. Leave this to people who know how to fight."

The boy was holding one of the stars like a spiked baseball.

Scirye gave a snort of disgust. "You don't even know how to use one of those," she snapped, and plucked one from the half dozen in his other hand. "You hold it by the tip." She held up the star between her index finger and thumb as Nishke had shown her. She had done well in practice, but she wondered how she would fare in real combat.

Leech's face grew stormy as he snatched it back. He looked as if he were going to argue, but froze when the dragon's laugh echoed around the dome like the rumbling of an avalanche.

The dragon's scar twisted his smile into a menacing leer as he leaned downward. "Do you really think any of you can stop me?"

Nishke's spear was a blur as she thrust it upward with lightning speed. If she hoped to catch him unawares, she failed. The dragon's long neck writhed out of the way as he hissed mockingly and then dodged her back swing just as easily—until he was almost impaled by a spear thrust from Lady Sudarshane. The spear point gouged a stripe across the dragon's scales, but the ancient wooden shaft broke before she could pierce home.

With an angry hiss, the dragon dove, feinting with his head while he struck with his claws, snapping the old wooden shaft as if it were a straw. Lady Sudarshane held the broken spear shaft like a club to defend herself.

The dragon dropped through the air again, paw upraised to smash Lady Sudarshane when Nishke darted in front of her mother and stabbed upward with her spear.

The dragon screamed in pain as he retreated upward, blood dripping from his paw; as he climbed to safety, the tip of his long tail flicked Nishke to the side.

Scirye shed her clumsy cloak. Then, with Kles still flying over-head, she ran over to her sister. Though hurting, Nishke handed Scirye the spear. "Mother needs this."

Inside, Scirye wanted to run away, but she knew that the true answer was not escape but Tumarg: to move forward straight into the violent, bloody confusion. So, with a nod, Scirye took it and raced into the heart of the battle. Even as the dragon rose to the ceiling, the gray dragonflies—that was the only thing Scirye could call the horrors—swooped downward past him, leathery wings pulled in tight, their claws stretched out to gouge and tear.

The museum guards, including the troll, were shifting their feet as if they were having second thoughts about staying. The Pippalanta and Kushan staff, however, were standing their ground.

"*Yashe! Yashe!*" they shouted defiantly as they thrust. "Honor! Honor!"

Several more spear and halberd shafts broke, but others remained true and whole. The metal blades forged by Kushan weapons-makers served their descendants well.

Terrified but determined, the girl dodged about until she reached her mother. Lady Sudarshane was standing with the spear shaft raised like a club.

She threw away the broken spear as she took the one from Scirye. "Thank you," she said with her usual manners. "Now duck, dear!"

One of the gray dragonflies dropped toward them. Deadly claws sliced toward them both. When her mother parried, sparks flew as the blades met the talons.

As Scirye crouched, she could hear the dragonfly panting, smell the hot stench of its breath, feel the wind raised by its beating wings. Though her mother was using all her strength, the spear blade was being forced slowly backward. It was an unequal contest between a single human and a beast with four sets of talons.

Frightened, Scirye forced herself to look upward, past her mother's straining face to the hideous gray dragonfly. The eyes glowed a brilliant red like burning coals and the mouth was drawn back in a hideous leer as saliva dripped from the sharp fangs.

Suddenly golden stars twirled overhead, their points flickering with light. *Thunk! Thunk! Thunk!* With a screech, the dragonfly flapped upward, blood streaming from wounds where the throwing stars had embedded themselves. More stars leaped from Primo's hands. And then even more from Leech and Koko, and for a moment all four dragonflies flew higher.

But the victory was short-lived.

The ruthless dragon grasped its own injured ally in its claws and then broke its wings. As the serpent shrieked in pain, the dragon flung it downward toward the man named Primo and the two boys.

Primo had enough time to throw himself against Leech and Koko and knock them to the side before the still writhing dragonfly fell on top of him. The floor shook and then buckled under the impact. As the dust settled there was no sign of the man, only the now dead serpentine carcass.

The three surviving serpents circled cautiously now that they were aware that these were no easy prey.

"Now go," Lady Sudarshane said to her daughter as she kept a wary eye on their enemies.

Scirye swallowed. She would have liked nothing better than to escape this deadly chaos, but she couldn't desert her mother and sister. "No. You need every defender you can get."

Prince Etre was bleeding from a cut on his cheek and his gray mustache was now tan with dust. "She's safer here with us than trying to cross the room by herself now," he said. From his belt, he pulled out a stiletto and held it out to Scirye. Jewels gleamed on the golden hilt, but the blade looked deadly enough. "I can assure you that this is more than decorative," he said. "Guard our backs, child."

Her mother stepped to the side. "Then inside the circle with you," she said.

Scirye slipped into the center of the tight ring formed by the Pippalanta and other Kushana as well as the museum guards, and her mother resumed her post.

From overhead, they heard hissing, spitting, and cursing as the dragon tried to force the three suviving dragonflies to attack again. It was only when the dragon lashed out with his claws and tail that one of them dove.

Scirye's stomach did flip-flops as she watched the serpent shriek down toward her, but she gripped the dagger tightly.

The Pippalanta shouted their war cry and the museum guards did their best to imitate them. Spear heads stabbed upward and the dragonfly hung in the air, snapping its jaws in frustration. Strings of saliva dripped from its mouth as its claws struck at the tormenting blades.

A museum guard cried out as the saliva touched his sleeve. The cloth began to smoke as he dropped to his knees.

"Its saliva is poisonous," Lady Sudarshane warned.

Another guard darted away from the circle. As he ran, he threw his halberd away.

"Get back in formation," Lady Sudarshane ordered him, for that had left a gap in the circle. Bravely Scirye stepped into the space.

Instantly, the dragonfly dove, talons scything the runaways down like weeds as he swept on toward Scirye. She clutched the stiletto as the dragonfly bore down on her. He was coming so fast! He seemed to be all fangs and claws.

With a scream like a griffin ten times his size, Kles darted straight at him like a furred and feathered lightning bolt. The gray dragonfly's claws whistled toward the pest, but Kles nimbly slipped under them. The next moment he was staring right at the monster's snarling face.

The little griffin did not hesitate but raked its enemy's eyes. Blinded, the giant dragonfly twisted frantically in the air as it tried to hit him. Kles, though, was as agile as a mosquito, dodging the blows as he struck its head with beak and claws. And Scirye felt her heart almost burst with pride and love, for he was her griffin and he was fighting to save her.

Finally, screeching in frustration and unable to see, the dragonfly smashed into the floor, skidding over the tiles and tossing chairs to the side in its wake.

Kles might have been trained for the niceties of court etiquette, but once again his primitive ancestry drowned out all other thought. His beak opened in the age-old scream that generations of his kind had used and he shot across the room for his opponent's exposed throat. The big vein pulsed, drawing him like a magnet. He didn't notice the injured dragonfly's claws waiting to strike him when he attacked.

Scirye started to run toward him. "Kles, come back! It's a trap!"

Her mother glanced fearfully after her daughter and then too late up above her when she heard the shrieks. A third dragonfly had seized its chance and was diving toward Scirye's unprotected back.

Stars and then spears rose into the air but the wounds only increased its rage, and the creature did not slow at all.

"Scirye!" her mother screamed.

The girl turned around in time to see the huge mouth bearing down on her, fangs ready to tear her apart.

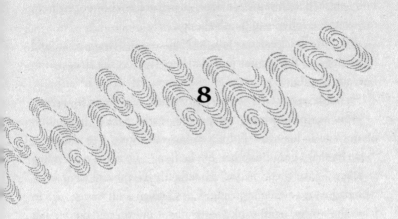

8

Bayang

Bayang had seen the foolhardy Kushan girl leave the protection of the circle to chase after her lap griffin. As the winged attacker dove, the girl raised a stiletto but she was trembling so much that the point wavered. She looked like a sparrow trying to fight off a falcon.

Bayang flung the chain through the air so that it wound around one of the monster's forelegs. Then, standing with her legs spread, she tugged with all her might. She had no hope of dragging the large attacker to the floor, but it was just enough to break its descent.

It flapped its wings frantically, screeching in anger, as it tried to free itself. The desperate girl thrust upward clumsily, the blade biting into its hind leg. The next moment a tall Pippal whipped a halberd through the air, burying the blade in the beast's chest. The gray body crashed against the tile floor, an evil green ichor oozing from the wound as it began to thrash about wildly.

When the flying creature fell, the chain was still wrapped around its foreleg and Bayang was pulled off her feet. As she struggled to rise, she heard the last flier descending toward her for revenge.

So, she thought, *this is how everything ends—I've failed my people.*

From out of nowhere, her prey appeared next to her with a golden star in his hand. For a moment, she thought he was going to jab its sharp points into her, but he flung it up at the descending attacker. "Take that!" he yelled defiantly. His throw went wild, whizzing a yard away the creature's head. Even so, it was enough to make the winged beast bank away from the unexpected danger and straight into a hedge of the defenders' spears.

It shrieked as it twisted about, impaled on a half dozen spear heads.

Bayang straightened up. Dust matted her hair and clothes. "You saved me," she said in shock. From the legends, she had believed her prey to be a vicious killer, not someone who would risk his own life to rescue a stranger.

"Of course." He flashed a disarming grin at her. "We're on the same side."

She stood in confusion. He wasn't acting like the evil monster of the legends who killed with such casual cruelty. While she was trying to decide if he was attempting to lull her into a false sense of security, he did something even more shocking: He turned his back on her!

As her prey craned his neck, searching for the next target, it would have been so easy to snap his neck and then rejoin the battle against Badik, but Bayang prided herself on being a warrior first and last. In carrying out her assassinations, she had never struck her targets from behind.

However, even if her assigned prey faced her again, tradition now demanded the opposite of duty. Her people lived by a complex code of honor but at its core was one basic tenet as old as her race: If someone saved your life, you must repay the debt. And her prey had just placed her under an obligation that was far older and more imperative than the elders' commands.

She could not kill her prey until she had repaid him. And then what? Once the debt was settled, once the scale of obligations was balanced, was she going to take the life she had just saved? That seemed too absurd.

What was she to do now?

9

Scirye

Heart thumping, Scirye turned from the woman and the boys to see Kles flying overhead, screaming defiance. His opponent lay dead with a bloody throat. Somehow he must have evaded the trap and carried out his attack.

"Stand back-to-back," Nishke ordered.

Scirye had been staring in horrified fascination at the dying dragonfly, but her sister's words woke her as if from a nightmare. She turned and pressed her back against her sister's when there was a gigantic crash.

Even shatterproof glass could not stand up to a dragon's tail. Everyone was hunching as bits of glass flew from the case that held Lady Tabiti.

As the dragon hovered, it reached a foreleg into the case. "I've got it!" With a cry of triumph, he held up the archer's ring clutched between his claws. "There's no stopping me now!"

And then, with a vengeful malice, the dragon brought his tail down upon the Jade Lady herself. Jade rectangles and gold wire flew in all directions as the dragon pounded the fragile body into dust.

"No!" Nishke cried.

While everyone else's eyes had been upon the dragon, Nishke had been the only one to charge forward. Desperately she raised the halberd over her head to fend off the thief.

With an evil laugh, the dragon swung his tail so that the heavy column of bone and muscle struck her, tossing her backward like a doll.

Still laughing, the dragon flapped his wings so that clouds of dust flew everywhere as he flew toward the domed ceiling.

He struck the shatterproof panes with his huge paws and his mouth bellowed magical spells that made the listener's hair stand on end. Finally, the glass broke in a rain of crystal shards and the magical wards dissolved.

With a cry of triumph, the dragon's massive body soared through the hole and into the sky.

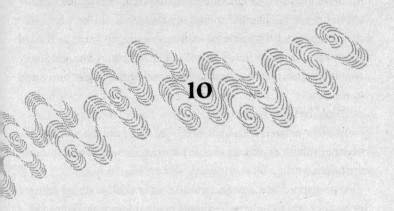

Scirye

Kles circled through the dusty air, the battle rage ebbing away, leaving only the taste of pulverized concrete thick in his mouth. The light flickered wildly as primitive fire elementals, their brains no bigger than gnats, darted about in the air from their broken homes. Voices moaned and a man was whimpering.

When Kles spotted his mistress, her face was white as chalk as she knelt besides her fallen mother. She had retrieved her discarded cloak and folded it into a pillow for her mother, who was unconscious but still breathing.

When the griffin settled upon Scirye's shoulder, he felt her body still shivering with anger and fear. So he wrapped himself lovingly about the back of her neck, crooning to her as he rubbed his soft feathered cheek against hers.

When she had made her mother comfortable, Scirye turned toward her sister. Nishke lay crumpled against a wall like a broken doll. Her eyes stared blankly, never blinking.

Scirye got up to go to her but saw Prince Etre. A banner proclaiming the glories of the Kushan Empire dangled down from one end just above his head. He was making no effort to stanch the blood flowing from his shoulder, but was staring with a vacant look instead at the shattered case where the Jade Lady had once rested. The other survivors also sat in shock within the wreckage. No one was doing anything. They might as well have been statues.

Scirye glanced at Lady Sudarshane, who was breathing softly. Her mother was the one who always made things right; since she was unconscious, Scirye would have to try her best to take her mother's place. And she knew what her mother would say: Their family always put others before themselves.

So Scirye forced herself to rise to her feet. Half in a daze, she walked as slowly and stiffly as a zombie. Her boots crunched across broken glass and shattered antiques until she reached a Pippal who was lying down, gazing at the blood streaming from a gash in her arm.

Tearing off a strip of cloth from the hem of her tunic and with a piece of broken spear shaft, Scirye fastened a rude tourniquet above the injury. When she twisted the wood, the flow stopped. From far away, she could already hear the sound of ambulances rushing to the museum. This would do until they came.

When Scirye tried to speak, her first words came out as a croak so she made herself swallow. "Can you move?" she asked the Pippal.

When the Pippal nodded, Scirye used the same commanding tone her mother used when she wanted Scirye to do something without any argument from Scirye. "Then take care of Prince Etre."

To Scirye's relief, the Pippal dipped her head respectfully and got up to do what she had been told. The girl went among the

Kushana and the museum guards, rousing those with minor injuries to tend to those who were worse off. To Scirye's surprise, they all obeyed.

Finally, she reached the two boys. They had braced their feet while they tried to shove the fallen monster off of their friend. Despite their best efforts, the monster's corpse didn't move at all. There was no sign of the man and Scirye was sure he could not have survived the crushing impact.

The brown-haired boy was panting as he pushed, calling out "Primo!" over and over. He ignored the blood pouring from the cut on his cheek.

Scirye grabbed the larger boy's shoulder. "Stop your friend's bleeding."

The larger boy spread out his arms in frustration. "I've tried. Leech won't let me."

The brown-haired boy looked furiously over his shoulder at them. "Koko, we have to save Primo!"

Scirye was finding it hard to control her own hysterical grief. She grabbed hold of the frantic smaller boy and shook him. "You have to take care of your injury or you'll hurt yourself worse. That's what Primo would want."

The boy stood stunned, as if she were speaking a foreign language. Taking advantage of the lull, Scirye tore a strip from her sleeve and pressed it against his wound. Luckily it did not seem to be very deep and the pressure stopped the bleeding. He stared at her with a sorrow so great that it made her forget her own losses for a moment. "Here. Hold this."

He let her guide his hand to the temporary bandage. When she let go of him, he burst into tears. "He gave his life for us."

His words renewed her own fears. "So did many others," she said.

Checking the gallery, the girl saw that the rescue effort was well under way. The severely injured were being taken care of and made comfortable. They no longer needed her.

Now came the moment she had been dreading. Pivoting, she headed over to Nishke.

Her sister's eyes, which had once danced with such life, were now dull. Her face was a mask of anger and despair.

Hoping against hope, Scirye knelt and took her sister's wrist to feel for a pulse. She waited a minute. Then two. Then three. Then she stopped counting.

She wished with all her heart that Nishke would suddenly smile and tell her gullible little sister that she had fallen for yet another prank. But Scirye knew that Nishke never would. The girl's shoulders sagged as she gently placed Nishke's wrist over her stomach. Then she closed her sister's eyes.

Scirye faced Nanaia. The goddess's statue had become twisted around somehow during the battle so that she tilted at an angle, staring sorrowfully at the carnage.

In her lower right hand, Nanaia grasped a scepter with a flowering head to symbolize the power she had over the dead, for the same earth that gave its bounty to the living also embraced the dead. Nanaia the Peaceful also granted eternal sleep and renewal.

Scirye asked the goddess to grant her sister peace, but as she used what remained of her sleeve to clean the dust from her sister's face, Scirye knew that Nishke could have no rest until the dragon was killed and the ring recovered.

Kles straightened upon his mistress's shoulder as he folded his wings and brought his forepaws respectfully together. "It was the way she would have wanted to die," he said, "keeping faith with her duty."

"I was looking at her just before the monster fell on her. I saw her face, Kles. Nishke thought she had *failed*." The realization made Scirye double over as if a knife had stabbed her.

The girl rocked back and forth for a moment as she covered her ears. "And I can still hear that dragon mocking her." She shook her head violently as if trying to toss the sound out of her memory. And inside her, she could feel the anger swelling until she thought she would burst.

Nishke could not recover the ring. She could not restore the honor of the Pippalanta or her family. Well, then, Scirye would just have to do it for her. For all of them.

Scirye turned to Nanaia yet again. Sometimes she was the Kind and sometimes the Peaceful. But her upper left hand clutched a bow, for when the laws of Kindness and Peace were broken, Nanaia became the Hunter. Terrible, unforgiving, and above all relentless until she had exacted her revenge.

And now Scirye's heart asked the goddess for a second boon: *Make me like you until I've punished the dragon*, the girl prayed. *I don't care what happens to me afterward.*

A breeze blew in from the broken skylight, brushing the dust before it. Scirye's eyes followed the little white cloud along the floor until it stopped against the wall just beneath the flying carpet.

Was it a sign or a coincidence? Whichever it was, she knew deep in her heart that this was Tumarg. Afraid, yet determined, the girl rose and walked toward a corner of the room.

"Where are you going?" Kles asked as he adjusted to her getting up.

"I wanted to be a warrior," Scirye said. Angrily, she remembered Leech's harsh words to her. "Well, pretending *is* for children. There's only one thing to do."

"This is no time to do something wild," Kles said.

"If my ancestors hadn't been a little wild, they couldn't have fought their way across a wilderness and taken an empire," Scirye said as her eyes searched the room.

"That was all very fine for a band of refugees, but it's completely out of place in 1941," Kles argued.

Energy suddenly surged through Scirye, warm and electric. She went over to the goddess, and with a bow to Nanaia, picked up the halberd that Nishke had tried to use in her last desperate attack. Scirye thought the shaft was still warm from her sister's hands. It was so heavy that she dragged the shaft behind her until she reached the old flying carpet still hanging within its gold frame.

"You don't know how to fly," Kles objected.

"When we were at the Paris embassy, I rode a griffin," Scirye countered. The Kushan ambassador there had been fond of flying about the city on his griffin, to the delight of the Parisians. As a bribe for behaving at an important reception, Lady Sudarshane had gotten the ambassador to reward Scirye with a ride.

"Only in the embassy courtyard," Kles pointed out, "and no more than a meter up. A carousel horse could have taken you even farther above the ground."

She had, indeed, only gone about in circles, but even so . . . "It still counts," Scirye insisted, and shifted her grip on the shaft so that she was gripping it near the halberd blade.

Kles gave a startled cry and flapped away from her as Scirye swung the halberd up clumsily. The gauntlet was still on her hand and she held it up to protect her eyes as her other hand swung the halberd against the glass.

The tempered glass cracked but did not break, crystalline lines spreading across the surface.

"That's a priceless antique!" Kles gasped as he hovered near her.

"I need it to go after that dragon." Scirye struck furiously at the glass over and over until it finally shattered into small bits.

The brown-haired boy called Leech had come over to see what she was doing. His wound had stopped bleeding but blood had smeared with the dust so that his face had become a gruesome mask.

"That rug'll never fly," he said.

He was just so typical of the brash, overconfident idiots in school that she did not even bother glaring at him. "It did once," she countered. From past experiences, she knew it would be a waste of time to try to correct someone who was as happy wallowing in ignorance as a pig in mud. So rather than explaining more, she went on hacking the carpet from the frame with the halberd blade. The old, brittle threads broke easily and the carpet was curling down on her before she realized it.

She was surprised when she glimpsed another pair of hands catching the top of the rug before it could engulf her. Leech said nothing as he helped her lower it to the floor.

Koko was wiping the grit from his face with his handkerchief as he came over. "The girlie's gone cuckoo."

Kles snapped his beak haughtily. "You will address the Lady Scirye properly and keep your insults to yourself."

"Calling her a lady doesn't make her one." Koko smirked. "And she's still crazy."

"Shut up, Koko," Leech said, but he seemed to share the opinion because there was pity in his eyes as she spread the carpet on the glass-covered floor.

Scirye did her best to ignore them. "Can you read the spell, Kles?" she asked her griffin.

Kles had earned the knowledge painfully enough after all the pecks from the eyrie keeper. "Yes," he said as he settled again on her shoulder, "at least I think I can. But is there any point in trying to talk you out of this?"

"No."

"I didn't think so," the griffin said regretfully. "Then we'll need a small bit of your life flow."

Scirye cut a finger of her free hand with the stiletto Prince Etre had given her and squeezed a ruby drop out onto the fingertip. "What next?" she asked, holding her finger poised over the rug.

"This is madness." Kles sighed. But he pointed a claw at the upper left corner. "Let the carpet drink there. And then say the words after me."

Scirye was startled when she touched the spot and felt the carpet almost kiss her finger. The gold threads around her fingertip began to burn with an inner fire.

"*Ytarte yentantse,*" Kles began in the Old Tongue.

When Scirye repeated the words, the carpet's edges began to flutter slightly. Within the center, the image of Oado, the god of the wind, seemed to waken as if from a long slumber.

Koko sidled in close to his friend and whispered, "Let's go." He looked about the room and then said conspiratorially, "We'll cram what we can into our pockets and put the blame on the dragon and his buddies."

Leech shook his head. "I'd feel too rotten inside if I ran away now. If she can get this thing to fly, I'm going with her."

Scirye shook her head. "You'll only get in my way."

"The dragon killed my friend, Primo," Leech said. "Primo saved our lives. I never knew anyone so kind as him."

Scirye saw the determined look on his face. Just like her, he had a purpose now. A hunger for revenge was so much better than wallowing in their earlier despair. Whether he knew it or not, he had given himself over to the goddess so, for Nanaia's sake, she would have to put up with him.

She pointed to the shattered window on a nearby display. "Then get the throwing axes. They won't travel as far as the stars, but they'll do more damage when they hit."

He nodded patronizingly. "Not a bad idea."

Koko followed Leech over there and watched as his friend reached carefully through the window and took out six of the small gleaming axes, the rubies and diamonds on the shafts gleaming as they caught the light momentarily.

"Okay, okay," Koko said desperately, "I'm sorry about Primo, too, but this won't bring him back. Let's just take the axes and get out of here." He seemed disappointed when Leech stuck them in his belt and headed back for the rug. "There's nothing you can do against that monster."

"We can try," the girl said grimly as she took a pair of axes and slung them in her belt.

Leech stared at Koko challengingly. "We've always had one rule: No one hurts one of us. If they do, we get even. Well, Primo was our friend."

Koko looked yearningly at the exit but his eyes came back to his friend. "I knew you were trouble when I saw you in that alley just after you ran away from the orphanage. I should have left you there."

"Why didn't you?" Leech asked.

"Because I felt sorry for you. You were shivering and scared of your own shadow. So I broke my own rule about thinking of my own skin first." Koko tugged at his hair. "And now I'm going to do it again." Disgusted with himself, Koko picked up an axe, too. "Argh, I'm such a moron."

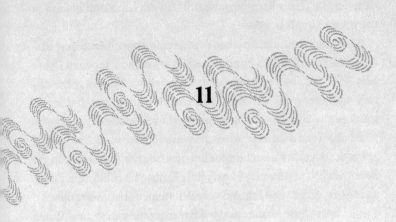

11

Bayang

Bayang trembled with rage and frustration as she watched her enemy escape. Her hatred for Badik was so deep, she felt it in the very marrow of her bones.

Get a hold of yourself, she scolded herself fiercely. *Mindless fury won't help your people. Badik is gone so think about what to do about the remaining target.*

She took several deep breaths, rejecting all emotion and focusing on the hard facts as she had trained herself to do.

Her prey had saved her, a complete stranger, and later had been so heartbroken when his bodyguard had died. These were not the actions of a heartless monster who murdered brutally and wrecked so many innocent lives. Instead, he had shown a hatchlinglike trust when he had turned his back on her. She found it touching that, despite all his hardships, he still had the same kind of faith of the young: simple but deep.

Many believed that a person could improve with each new lifetime. She found herself hoping that was what had happened to her prey—the cycle of deaths and rebirths slowly washing away the callous murderer from his soul like dirt stains from a shirt. If that was true and she killed him, who would be the real monster then?

As she wound the discarded chain around her waist, she looked about the wreckage, searching for her prey. She saw him sitting on the floor with his friend and the bossy little Kushan hatchling. They were all looking very scared but also very determined about something.

The bossy little Kushan noticed Bayang at the same time. "When my mother wakes up," she called to Bayang, "please tell her that I've gone after the dragon."

The dragon? Bayang stared at the hatchlings skeptically. *Had they all taken knocks to their heads during the battle?* Then she noticed the rug for the first time. Its edges were rippling, curling, and then straightening out as if it were alive. The Kushan hatchling must be of the Old Blood and either she or her griffin could read the Old Tongue.

Bayang had thought there was only one flying carpet left in the world and she had flown on it several times while on a mission in disguise in the New Persian Empire. The secret of their creation had been lost centuries in the past, and since then no one had been able to figure out the complicated process of simultaneously casting the complex spells as the threads were woven.

This one might have flown when it was new, but slashed from its golden frame and lying on the floor, the threadbare rug looked more like trash than a valuable antique. She was sure that it would fall apart at the first attempt at flight, but even if it held together by some miracle, these hatchlings had no idea of the trouble they were getting themselves into. Carpet flying was not for amateurs.

Of course, one way or another that would eliminate her prey and solve her problem. However, Bayang prided herself that when she carried out a mission, no harm came to bystanders even if they might be as obnoxious as the Kushan hatchling.

She strode over to them, gesturing for them to stand up. "That old antique won't take the strain of a chase. It'll fall apart in no time." She deliberately added, "*Little* girl."

The young Kushan's head jerked up as if Bayang had poked her with a sharp stick. "I fought just as hard as you did." She paused as irritation and manners warred with one another. In the end, politeness won out. "But thank you for distracting that monster." The Kushan hatchling's shrewd eyes studied Bayang. "San Francisco certainly breeds muscular little old ladies."

Her prey nodded. "You swung that chain like a piece of rope."

Bayang took a breath and fought down her panic. The important thing was to keep her actual identity from her target.

"My name is Bayang Naga," Bayang said. "I'm with the Pinkerton Agency, Special Operator for the Magical Division." Somehow her purse had managed to stay strapped to her shoulder. She snapped it open now and took out her wallet, flipping it open to show the fake badge.

It was a magical object that became whatever she needed. If she had called herself a Canadian Mountie, the badge would have become that. She could also have been an Interpol detective, a chicken inspector, or any one of a dozen other professions and with an equal number of false identities. However, since she didn't expect to be with the children long, she used her own name since that would reduce possible mistakes.

Together, the hatchlings stared at the shiny gold badge and then her prey's friend swung his gaze up toward her. "So you're in disguise."

"That's right," Bayang said, relieved that the fake badge seemed to be holding up.

"The Pinkertons have a magical division?" the Kushan hatchling asked.

"We don't operate openly, but then usually neither do magical criminals, so we like to operate behind the scenes," Bayang explained. "I was sent here as backup."

"How come no one warned the consular staff?" the Kushan hatchling demanded.

"I don't know. You'll have to ask whoever hired the agency," Bayang ad-libbed quickly.

The Kushan upstart gave an amused sniff. "Well, I'll repay you somehow after we get back."

Bayang opened her mouth in astonishment, unable to believe any hatchling could be so mad. "I'm trying to save your life again. Only an idiot would try to fly this"—she waved a hand as she tried to find the right term—"this overgrown rag."

The little twit stuck out her chin defiantly. "They hurt my mother and killed my sister. The carpet only has to hold together long enough to let me get even. So I don't have any use for advice like yours if it's just excuses to do nothing."

"I couldn't stay here either," her prey said, sitting down behind her. "They murdered my friend."

"And me, I'm just a fool," Koko said, plopping down on the rug.

Bayang made a frustrated sound at the back of her throat. Why did the Kushan and her prey have to remind her about debts?

Until she had repaid her prey for saving her life, she would have to accompany him. Anyway, it suited her own purposes to pursue Badik, as well. If she saved her prey's life during the hunt, well, she would wait until that happened before she worried about what to do about him.

Motioning the hatchlings to back away from the head of the carpet, Bayang said, "All right then, move back. I owe the boy my life."

The Kushan hatchling stayed where she was. "Are you of the Old Blood?"

"No," Bayang said, "and I know only a smattering of the Old Tongue. But that's enough to provide something that you'll really need."

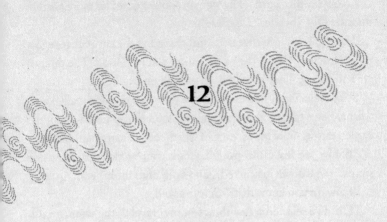

12

Scirye

"Touch there," the little elderly woman commanded. Her shoulders were no longer stooped and her back hunched. Instead she was standing as straight as a Pippal with a fierce look in her eyes.

"Why?" Scirye demanded suspiciously.

The woman raised one eyebrow in a superior attitude. "Have you thought about how you're going to hold on when you're maneuvering that rag hundreds of feet above the ground?"

Scirye hesitated, reluctant to give this Miss Know-It-All any satisfaction, but Kles tapped her. "Go ahead. It's better to damage your pride rather than your head."

Doubtfully, Scirye squeezed her finger until a drop of blood balled on its tip, then traced an ornate curlicue woven into the carpet's design.

"Now say this word." The woman spoke a word far more ancient than the Old Tongue. "*Dherkik*."

"*Dherkik*," Scirye repeated, and gasped as the curlicue rose in a loop. Reaching down, the woman tugged at it. "Good. The threads are still strong. They should hold our weight."

Scirye reluctantly had to admit that this woman might really know what she was talking about, so she and the stranger paced about the carpet, raising more loops, each of which the woman tested carefully.

"Before we leave the ground, hook your ankles through these straps," the woman instructed, "and hold onto the others."

"How do you know that?" Scirye asked.

"Oh, I've learned a few things in my travels," the woman said, bumping into Scirye when they both tried to sit at the head of the carpet.

Scirye didn't like how the stranger was assuming command of *her* expedition. "It's my carpet." The girl glowered.

The woman put an exasperated fist on her hip. "But I've actually flown one. Have you?"

Kles tugged at her ear. "Let her try. She's proved she's on our side, and she knew about the loops."

Reluctantly, Scirye stepped back and plopped down on Leech's left. The woman supervised them as they set their ankles through a pair of loops and gripped the long steering loops like the reins of a horse.

From the epic poems Scirye had read, she knew it was only proper to introduce herself to her fighting companions. As scared and angry as she was, she also felt a little thrill at having her own adventure.

"My name is Scirye and this is Kles, my lap griffin," Scirye began, nodding to Kles, who sat on her shoulder.

"Oh," Koko said, "is that what that thing is."

Kles bristled. "I am not a thing, you fat toad."

Scirye pulled at his leg. "You're the one who's always reminding me to mind my manners," she scolded.

"My name's Leech," the smaller boy said and jerked a thumb at the bigger, chubbier boy. "And this is Koko."

"He's the brawn and I'm the brains," Koko added.

"We'll need both before we're done," the woman said curtly. "Say the spell."

Kles haltingly read the long forgotten words. But at first nothing happened.

Relieved, Koko began to slip his ankle from a loop. "See, the sign was right—Hey!"

The front of the carpet jerked into the air and then lowered itself again. Kles read the spell more confidently now. This time the carpet rose, bucking and twisting like a living thing, tossing Scirye and the others against the straps.

"Easy," Koko yelped, hastily securing his ankle.

"It's not like I'm flying a dirigible, you know," Bayang shot back. "Carpets have wills of their own."

She strained at the steering loops as they almost crashed into a wall, banking sharply to the left.

Scirye had had her doubts about the ankle loops, which she expected to be as weak and frayed as much of the carpet, so she was grateful that they felt as strong as they still were.

She watched the opposite wall rushing toward them, but in the last few seconds, the woman managed to level the carpet off and sent it circling the gallery.

"See, there's nothing to it," Bayang declared triumphantly.

As if annoyed, the carpet suddenly sagged in the middle so that Scirye bumped against Leech.

Angrily, Bayang grabbed the fringe of the rug as if it were hair. "Behave yourself," she commanded the carpet, "or I'll hand you over to the moths."

The carpet flattened out—though it rippled defiantly when they least expected it.

With a tug at the steering loops, Bayang sent the carpet spiraling upward toward the jagged hole in the skylight.

13

Bayang

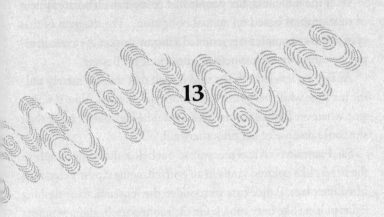

As they shot through the jagged hole in the skylight, Bayang's prey let out a whoop of excitement, as if he were having the time of his life.

"I've always wanted to fly! I dream about it almost every night," her prey exclaimed happily. "This is wonderful."

What am I doing? she asked herself. *I'm not supposed to be teaching him to enjoy flying again. I should've killed him and left in the confusion.*

Even now, it would be so easy to arrange an accident up here. But she couldn't. Not after her prey had saved her life.

Why did he have to complicate what should have been a simple assassination? she complained to herself. *In the old days, prey knew their place. They didn't save their hunters in the middle of a pursuit.*

Over the millennia, her people had created an elaborate system of relationships based on mutual obligations. The diagram of that system was so complex it resembled a thorny thicket. As a result, repaying a debt was as instinctive as breathing for Bayang.

As Bayang leveled off, she told herself that she was merely biding her time while her primary mission had changed. Now it was to stop whatever Badik's scheme was. Once she had taken care of that, she could dispose of her prey afterward.

San Francisco's civic center spread out below them, the people in the streets like colored knots in an ever-changing tapestry that now filled the plaza. Police cars surrounded the museum, their flashing lights pulsing like fiery rubies. On the rooftop itself, gnome janitors gaped at them with scrub brushes in their hands, having momentarily forgotten their job of cleaning the pigeons' mementoes from the balustrades—a task that guaranteed eternal employment since the pigeons simply shifted to the areas the gnomes had already cleaned.

"Where are they?" asked her prey. Bayang sighed inwardly to herself. This was awkward, wasn't it? She supposed she had better adjust her labels and temporarily call him by name—Leech.

In the back of her mind, there was a small worm of doubt now. She could kill prey as long as they were just hateful things. It would be harder to murder someone she knew. When the time came to resume her original mission, would she be able to?

In the last century, humans and magical creatures alike had packed San Francisco's hills and valleys. Naturally, when they built their homes, they had constructed structures like the ones they had left behind in the old country. Minarets competed with pagodas for the title of the tallest building, stolid emporiums stood across the street from canvas-roofed bazaars. The sheer volume of noise, color, and smells was known to overcome the unprepared tourist and guidebooks advised visitors to acclimate themselves for a couple of days before venturing very far into the city.

Bayang, the griffin, Leech, and—she cursed herself in exasperation, she might as well use the wretched hatchling's name as well—Scirye scanned the surroundings. From the groans, her prey's friend, Koko, seemed to be sick.

"There!" Scirye said.

Bayang's people prided themselves on their keen eyesight but the girl's was far sharper. *Perhaps,* Bayang thought, *she gets it from generations of desert dwellers.*

The girl leaned forward so that her hand was pointing over Bayang's shoulder toward the northeast. Finally, Bayang picked out the speck that was Badik flapping toward the skyscrapers along Montgomery Street in the heart of the business district.

She felt anger surge through her. She had waited centuries to settle this debt with Badik.

"Hold on," Bayang said, and banked the carpet so sharply that the Kushan's pet griffin was thrown from her shoulder.

"Oog." Koko made gulping noises as if he was trying to hold back his breakfast, but the girl let out an exhilarated whoop that Leech echoed.

"Is this also your first time flying?" Leech asked her as the wind whistled about them.

"No," the girl said. "My mother's last post was at the embassy in Istanbul, and the ambassador maintained his own stable of griffins," she explained. "He took me for a flight on one. I loved it."

Bayang glanced over her shoulder to see the girl's hair streaming wildly behind her. She was grinning.

"I'm surprised someone of the Old Blood is in the consular corps," Bayang said. "I've heard Kushan nobility are famous for their pride and don't like to mix with 'commoners.'"

"The Old Blood belongs to my father's side," the girl explained.

"And his is so diluted that we have only a distant claim to the lion throne."

Knowing how murderous Kushan politics could be, Bayang reflected that perhaps that was the reason why the girl and her family were still alive.

The hatchlings' enthusiasm must have pleased the carpet because it seemed more responsive to Bayang's commands. Having tamed it, Bayang thought they could risk going faster.

"Lean forward," she ordered. "It will cut down on resistance from the air. And hold on tight."

She had been eying the flagstaffs on buildings of various heights, trying to judge the best winds. The one she wanted was a bit lower than she would have liked, but she angled into it. It caught the carpet, sweeping it along like a leaf on a stream.

They flew over the rooftops, barely skimming over the huge water tanks that would be used in case of fire. When they startled a flock of pigeons, for a moment they were surrounded by flapping gray and black scruffy bundles.

The small griffin shot over Bayang's head, aiming for the nearest bird.

"No, Kles!" Scirye commanded. "We don't have time for that."

The griffin flapped his wings to stay in place, his eyes fastened on the fleeing birds. His movements were stiff and jerky as if he were fighting his own instincts. "It's not like I was picking on them, you know. The pigeons here are vicious. They probably mug any lost tourist. Besides, I'm hungry. I would have shared."

Koko had turned an interesting shade of green. "How can you think about eating?"

As the carpet passed beneath him, the griffin dropped back down to join them. "If you throw up," Kles said unsympathetically, "remember not to face the wind."

"Yeah, Koko. You're the one who's been complaining about doing the same things lately," Leech said. "Enjoy it."

"Oog, and double oog," was all Koko could say.

The buildings in the business district were so tall that they acted like mountain ranges with the wind howling through the artificial canyons. Spires aimed at the sky like lances, while carvings of flowers, eagles, and grape vines decorated the buildings' shoulders. Granite, marble, and brass were everywhere.

As the carpet settled into one of the currents, the air seemed to come alive around Leech, whipping at his face and trying to tug him from the carpet, not even caring that bits of fringe and fabric were flaking off the rug's edges.

The carpet bucked and writhed now in the wind's grip, as if the rug were a saddle cloth on the back of a wild stallion. People on the upper floors of buildings looked up, startled from their desks as the carpet sped by.

"Hey, the carpet's getting warm," Leech said admiringly. "It comes with a heater. Those old-timers thought of everything."

"No," Bayang said in a worried voice. "The original spells woven into its threads were never designed for this speed."

"Keep going," Scirye urged. "We're closing the gap." Badik had grown in size from a speck to a bumblebee.

They streaked past an old building whose owners had used all of their triangular lot by creating a skyscraper with three sides and then filling the ledges and corners with scowling gargoyles.

From the corner of her eye, Bayang thought she saw one of them lean forward. "Did one of those things move?" She had just started to nod her head in that direction when a gargoyle rose on four legs and spread its wings. It was one of Badik's gray fliers, hidden among the statues. It had crouched down and remained still to set up this ambush. A little farther away on the ledge, another stood up.

They flung themselves downward, plunging with outstretched talons.

"Hold tight," Bayang warned and sent the carpet into a steep dive.

As the wind tore at them, the griffin lost his grip and was pulled free. With a squawk of protest, he disappeared behind them.

"Kles!" Scirye cried in alarm. She turned to see him flapping his wings frantically to catch up with them.

"Don't worry," Bayang said. "Those are Badik's creatures. It's not your griffin those things want."

"*That* doesn't help my peace of mind any," Koko moaned.

Flying on a carpet was not the same as flying in her true form. The carpet would be sluggish when it came to pulling out of a dive. And she had her passengers to think of, so she adjusted her tactics to fit the situation, trying to level off sooner than she would have liked.

The carpet tried to respond, but as Bayang feared, it was difficult. It took several frantic tugs at the steering loops before the rug flew horizontally again. They wound up much lower than Bayang had intended, skimming over the startled patrons in an outdoor café. A lizard waitress lashed her tail at them so violently that the tail itself detached and crashed into a buffet table.

"Sorry," Scirye called as they left the restaurant.

Bayang looked back. Their plunge had opened more distance between them and their pursuers, and Bayang flew over the tops of the cars, buses, and trucks waiting their turn to go as an air sprite hovered above the intersection, directing traffic with a glowing wand. As they zoomed past the sprite, the creature put his large lips together and blew a shrill, piercing whistle.

Bayang stared steadily ahead and downward of their path, steering around a truck loaded unusually high with crates . . . watching . . . waiting . . . as the diving monsters' shadows swelled in size. And in the meantime, Badik was getting farther and farther away.

"They're practically in our laps." Koko gulped.

Bayang banked to the left so suddenly that it threw them all in that direction. Only the straps saved them from falling, and Bayang fought to adjust for the sudden shift in weight. But she had timed it perfectly.

A monster screamed past the spot where they had been and smashed into the top of a bus with a reverberating thump. Brakes screeched and horns blared all over the street as vehicles swerved and fishtailed, causing more collisions.

Bayang straightened the carpet out over the sidewalk, but they were now so low that they knocked the hat off a man. Pedestrians threw themselves to the pavement to avoid them as she unwound the chain from her waist.

She whipped the chain out so that it wrapped about a streetlight, arm and wrist straining to hold onto it. The straps cut into her ankles as the carpet swung violently around. She just hoped they were strong enough to stand the maneuver or Bayang herself would go flying from the rug.

When they had spun 180 degrees, she tugged the chain free and then angled the carpet upward. They had come up behind the remaining monsters, who were now hovering over the gigantic traffic jam as they tried to spot their targets.

"I got a shot," Leech whispered excitedly.

Scirye said in a low voice, "No, don't throw that axe!"

"Yeah, that axe is worth a mint," Koko scolded.

"No rich, spoiled girl is going to boss me around," Leech said rebelliously.

"No," Scirye said, "I guess I'm standing in for your conscience."

She had such a natural authority that Leech found himself lowering the axe.

Bayang rose up slightly, twirling the chain over her head as they charged forward. Her aim was true and the chain wound itself about one monster, pinning its wings to its back. With a jerk, she sent the monster spinning to the street where it smashed into a windshield.

With a shriek of rage, the remaining monster shot toward them, talons spread, fangs prepared to rip and tear. There was no time to get the chain ready for another strike so she turned the carpet. It would have to be up to the hatchlings to defend them.

Leech swung and missed as the monster slipped agilely to the side so that the monster was now over Scirye. The horrible creature ripped a chunk out of the carpet's edge, flinging the disintegrating fragment away as it slashed at Scirye. Instinctively, the girl raised the leather gauntlet, and though the talons scratched marks on the tough fabric, they did not pierce it. But the force knocked her down against the carpet, her elbow causing another piece to flutter away.

With a shrill cry, the griffin plummeted out of the air and straight onto the monster's neck. The startled monster dropped several feet before it bounced upward again. Hissing and snarling, it tried to twist so it could reach its tormentor.

Scirye swung the axe as she sat back up. The steel blade flashed in the sun as it bit deep into the monster's chest. Green ichor gushed from the wound.

As the monster fell with a thud on the roof of a taxi, Kles flapped free, trilling in triumph before he settled again on Scirye's shoulder.

Scirye, though, didn't seem to share in her griffin's jubilation. She was no longer the angry Pippal bent on revenge. Instead, she sat, staring in shock at the green fluid slowly trickling down her still outstretched arm. Nor did the boys say anything, their bluster all evaporated by the deadly flight.

As Bayang steered the carpet away from the street, she was already scanning for her enemy, but there was no sign of him.

Behind her, Scirye said in a small voice, "I never killed anything before."

"Really?" she asked, keeping her eyes overhead. "You could have fooled me. You kept your head during the battle—just like a veteran warrior." But the praise didn't produce the smile the way it would have with a hatchling of Bayang's people. Instead, it upset the girl to the point of tears. Bayang had no experience comforting human hatchlings so she tried to change the conversation's course. "I mean," she said lamely, "I thought every Kushan hunted. Half the objects in the exhibit were decorated with hunting scenes."

"We left the empire when I was little," Scirye said. "Most of my life, I've lived in foreign cities like this where hunting isn't allowed." She lowered her arm to her lap, where it stained her costume. "I wanted to be a Pippal so I used to read all the epics. Somehow in the novels and poems, fighting is always so glorious. My mother warned me that it was easy to want to be a hero, but it was difficult to actually be one."

Dimly, Bayang recalled her first kill. She had been just as disillusioned as the girl. Even now, after so many battles, Bayang felt no thrill, only a vague unease and distaste for what she was doing.

It was almost as if the girl were a younger version of herself, despite belonging to a different species. Bayang found the notion puzzling and mildly annoying, for humans belonged to one of the more troublesome lower orders.

However, the girl had fought as bravely as any of her people, so Bayang felt she should acknowledge that. "Well," she concluded clumsily, "your sister would have been proud."

"Thank you," Scirye said in a small voice. Her griffin had draped his lithe body about her neck and shoulders and was crooning to her as if she were his chick.

Curious, Bayang glanced at Leech. He seemed as shaken as the girl. Suddenly he seemed to notice the axe in his hand and a look of revulsion passed over his face. His hand jerked up to throw it away as if it were on fire, but he caught himself and lowered it again.

"We're fighting for your sister and for Primo," he said as if trying to convince himself that the pursuit was the right thing to do.

No, he was taking no pleasure in the death of an enemy—even though that monster had been trying to kill him. The lap griffin was more bloodthirsty than Leech. Bayang wished the elders could see the boy at this moment. They might change their minds, too.

That thought exploded her orderly world like a bombshell. She had been taught that the elders were older and far wiser than she was. For centuries, she had never judged the rightness or wrongness of her missions—only carried them out with ruthless efficiency. She was not supposed to question, only obey.

And yet she could not deny her own experiences with her prey—she corrected herself. No, he was a person. And his name was Leech. Could the elders be wrong?

Bayang had dedicated herself to building an orderly world in which she was always in control. Now she felt her carefully constructed world beginning to crumble into a confused heap.

When they were about sixty feet over the street, Bayang banked in the direction that she had last seen Badik taking.

"The fighting will only get worse," Bayang warned them, "so if any of you are having second thoughts, I'll set you down."

It would mean losing track of Leech for a while, but she owed him that much for saving her life.

Koko cleared his throat. "Maybe that's the smart thing to do."

Scirye wiped the back of a hand across her eyes. "I can't forget what happened to my mother and sister, but even if I could, I can't ignore the promise I made to Nanaia. I told her I would take her revenge if she would just help me. And so far she has."

"Ah," Bayang said. When she had been young herself, she had wanted to punish Badik just as much—no, wanted was too pale a word. The need for vengeance had burned white-hot in her. However, she had never faced such a heavy fate as Scirye's. "When a goddess grants your wish, it's hard to tell her that you've changed your mind. But perhaps you could make it up to her in some other way."

"And I have to get even for Primo," Leech insisted. "If I run away, it would be like saying he meant nothing to me. It would bother me the rest of my life."

"Then we hunt," Kles said, sounding pleased.

Bayang weighed what was the right thing to do. She knew what tradition would demand of her people's own hatchlings. They would be expected to take revenge on those who had killed their kin.

These were human children who lacked the talons, fangs, and muscles of her people, and yet, as fragile as they were, they had boldly faced danger. Their vulnerability made their resolve all the more admirable—even if one of them was her intended prey. Through all the centuries, she had paid no more attention to humans than she would have to short-lived but pesky mosquitoes. But she found herself liking Scirye—and even Leech as well.

Reluctantly, Bayang decided that she had to treat their wishes with the same respect that she would give to those of her people.

And so, still despite strong misgivings, Bayang took them higher in search of her new prey, Badik.

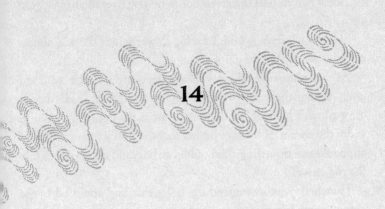

14

Leech

Her short gray hair whipping behind her, the tiny woman named Bayang took them high above the skyscrapers, away from the honking cars and police sirens, until they circled slowly over the building tops. At this height, it was an all new San Francisco inhabited by pigeons and air sprites, tiny creatures that floated in the winds like dandelion fluff, in and out among the flagstaffs and water tanks. Here and there was an occasional windblown rooftop garden with bent shrubs.

Leech searched the skies for any sign of the dragon, eyes skipping over the gleaming nozzle-shaped column of the newly built Coit Tower on Telegraph Hill and the houses clinging to the hill's side like rectangular beads on a cloak.

"He's gone," Leech said in frustration.

"No, he changed direction," Scirye said, pointing eastward.

Leech had missed the green dot skimming over the hangar roof on a pier.

"Hold on," Bayang said. Leaning forward until she was almost double, she banked the carpet.

As they plummeted downward at a steep angle, Leech crouched over, feeling the carpet's straps cut into his ankles. His hands grasped what he could of the carpet just as the others were doing. From the corner of his eye, he saw that the pesky little griffin had slipped down from the girl's shoulder so he could dig his talons into the rug, as well.

Hunched over, he noticed the holes that had appeared in the carpet, some big enough to watch the city passing beneath them. *How long will this thing hold together?* he wondered. But then he told himself to focus as Primo had constantly told him to do.

But as they whizzed over the long, dirty warehouses that squatted right by the edge of San Francisco Bay, Leech felt the exhilaration rush through him like a wind blowing away all his fears.

There's nothing like flying, he thought to himself. *The funny thing, though, is that this pleasure is so familiar—like I've flown a lot of times before and yet I know I never have.*

He couldn't wait to tell Primo about his first flight, and the memory stabbed him like a knife. He couldn't. His friend was gone. Once more, anger overcame sadness. He'd make the thief pay.

They soared toward piers and wharves jutting out from the sides of San Francisco like teeth; boats of all sizes were tethered to them by thick cables.

The area was buzzing with activity, as usual. Troll stevedores hefted huge stacks of crates down the gangplank of a tramp steamer while, sparks flying from his wand, a third-class wizard repaired a hull plate. The water frothed around a moored tugboat as water elementals cleaned off the rust and barnacles.

Farther out on the harbor, a merman shouted instructions to a slick, broad-backed leviathan, nudging a red and black merchant ship toward a wharf while ferries churned back and forth, leaving huge white wakes behind them. A Navy destroyer glided underneath the recently opened Bay Bridge that connected San Francisco to Oakland. The cars and trolleys on its two decks looked like toys. Sailboats slid through the white caps, their triangular sails gleaming in the sunlight, accompanied by flocks of hired air sprites.

Against the greenish water, though, it was hard to see Badik until he made the mistake of going too low. When the water heaved up, his passage left a telltale white streak on the surface.

"He's making a beeline for that boat," Koko guessed.

About a hundred yards ahead of Badik was a large yacht with an immaculately white, angled hull and polished mahogany cabin and decks.

"What would a dragon need with a boat?" Leech wondered.

"Why indeed?" Bayang asked. "But he's definitely aiming for it so let's find out, shall we?"

She sent the tattered carpet into another steep dive, leveling off as low as she dared as she tried to avoid being seen by the yacht's crew. Near the surface, the air was misty with spray and tangy with salt, and she just hoped there would be no sudden high billows that could knock them from the air.

As they watched, Badik plunged into the water, white foam splashing from the spot. Then a blurred form continued beneath the water underneath the yacht.

Koko scratched his head. "What's he up to now?"

Bayang saw two sailors in crisp white uniforms standing on the deck. "There's a ladder on the other side. I bet that's where he's going."

Even as she said it, the pink form of a man appeared on the deck, and the sailors quickly covered him with a blanket.

"He's disguised himself as a human," Bayang said.

Immediately, the water churned at the boat's stern. The anchor slid up, water dripping from its flukes. The yacht began to move straight ahead toward Treasure Island and the International Seaplane Terminal that the artificial island housed.

"I've heard some collectors pay thieves to steal art treasures for them," Leech said.

"They'd never be able to show it," Scirye objected.

Leech had heard rumors about that on the street. "They don't care," he said, trying to sound worldly-wise, "as long as they get to enjoy it in private."

"But why the ring?" Koko wondered.

Scirye touched the axe in her belt. "We'll ask him when we catch him," she said grimly.

As they sped after the yacht, a water sprite turned from his chore of cleaning the rust from a buoy to watch them pass. Leech waved in greeting but twisted around and looked up excitedly when he heard a roar of great propellers. A plane was sliding slowly out of the sky like some lovely silver bird. Its wings stuck out from the plane's top with four propellers spinning so fast that they looked more like flashing disks. Smaller wings extended from its belly and its body tapered gracefully into three tails.

"It's a Pan American Clipper!" he said, pointing. "I was hoping we'd see one. They say the Germans have a bigger one now, but they don't crisscross the world like the Clippers do."

Koko rolled his eyes. "Why do you have to be so bonkers about planes?"

Leech was capable of talking about planes for an hour, but his friend had made him feel self-conscious so he shut up, watching instead with gleaming eyes as the Clipper landed. Its elegantly curved hull skipped across the surface like a stone, leaving white splashes in its wake, the distances shortening between the touchdowns until the seaplane finally stayed on the surface. The bottom pair of wings steadied it as it glided forward, once again a thing of grace. The pilot killed the engines on the left wing so that it turned in a circle, aiming toward the pier ahead.

The whole world seemed to be arriving at or leaving Treasure Island, which had taken six years for engineers to create out of the bay. Seaplanes of all sizes bobbed up and down at the other piers, for this was a hub. Here passengers could transfer to smaller seaplanes to fly on to other destinations or use the bridge to go into San Francisco to the west or Oakland to the east. Trucks loaded with crates and luggage trundled back and forth among the streams of people bustling to and from the large terminal.

At the northernmost pier, tractors hauled a seaplane onto a submerged, wheeled trailer so that they could roll it onto dry land and into one of the huge rectangular hangars. The tractors looked like little yellow chicks fussing over a plump mother hen.

Farther south, connected by a road, was the smaller Yerba Buena Island, formerly Goat Island, where commercial ship piers had been added to the Coast Guard Station. The beacon in the lighthouse and the foghorns had all been turned off in the bright, clear sunlight. It was here that the surface ships landed, their passengers traveling over to Treasure Island by means of a narrow causeway. Piers and wharves jutted from the sides of the island as thick as whiskers where dozens of sea taxis and private and public boats and ferries bobbed up and down, but they finally picked out the dragon's yacht.

"Keep an eye out for incoming boats and planes," Bayang warned.

There was a shout and a loud, angry squawk. She turned to see Leech lying on his back as feathers fluttered down on his chest and a large, indignant seagull flapped away.

"And seagulls," Scirye said, trying her best not to laugh.

Koko had no such inhibitions. "He must've thought you were a hamburger," he teased. "Come to think of it, there is a resemblance."

"Ha, ha. Very funny." The carpet shook as Leech righted himself.

Through a hole in the fabric, Bayang nervously saw the choppy bay waters slide past. "All of you, don't move!" she warned. "I don't know how much longer this carpet is going to hold together."

Even as she spoke, a foot-long strip ripped off from the left edge and fluttered away across the water. The next moment, Koko gave a frightened whoop as a piece disintegrated underneath him.

Leech was laughing even as he hauled Koko onto a still intact section. "Time for a diet, pal."

Kles petted the carpet as if it were alive and pleaded as one flying creature to another. "Hold, please, hold. Oado of the Winds, help us," Scirye muttered hastily. Bayang did some praying to her own deities.

Despite their pleas, patches, some as large as a fist, began to break away and loose threads whizzed past in a haze. The more they lost of the carpet, the harder it became to fly. A rogue wave slapped at them so that they bounced upward, and the now sodden fabric became sluggish. The rug no longer responded quickly to Bayang's corrections, instead rising and falling like a roller coaster car despite all her attempts to hold it steady.

"Why does it smell like wet dog all of a sudden?" Leech wondered.

"Actually, more like wet griffin," Scirye teased.

"I beg your pardon," Kles said stiffly. "Griffins don't smell like dogs, wet or dry."

Bayang fought the carpet as it tried to nose into the water. Thirty yards, twenty, ten, and then they were over the surf line where the spray rose, wetting their clothes in a fine drizzle.

Having carried out its last duty, the carpet seemed to disintegrate into a cloud of fragments and thread, and they pitched forward onto the sand of a small beach.

Koko sat up, spitting out sand. "Let's take the bus back."

"After we've had a chat with that dragon," Leech said, slipping the unattached loops from his ankles.

"I was afraid you'd say that," Koko groaned.

15

Scirye

Kles spat out a leaf of seaweed. "I've seen rocks make more graceful impacts," he said to Bayang. "The clumsiest fledgling from my eyrie—!"

"Now, Kles," Scirye said as she brushed sand from her clothes, "I couldn't have handled the carpet as well as she did." She added in a voice that suddenly dripped with mock sweetness, "After all, she only said she knew how to fly a magical carpet, not land one."

Momentarily blinded by strands of seaweed that hung down from her head like a damp green wig, Bayang parted the strands and peered at the pair. "Without me, the only thing you could have done with that rug was use it for your naptime, *little girl*." The last two words had the desired effect as both mistress and griffin bristled. "And let me point out that any landing you walk away from is a good one."

"Says you." Koko wrung out his handkerchief. "I got to get me a new one of these if I'm going to travel any further with you."

"You can be as fussy as an old cat sometimes," Leech said in exasperation. "Put up with it like the rest of us." Then he pointed at Scirye, Kles, and Bayang. "And as for the three of you, remember that the dragon is our enemy, not one another."

Bayang grunted her embarrassed agreement and pivoted, flinging the seaweed from her head, and Scirye turned her back on the woman.

While Kles rose into the air and shook sand from his fur and feathers, Scirye retrieved a piece of the carpet about two feet square. On it, she lay her remaining axe. "We'll hide our weapons in here," she said. The boys placed their axes on top of hers but the elderly woman threw her chain away.

Scirye didn't ask her why. As annoying as Bayang could be, the Pinkerton agent had a confident air that suggested she could handle anything—from flying a carpet to improvising a weapon from whatever was near or simply fighting with her hands. And she found herself envying Bayang, for Scirye knew she lacked the skills that justified Bayang's arrogance.

When Scirye rolled up the rug into a cylinder, she lifted it effortlessly and then took her hands away. The rolled-up carpet began to drift in the breeze until she stopped it with a palm. "I thought there'd still be some magic left in the fabric." She put it under her arm, more to keep it from floating away than to support it. "It's not any heavier than a pillow."

With Kles upon Scirye's soggy shoulder, they slogged above the surf line through the sea wrack heaped upon the narrow, sandy beach and climbed the wooden stairs to a boardwalk that linked the piers. The planks shook as a bus rumbled past.

As they walked along the boardwalk, Leech spotted a shirt that some worker had left on a bench.

"Koko?" he asked quietly.

Koko glanced around. "It's clear."

Keeping his eyes ahead of him, Leech smoothly swept the garment from the bench. Then, folding up the clothing, he rolled it up and held it against his stomach.

Scirye was scandalized. "Put that back," she ordered.

"Shut up," Leech said. "I took it for you. You can't walk around in that get-up."

Though Scirye herself had objected to the costume, she wasn't about to allow this arrogant boy to tell her what to do. "I'll wear what I like."

He grinned in that superior manner of his. "We want to be able to sneak up on the dragon before we attack. Don't you think he's bound to notice someone in an ancient Kushan costume?"

Scirye bit her lip, annoyed that she had missed the obvious—and worse that it had been this boy who had pointed it out to her. That made her reluctant to give in. "But it wouldn't be Tumarg."

"You got guts, or you couldn't have killed that monster," Leech conceded, and shook the sweatshirt at her, "but it's going to take more than guts to beat that dragon. We've got to be smart, too."

Her eyes narrowed. "Are you saying I'm stupid?"

"Look, girlie," Koko chimed in, "this isn't like passing exams in your hoity-toity classroom. You're in the School of Hard Knocks now. Flunk a test here and . . ." He drew the edge of his hand across his neck like a knife.

Leech dangled the sweatshirt at her again. "Listen to us. It's our turf."

Kles crooked a foreleg around Scirye's head and pulled her head close to his beak. "We can always try to pay the owner later," he advised her in a soft voice.

"All right." She finally stretched out a hand.

As she took it from him, Koko shook his head. "With that prissy attitude of yours, you wouldn't survive more than a day on the street, girlie."

"Lady Scirye usually doesn't have to worry about things like this," Kles countered. Fluttering into the air, he grabbed a sleeve in each hindpaw and helped his mistress tug it on over her head. When he had settled back there, he carefully brushed her hair back into place. "You look a frightful mess. Whatever will your mother say?"

Scirye bit her lip guiltily. "I just hope she's all right. I should call the Consulate and find out how she's doing."

"I'm sure she's getting the best of care," Kles assured her.

"She'll just feel awful if she can't be at my sister's funeral," Scirye said. The corners of her eyes stung as she realized she was going to miss it herself. It would be horrible if there were no family to say good-bye to Nishke.

As the first tears appeared, Kles brushed them tenderly away from her cheeks. "Nishke would want you to get back the ring."

"I know," Scirye mumbled, and then squared her shoulders. "So that's what I'm going to do."

As they walked along, Leech looked at her sympathetically. "Everything was so crazy at the museum, I didn't realize your mother had gotten hurt. Sorry to hear about that. It must be rough."

Scirye glanced at him suspiciously, wondering if he was being sarcastic since he seemed to dislike her so much. But his concern seemed genuine. "Thanks. I know you'd feel the same way if it was your mother."

He jammed his hands into his pockets. "Not a chance. I don't remember her at all because I was just a baby when she left me at the orphanage."

"Oh," Scirye said in a small voice.

"Don't feel sorry for me!" he shot back defensively. "Me and Koko do fine on our own."

"You don't need to jump on me," Scirye said, annoyed. "What

do you expect someone to say when they hear what you just told me?"

Koko sidled in between Scirye and Leech. "Sorry about my buddy." Koko smiled apologetically. "He's got a stiff neck, all right. But sometimes pride's all we got."

Embarrassed, Leech scratched the back of his head. "Yeah. I guess I get carried away, but in the bunch we hang out with, you can't seem weak or they'll jump all over you."

Scirye said nothing. She'd been wrong about Leech. He wasn't like the other students in her various schools. It wasn't privilege that had made him arrogant but necessity. However, it didn't make him any less obnoxious.

After a quarter of a kilometer, they came to where the yachts were berthed, some big enough to be cruisers. They found the boat behind a locked wooden gate with a guard posted there.

Bayang strode up to him officiously. "We have an urgent message for the yacht."

The guard squinted suspiciously. "That must be some important message if it takes four—?"

"Five," Kles corrected him.

"It takes all four of you and a funny parrot to deliver it?" the guard said.

"Parrot?" Kles asked, outraged, but he could say no more because Scirye had clamped her hand tightly around his beak, holding it shut.

"Not now, Polly," Scirye improvised. "You'll get your cracker later."

"My mother couldn't take care of my children." Bayang shrugged.

The guard regarded the slightly soggy boys and girl and then folded his arms across his chest. "I don't blame her. I bet she's escaped to Canada by now. Well, you wasted a trip. There's nobody on board this ship. Mr. Roland and his party already caught the shuttle bus to the Honolulu airport terminal."

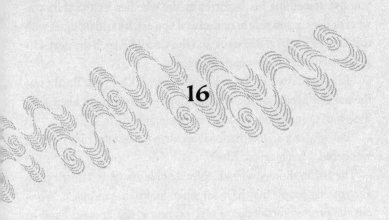

16

Bayang

Bayang thanked the guard and ushered them back the way they had come. When they were out of earshot, she shook her head in self-reproach. "That was my mistake. We should have headed for the terminal."

"Well, that was a waste," Koko complained. "First, you crash-land us and then you take us on a wild-goose chase."

"Leave her alone," Leech said. "We agreed with her, didn't we?"

"Why are you taking her side?" Koko asked, hurt.

It was a small thing, but Bayang hadn't expected her prey to defend her. *Blast him! Why does he have to be so likeable?*

"Who's this Roland guy anyway?" Koko asked.

"One of the richest men in the world." Bayang frowned. It was even worse news to hear that Badik was allied with such a powerful human. "He's got a finger in everything, so chances are every day you use something his factories made, whether it's the shirt you wear or the car you ride in or the meal you eat. It's said he dines with the King of England one week and the Czar of Russia the next. His nickname is the Uncrowned Emperor."

"I saw him once in the palace in Bactra," Kles said. Bactra was the ancient capital of the Kushan empire. "He was on his way to dine with the emperor. He must be behind the theft."

"But why risk an international incident to steal the ring?" Scirye wondered. "Is it magical, Kles?"

The griffin shook his head. "Not that I know of, but the ring's so ancient that people may have forgotten how to use its magic. Without the proper knowledge, a magical ring is just another band of stone. However, I doubt if there's anything supernatural about the ring. It's priceless because of its symbolism and the fame of its previous owners."

Badik, though, was only interested in power, not money, so he would never hire himself out as a mere thief, Bayang thought. "The ring has to be more than an antique. If it's not magical, perhaps showing the ring to the right person will give Roland access to a special treasure."

"Oh, like a pawn ticket lets you claim something," Koko said.

"But whatever the purpose," Bayang went on, "you can bet the ring is part of some major plot."

The hatchlings stopped walking, digesting that news uncomfortably, and Bayang thought how small and young and helpless they looked at that moment. Perhaps this would discourage them enough so that they would no longer get in her way.

But then Scirye lifted her head. "We could talk all day and never figure out why Roland wants it. So why don't we go ask him?" She added grimly, "Once we get back the ring."

Despite her determined words, the hatchling's voice trembled slightly, and Bayang found herself admiring the little human's courage, if not her sense.

"It's the only way." Leech nodded.

Koko tapped the side of his head as if trying to unclog his ear. "There must be something wrong with my hearing, because I just heard you saying you were willing to take on a dragon and one of the most powerful men in the world."

Leech grinned infectiously. "You were the one who said you were getting bored." Grabbing Koko's arm, he broke into a run. "Come on," he urged, dragging his friend along.

"This is not a game!" Bayang called in exasperation.

Leech turned around, backpedaling as he answered Bayang. "I know, but we still might as well have fun."

Despite herself, Bayang found herself enjoying his spirit—Scirye's, too, for she was racing alongside them, laughing as if they were on a holiday at the beach. These hatchlings made her feel young and carefree again in a way she had not felt since the days long ago before Badik had attacked her clan.

After that terrible battle, her one thought had been to turn herself into a warrior capable of destroying Badik. In that single-minded pursuit, she had shed such notions as enjoying herself. Seeing the hatchlings now, though, she began to wonder if she had missed something.

Her longer legs would have allowed her to catch up to them, and she almost gave in to the temptation. However, she caught herself just in time. What if Roland had spies out? So she stayed in disguise by hobbling along. She had been Bayang the Assassin too long to change now.

Which meant that Leech would have to die sometime.

17

Scirye

Driven by a strong sense of urgency, Scirye and the others didn't stop where travelers were gathering to wait with their luggage for the bus shuttle. Instead, they kept on going, almost jogging along the causeway and then northeast up a broad street called California Avenue.

At the same time that Pan America had opened its terminal on Treasure Island, San Francisco had also staged a world's fair there. Most of the fair's structures had been constructed with cheap materials because they were only meant to be temporary, but the seaplane port's buildings had been more permanent. The semicircular building on their immediate right had been the fair's administration building but now served as a control tower and terminal. Farther up the road were two former exhibit halls whose graceful arches and tall windows made them resemble cathedrals, but which were now hangars.

The rest of the fair's exhibits and gardens were being replaced by other airport facilities and additional hangars. Clearly, business was booming at the seaplane port.

Passengers were bustling in and out of the terminal, the walls of which curved like a giant smile, and they entered through the main doors into a high, spacious lobby. A huge aluminum mobile hung from the ceiling. A globe with the skeletal framework of the continents symbolized the earth. About it bobbed huge rings on which seaplanes had been soldered, suggesting the different flight paths of the airlines. More bold metal artwork adorned the upper part of the surrounding walls, while flowers and small trees served as ornaments to decorate the lower areas.

The noise inside hit them with the force of a tidal wave. Hundreds of people were all chatting in dozens of tongues above the slapping sound of shoes, boots, and sandals on the marble floor. There were diplomats from the Dahomey kingdom, Azteca from the southern realms, Turkomans in fezzes and with mustaches large enough to damage an eye. Brushing shoulders with them were furry kobolds from the Russian steppes and airy ifrits from the Saharan deserts. All that was missing were penguins from Antarctica.

Kles gazed at the different colorful costumes passing by. "This is just like back in Bactra. It almost makes me homesick."

Scirye, who barely remembered her life there, made a vague grunt.

"Pan American Flight 54 to Honolulu will be leaving shortly," a voice boomed from a loud speaker.

Bayang scanned the people hurrying by. "I've seen Roland's face in the newspapers and newsreels, but there's just too many people."

"Couldn't we page him?" Scirye offered.

"He'd just send one of his underlings," Bayang said.

"Sometimes two nostrils are better than a pair of eyes," Kles said. He turned his head in a slow circle, sampling the air until he straightened. "I've caught the thief's scent." Then he rubbed his beak with a forepaw, suddenly puzzled. He sniffed again and his gaze fell on Bayang.

"What's wrong?" the woman asked. "Did you lose the trail?"

Kles's eyes narrowed suspiciously but all he said was, "No. The thief's over there." And he pointed a claw.

"What if he's already handed the ring to Roland?" Scirye asked.

"Then we'll see if the thief knows where his former employer is going," Bayang said, "before we take care of him."

They followed Kles's directions through the crowd to the huge Pan American counter where uniformed clerks were taking care of the passengers.

"That's Roland," Bayang said in a low voice.

Scirye had been expecting some slick-haired, pencil-mustached villain like in the movies. However, Bayang nodded to a tall, well-built man with long blond hair and delicate features—the kind who might have been seen conducting an orchestra.

He was dressed in a cream velvet coat with wide lapels and white pants. In his hand was a straw panama hat. Scirye had been at enough diplomatic receptions to recognize simple but elegantly tailored clothes.

There were a half dozen suited men and women with him, one of whom was handling the actual tickets.

Kles pointed his beak toward a young man in the back. He might have looked handsome if he didn't have such a sour expression on his face. "He's the thief."

"Keep an eye on them," Bayang murmured to the children, and then surveyed the terminal until she saw a uniformed airport policeman. A veteran would have slouched comfortably, but this one stood at ramrod attention. Hunching over again like an old woman, she walked toward him. As she drew closer, she saw how young he was—and also eager to prove himself.

"Did you hear about the theft at the museum?" she asked.

The officer nodded toward a bank of lights where new headlines streamed across. "We just saw it now."

"Well, the thief is right here trying to escape," she said.

The children were still where she had left them and they signaled to her.

Roland had only moved a few paces away from the counter and was now talking with a beaming, bald-headed man.

Bayang pointed at the disguised dragon. "There's the thief."

Roland turned as the determined young officer bore down toward him. "Is there a problem, Officer?"

When the bald-headed man turned, the officer stopped in midstride. "What's the meaning of this, Jenkins?"

Jenkins touched the visor of his cap respectfully. "This lady"—he indicated Bayang—"says that this gentleman"—he waved his hand now at the shape-shifting dragon—"is the museum thief."

Roland seemed amused. "What sort of prank is this, Pete?"

"One in very poor taste," Pete said.

It seemed clear to Scirye that Roland's money was protecting the thief as well as himself. It was too much for the girl to stand and she charged over.

Scirye drew herself up and tried to sound like her mother when she was carrying out official business. "I represent the Kushan Consulate," the girl announced. "They've got the ring." As she waved a hand at them, the bundle of axes clinked. "Search them all. And their luggage, too."

"I am the manager of this seaplane port, young lady," Pete spluttered. "Don't tell me what to do. And don't go about making such wild accusations."

Jenkins looked as if he were having second thoughts. Even so, he stuck to his guns. "Maybe so, sir. But we can't let them go until we find out the truth."

The dragon must have had heard the clinking noise from within Scirye's bundle and took the opportunity to whisper his suspicions in Roland's ear.

Roland raised his cane and knocked the rolled-up carpet from her arm. Though the fragment hung in the air, the axes with their golden shafts clinked loudly on the marble tiles.

"I believe, Officer," Roland drawled, "that you'll find the axes were stolen from the museum." He motioned his cane toward Bayang and the children. "There are your real thieves."

Scirye was furious when she saw that Jenkins was staring at them angrily. "He's lying."

"I'm so sorry, Mr. Roland," Pete apologized.

Roland raised a hand and fluttered his fingers. "No need. The poor granny must have gone senile, and she's convinced her half-wit grandchildren about her fantasy." Though he had spoken in a breezy tone, his eyes were hard.

"Jenkins," Pete said, "take this crazy mob away."

"Yes, sir," Jenkins said miserably.

18

Scirye

When Kles wanted, he could be as huffy as a grand duchess who had just found a bug floating in her tea. He clapped his wings together with a loud snapping sound for emphasis. "How *dare* you arrest Her Ladyship?"

Jenkins cut off the griffin. "No kidding? And just last week we had a screwball saying he was the King of England." He smirked at Bayang. "And what are you? Her nanny?"

Jenkins's supervisor, Captain Honus, was a short, brown-haired man with a large head that seemed out of proportion to his body—almost as if someone had stuck a pumpkin on a body made out of wire. He turned his large head wearily so he could look at Jenkins. "What did you want to be when you were a kid?"

Jenkins scratched his cheek. "I dunno. Maybe a cowboy?"

"My mother told me to become a wizard," Captain Honus

grumbled, "but did I listen? No, I became a cop. And then when I retired, my wife told me to get a hobby, but did I listen again?"

Jenkins grinned crookedly. "It doesn't look like it."

"I took this job because I thought it'd be easy." He gazed glumly at Prince Etre's stiletto on his desk as if he wished it and his prisoners would vanish. "But every day seems to bring a new mess I have to clean up."

"Geez, we had no idea we were spoiling your day. So we'll just leave," Koko said, starting to sidle toward the door.

Captain Honus jerked his head and Jenkins hauled Koko back where he had been standing. Then the captain picked up the telephone receiver. "I guess I'd better check this out with the consulate," he said sourly and dialed the operator, asking her to get the Kushan consulate. After a moment, he put the receiver down. "The line's busy."

"It's probably all the press bombarding the consulate with questions," Bayang suggested.

The captain drummed his fingers on the desk. "Well, better put them in the cells until I can get through."

Scirye was disgusted. "But you're letting the thieves get away."

"That's a matter of opinion." The captain shrugged.

Suddenly Koko launched himself forward, knocking pens and papers to the floor as he slid across Captain Honus's desk. The boy stretched his hand out imploringly. "Don't throw me into the hoosegow. They made me do it."

Scirye muttered disgustedly under her breath. "What an *akhu*."

Leech was more open with his scorn. "Don't you have any pride?" he demanded. "You knew what you were getting into it." Seizing Koko's collar, he tried to pull him from the desktop.

When Koko twisted around on the desktop, pens, files, and framed photos crashed to the floor. "Don't touch me."

The two boys rolled around, clutching at one another and swinging wildly, but they were so close the blows were ineffective. One of them, though, managed to knock off the captain's cap.

Captain Honus and Jenkins dragged Leech off of Koko and threw him roughly to the floor. "Put them in separate cells," the captain panted. "They can cool off there while they're waiting for the police to come from San Francisco."

Koko was in tears as he babbled for mercy, but the captain contemptuously pulled him off his desk.

And though Leech was sporting a scraped elbow, he smiled briefly as he stood up.

Koko was still complaining as Jenkins shoved all of them rudely out of the captain's office and into a corridor. Barking came from behind a closed doorway. A sign on the door read, "Animal Quarantine."

The officer held out his hand. "And your bird—" He corrected himself as he gazed at the griffin's fur. "I mean, your dog goes in there."

Kles's wings snapped open and his beak parted to bite him.

For once, it was Scirye who got to remind her griffin to behave properly. "Manners. We represent the Kushan Empire."

Kles settled back onto her gauntlet. "I beg your pardon, but I'll have you know my ancestors were thinking and talking long before yours descended from the trees."

"He is also my companion," Scirye said with great dignity. "Are you willing to risk a diplomatic crisis by treating him like a dumb beast?"

"Well, no." The officer scratched his ear. "But your dog . . . or is it a bird?" He settled for a more generic word. "I mean, your thingamajig can fit through the cell bars."

"He would never leave my side," Scirye insisted.

Captain Honus must have overheard through his open office door because he stepped into the corridor. "Handcuff that little windbag to her then."

The officer took out a pair of handcuffs. He snapped one around Scirye's wrist and, after some head scratching, the other around the griffin's waist.

Now that justice was satisfied, Jenkins led them through a second doorway into a room with two holding cells on either side. The officer put Koko into a cell and Leech into the one next to him. Scirye, Bayang, and Kles all went into a cell opposite the boys.

Koko threw himself at the bars, begging the officer to let him go.

Kles gave him a contemptuous look and muttered darkly about cowards to Scirye.

Leech sat on a bench, pretending to be in despair as he rested his head in his hands. He didn't break the pose until the officer had left.

"Did you get something?" he asked softly.

Koko kept right on shouting his pleas for freedom as he reached his right hand up his left sleeve and produced a large paper clip. Then, with an elaborate flourish, he took a letter opener from his right sleeve.

"You've done this before," Bayang observed drily.

"A few times," Koko agreed amiably. He resumed his loud pleas for mercy as he began to pick the lock with the clip and letter opener, working with all the precision and concentration of a surgeon.

He bowed as his cell door swung open. "My, what a varied education," Bayang grunted. Behind her, Scirye stood up and came to the bars to watch.

"So have you," Koko replied as he set to work on Leech's cell. "You can learn lock-picking in a lot of places, but who teaches carpet flying?"

"Who, indeed?" Bayang said carefully.

Koko shot the woman a suspicious look and then went back to work. The next moment there was a click and the door swung open. "You'd think a new place like this would have better locks, wouldn't you?"

"Just be glad they cut costs somewhere." Leech chuckled as he stepped into the corridor.

As Koko and Leech started to walk past her cell, Scirye whispered, "What about us?"

Leech shook his head. "You're strictly dead weight. You couldn't even outsmart a couple of airport flatfoots."

Scirye gripped a bar of her cell. "I would've come up with something."

"When are you going to realize that a spoiled rich girl like you just don't belong with us?" Leech sighed. "Look. We're doing you a favor by leaving you behind," he said. "Go home and check on your mother. You're lucky to have her. Leave the revenge to Koko and me."

Scirye felt a momentary twinge of guilt at the thought of her mother, but that was overwhelmed by the anger she felt at Leech's arrogant attitude. Even though she knew she shouldn't antagonize him, she snapped, "All my life, people have been telling me what to do, and you're no different. Well, for once, I want to make my own choices."

Leech nodded slowly. "I guess I can understand that."

Scirye went on urgently. "If we hold you back, you can forget all about us. It'll be our job to get ourselves out of trouble."

"Okay, we'll get you out of the cell," Leech said, but he sounded as if he were already having second thoughts.

"Hold your horses," Koko said and stared at the girl. "Who called me an ah-choo?"

Scirye flushed. "It was *akhu*, and I . . . I judged you too harshly. I'm sorry."

"What is an *akhu* anyway, girlie?" Koko demanded.

"A sort of rat," Scirye confessed. "But I realize it wasn't true." She thought to herself, *Yes, it wasn't fair to the akhus.*

"Apology accepted," Koko said, and swung his eyes toward the griffin on her shoulder.

Kles's feathers bristled on his head. "I have nothing to apologize for. And her name is not 'girlie,' it's Lady Scirye."

Koko shrugged. "It's no skin off my nose if you two are twins for the rest of your life."

Scirye reached behind her back and gave Kles's tail a warning tug.

Kles flung up a paw petulantly. "Oh, very well, a thousand apologies, et cetera, et cetera."

"I'm sorry, too," Bayang said. "Now release us."

Koko swung his index finger back and forth like a metronome. "Ah-ah-ah, toots. First, tell us why you didn't identify yourself to Captain Honus right away?"

"The agency wants to keep the magical division a secret, so we don't advertise the fact it exists," Bayang said. "I'm expected to get myself out of situations like this."

Koko gave a skeptical snort and jerked a thumb toward the door as he said to Leech, "Let's go. Her story stinks to high heaven."

"You're not going to leave us in here," Scirye protested.

"Once they get the consulate, you'll be okay," Koko said to her.

"We have to help them," Leech insisted. "They're our friends, too, now."

"I am?" Bayang asked.

"Don't look so surprised," Leech said.

"My . . . profession's a rather solitary one," Bayang said thoughtfully. "It doesn't lend itself to friendships."

Koko wrinkled his nose in disgust. "What have I always said about sentimental stuff?"

"It's a waste of time." Leech shrugged.

"Right," Koko agreed. "It's a luxury smart guys like us can't afford."

Leech gave him an apologetic smile. "Sorry, buddy. I guess I'm just not as smart as you. Anyway, we're going to need their help to get that dragon."

"Look, I'm sorry Primo's gone," Koko argued. "We tried to get his murderers and nearly got ourselves killed instead. Enough's enough."

"Once you unlock their cell"—Leech looked sad but determined—"you can go your own way, Koko."

Koko rocked back on his heels, surprised and hurt. "But you and me are partners."

Leech leaned against the bars. "I can't ask you to do something this dangerous."

"That's for sure." Koko began working on the lock, grumbling all the while. "You're still just as wet behind the ears as when I found you. What's the use of teaching you anything if you won't listen?" In a minute, there was a click and the door swung open.

Leech stuck out his hand. "Thanks, pal. When this is done, I'll catch up with you sometime and somewhere."

Koko grabbed his friend's wrist and tried to pull him along. "And I'm telling you to go with me."

Leech pulled free from Koko's grip. "I didn't leave one set of bullies behind at the orphanage to get under the thumb of another one."

Koko looked hurt. "You didn't used to mind me telling you what to do."

"And I was grateful," Leech said quietly, "because you taught me how to stand on my own two feet. So maybe I'm finally listening to my own mind and not other people's."

"I never meant for you to ignore me, though," Koko said. There were tears at the corners of his eyes as if he were ready to cry out of sheer frustration.

"I don't think Leech is as scared to be alone as you are, Koko," Bayang said shrewdly.

"All of you, quit your yapping. Everybody's got to have a hobby, and mine's keeping Leech out of trouble." He rubbed his forehead. "But I ought to have my head examined."

"Ahem," Kles coughed, and then tapped a claw against the hand-cuff cinched about his stomach.

"Please," Scirye added.

"Okay, because you asked so nice," Koko said, and had them free of the handcuffs the next moment.

"Now I'll need one of your hairs in addition to yours." Bayang waved to the two other children.

"What for?" Leech asked.

"Ow!" Koko said as Bayang impatiently plucked a hair from his head. Entering his former cell through the open door, she laid the hair on the bench. Breathing on it, she muttered a spell and the next moment there was a replica of Koko sitting with a vacant expression.

"For this," Bayang said with a flourish.

"Did you have to make me look so dumb?" Koko complained.

"I think it's an amazing likeness." Leech grinned.

"Of the harmless sort," Bayang said, closing the cell door behind her as she stepped back into the corridor. "But even simple illusions have their uses."

Leech and Scirye voluntarily took hairs from their heads and Kles sacrificed a feather. Quickly, Bayang had images of all three acting like model prisoners in their cells.

Moving quietly to the doorway of the holding cells, they peeked out and saw Jenkins feeding a form in triplicate into the typewriter. "Darn red tape," he complained as he began to hunt and peck with his two index fingers.

Bayang motioned them to step back. "What we need is a distraction," she said. They backtracked to the Animal Quarantine room.

Shelves filled two walls with small cages on each. A regular menagerie of cats, dogs, snakes, and parrots immediately greeted them. In a larger cage against the third wall was a kangaroo.

Bayang had no sooner opened the first cage before the children were helping her free the other animals. When even the kangaroo had been freed, Bayang opened the door and they shepherded the creatures outside.

The freed animals erupted into the corridor, barking, meowing, squawking, and hissing with delight after their confinement. Bayang and the others made sure the creatures were heading toward the front door, listening to Jenkins and then the captain shouting.

A few minutes later, they snuck back into the front room. The front desk was unoccupied now and through the doorway they could see Captain Honus's office was the same way. While Scirye tried to call the Kushan consulate in San Francisco again, the others helped themselves to their belongings, which had been stuffed neatly into envelopes.

Koko grunted to Bayang. "I still don't trust you."

Bayang retrieved her purse. "We don't have to be friends. We just have to be able to work together."

Frustrated, Scirye set the receiver back into the cradle. "Something's still wrong with the consulate's telephones." Retrieving her stiletto from the envelope, she slipped it into her belt and then rolled up the axes in the carpet fragment again so she could carry it under her arm.

She debated what to do with the gauntlet but slid that into her belt, letting Kles ride on her shoulder, which was his usual perch when her mother was not watching. With long practice, the griffin's talons gripped her shoulder lightly but firmly.

Then they walked out of the police station, trying to look more nonchalant than they felt.

Bayang pointed inland to the recently built warehouses and

hangars where there were as many trucks and people as in downtown San Francisco. "We can get lost in the crowd there."

If the terminal was the clean, pretty face of the seaplane port, the maintenance area where the seaplanes were serviced was its noisy, messy guts. Gone were the sculptures and flowers. New structures of a more utilitarian design had taken their place but were still huge enough to make the seaplanes seem like toys and the workers like ants.

They entered the broad expanse of concrete, already acquiring interesting patterns of stains as trucks and tractors flowed back and forth. The noise of excited fairgoers had been replaced by the rumble of engines being tested, and suits and dresses by greasy coveralls.

This was more a shrine to technology than to magic. With one hangar, a troll strolled along as if the massive pontoon on his shoulder was a mere stick. In another hangar, a gnome directed an imp in welding two plates together while a few feet over, six more imps sat around a seaplane's exposed engine, listening sullenly as a second engineer tried to convince them to honor their contract and go back to work.

Fortunately, everyone was too busy with their tasks to notice Scirye and the others.

She was tempted to try to call again and find out how her mother was doing. But that would probably lead to her capture and, worse, her companions might also be caught. Worried and guilty, she decided to stay with them.

"We should find out what flight Roland is on and when it's leaving," Leech suggested.

"We'll still have to find a way to follow him," Bayang said.

"Then call your Pinkerton agency for help," Leech said practically.

"I'm supposed to operate undercover," Bayang improvised.

Then a green creature wheeled a box on a hand truck around the corner. Mechanic's coveralls had been pulled around his carapace, the sleeves and trousers rolled up over his short limbs. He plodded along on his stumpy legs to the rhythm of his tune.

Koko suddenly grinned. "Well, our luck must be changing. Leave everything to me."

"Where are you going?" Bayang demanded.

"You might know all about high-flying, but *I*," Koko boasted, "know all about lowlifes." Popping upright, he leaned casually against the top of an oil drum. "Still can't carry a tune, can you, Mugwort, old chum?"

At the sound of Koko's voice, Mugwort jerked to a halt as if on an invisible leash. Instinctively, his head disappeared into his shell. When he peeked out cautiously, he caught sight of Koko. Immediately Mugwort tried to plod away, but his heavy body could only move at a pace that even a snail could beat. "There's nobody here by that name," he called over his shoulder.

As Koko moved around the drum, his handkerchief fell out of his pocket. Peering out of Scirye's sweatshirt, Kles whispered, "We'll show him what he gets for nearly leaving us in the jail. Get that."

Scirye didn't question her griffin's order. Both schoolmates and staff members on three continents had learned that their lives ran much more smoothly if they were polite to Scirye and her griffin. Usually they liked to plan their revenge as meticulously as a military campaign, but there was no time for that.

There had been the time when the school bully had been tricked into putting talcum powder on his French fries and become a laughingstock, or the time that the military attaché in the Kushan embassy in Istanbul had found himself chewing on his own toupee at a banquet for the grand vizier.

Scirye glanced at Leech but he was busy watching his friend. Stooping, she picked up the handkerchief.

"Now get some of that grease on it," Kles instructed in a low voice.

Bayang wondered what the two were up to but said nothing while Scirye smeared some grease from the concrete onto the handkerchief and then folded the handkerchief into neat squares. And then she waited.

In the meantime, Koko had dashed across the concrete to grab Mugwort's arm. "Well, fancy meeting you here, old buddy, old pal."

Mugwort pivoted ponderously and shoved Koko's hand away. "You got the wrong guy." He tapped a claw at the name stitched to his coveralls. "I'm Aloysius Smith."

Koko winced. "And you still aren't any better at coining aliases. Aloysius? Really, come on."

Mugwort put a hand protectively over his name. "I got a good thing going. Don't spoil it."

Koko cupped his chin speculatively. "What's the scam? Skimming stuff from the cargo? Or is it old-fashioned smuggling?"

"Not me. My only crime nowadays is murdering a song. I turned over a new leaf, see?" Mugwort insisted, but there was something about his indignation that reminded Bayang of a hatchling who had been caught stealing candied eelings from the pantry.

Koko folded his arms skeptically. "I didn't know they had invented spot remover for leopards. What about if I do some reminiscing to your boss?"

Mugwort sighed as he dug his wallet from his coverall. "How much?"

"Put it away." Koko polished his nails against his chest. "I took up a new career, too. I'm a travel agent now, and I got some customers who've decided they need a nice Hawaiian tan and they need to catch the very next flight out."

"The ticket counter's in the terminal." Mugwort pointed out the direction.

"Sure, sure," Koko said breezily. "I'll go there right after I see your boss."

Mugwort shut his eyes as if he had abruptly developed a splitting headache. "If I do this for you, we're quits, understand? I can get you on and off the plane, but then you're on your own, all right?"

Koko wiped a hand across his forehead as if it were a slate. "Right. And I totally erase the name of Mugwort from my brain," he promised.

Mugwort seemed a little surprised to see that Koko's clients were children and an elderly woman, but he shuffled into a locker room.

Palming the handkerchief, Scirye hooked her arm through Koko's. "I guess we were wrong about you."

Koko freed himself from her grasp. "Don't try to butter me up, girlie."

"It's Lady Scirye," Kles said from within her sweatshirt.

"She might be a lady to you." Koko placed a hand over his heart sarcastically. "But she'll always be just 'girlie' to me."

In their campaigns of revenge, Scirye had developed the quick, nimble hands of a pickpocket so it was easy to slip the handkerchief back into Koko's clothes. *Leave her and Kles behind, indeed!*

When Scirye saw Bayang looking at her, she winked.

19

Scirye

Mugwort shuffled back with an armload of coveralls. Bayang's would have fit her—if she had been 300 pounds. The others were also for large adults so they hung on Scirye and the boys like tents, which at least left plenty of room in which Kles could hide.

As they began to roll up their sleeves and pants cuffs, Mugwort shook his head. "Try to keep out of the direct light, okay?"

Their progress across the maintenance area was slow because they had to keep pace with the plodding Mugwort, but finally they arrived at a truck loaded with crates. From the hand truck, he took the box and added it to the flatbed at the rear. "Hop on," he said.

Bayang and the others managed to find places among the stacks of crates. All of them had labels which read:

Ship to:

Roland Enterprises

Houlani

When Bayang saw the children looking about, she hissed, "Quit behaving like tourists. Look like you belong here." She set the example by folding her arms and pretending to be bored.

Leech and Koko had no trouble copying her. To survive on the streets, they had learned how to act different roles—as they had just done in Captain Honus's office. Scirye, though, felt the opposite of boredom. Her heart was pounding; she expected any moment for the police to shout out, "Halt!" The best she could do was sit rigidly and hope staring at her toes would fool casual bystanders.

As the truck slowly wound its way through the warehouse traffic, Koko pulled out his handkerchief. "I hate work."

"We're just pretending to work," Leech corrected.

"It's still hard," Koko insisted and wiped his forehead. As he lowered the handkerchief, the others began to splutter, trying to control their laughter. "What's so funny?"

"You," Bayang said. "You've got grease on your face." She pointed to the stripe across his forehead.

"How'd that get there?" Koko said puzzled, but as he raised his handkerchief to wipe it off, Leech stopped him.

"You don't want to do that," Leech warned, trying to keep from chuckling.

Koko looked down at his handkerchief and then frowned. "Where'd that come from?" His forehead wrinkled as he considered the possibilities. His eyes settled on Scirye. "It's funny how chummy you suddenly got back there."

"I was just so grateful you didn't leave us in the jail," Scirye said innocently. She and Kles were usually more careful about making sure blame couldn't attach to them, but they'd been improvising.

"Maybe I should have," Koko said suspiciously, and his voice took on a menacing tone. "You know, girlie, I can play pranks, too."

"Our target is Roland and Badik," Bayang reminded them, "not one another."

Leech grinned, glancing back and forth between Scirye and Koko. "You may want to think twice about it, Koko. You just may be outnumbered and outclassed."

"Okay, okay," Koko grumbled, looking down sorrowfully at his stained handkerchief. "Let's have a truce for now."

Finally, the truck reached the piers, chugging along as the bay lapped at the big wooden tree trunks that supported the concrete platforms.

Service across the Atlantic had not started until this year so Scirye had come to America by ship. Despite Bayang's warning, the girl could not help taking a closer look at the passing seaplanes.

They seemed to come in all sizes and designs. Some floated on their bellies in the water like fat gulls. Others rode high up on pairs of big pontoons, looking like long-legged storks. There were sleek single-wing racers, two-winged air yachts all the way up to a monster with nine wings and eight engines, four facing forward and the other four faced toward the rear. With all the struts and crisscrossing wires, the craft looked more like a trio of mobile bridges than an aircraft.

Mugwort stopped the truck at the foot of the pier by several luggage carts. Close up, the Pan American Clipper was huge as it bobbed up and down, tugging at its mooring ropes as if impatient to be off. With its rounded hull over a hundred feet long, and wings over a hundred and fifty, it truly lived up to its name of "flying boat" and dwarfed the nine-winged sea plane. Even though the blades of the four propellers were enormous, they still didn't seem big enough to lift such a gigantic craft into the air.

Mugwort appeared at the back. With seaplanes arriving and leaving, there was almost a constant roar of engines so he had to speak loudly. "Here," he said, handing a suitcase to each of them. "Follow me."

They walked along the pier where the Clipper's triple tail rose high above them. Ahead of them, a broad wing cast a large area of shadow over the water and the pier. Scirye couldn't help feeling as if they were walking straight into the belly of a whale.

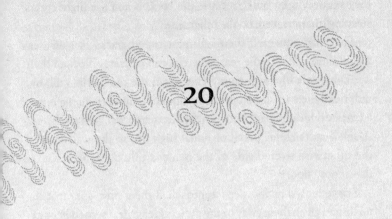

20

Scirye

Scirye pulled her gauntlet from a pocket of the coveralls and slipped it over her hand. "You can come out now, Kles," she whispered. With her free hand, she undid enough buttons on her overalls for Kles to slip out and light on her leather-covered hand on her lap. She held a finger up to her mouth in warning as workers loaded the starboard cargo hold on the upper deck.

When she had first entered the long, narrow hold on the port side, Scirye had felt like they were in a cave because it was so gloomy. It extended along the upper deck but also into the space inside the wing.

When they had stowed the suitcases away, Mugwort had pointed to a door on the front bulkhead and warned them in a soft voice that they needed to be quiet because the cockpit and the flight crew's sleeping quarters were on the other side.

They had squeezed their way past roped stacks of suitcases, trunks, and crates to the rear, where a wall of crates blocked their way. Mugwort lifted an empty crate from the top of the wall and motioned them to climb over. They found themselves pressed into a cramped hiding space between the rear cargo wall and the boxes. A small rectangular patch of metal high up on the wall marred the otherwise riveted side of the plane; a pile of blankets sat on the smooth floor.

Scirye tensed as footsteps approached them now, sure that the turtle had given them away to the police. Her griffin sensed her anxiety and crouched, ready to spring into action. The others must have thought the same thing because Bayang began to undo the bundle with the axes and Leech and Koko waited to take them.

"I knew we couldn't trust anyone with a name that sounds like a noise a sick mongoose makes," Kles grumbled.

But it was Mugwort's homely face that peered down at them from the wall of crates. He glanced over his shoulder to make sure no one was watching. "Here," he said in a soft voice, lowering a sack. "It's some food and water."

Koko took it with a nod of thanks. "Is this ritzy stuff from down below?"

"Don't push your luck," Mugwort grunted. "We'll be closing the hold in a moment."

"Any cops come asking about us?" Koko asked as he took them.

Mugwort nodded. "Sure, but I told them we hadn't seen anyone."

Koko handed the armload to Leech. "They took your word for it?"

"Me and them play poker every Friday." Mugwort chuckled. "I always make sure I lose some."

"You've done this before," Bayang observed.

Mugwort beamed with professional pride. "I make it worth everyone's while not to look in this nook. When you get to Honolulu and hear this"—Mugwort whistled a short tune—"you'll know it's my guy. He'll get you out of the clipper safely."

"Thanks, buddy," Koko said.

Mugwort grunted sourly. "We're even now, so drop the 'buddy' business."

Koko nodded agreement. "I meet you on the street and you're a complete stranger."

Satisfied, Mugwort started to slide away. "Bon voyage then."

"Who are you?" Koko said companionably.

A few minutes later, they heard the door clang shut on the seaplane. Leech had expected the hold to grow even darker, but oddly enough there were faint beams of light coming from around the edges of the oval patch.

Bayang stood up and examined it. "This is covering a porthole."

Suddenly the whole hold shook as the Clipper's propellers whined into life, deepening in pitch until they were a steady roar, making it difficult to talk.

When Kles shifted uneasily from one leg to another, Scirye set him upon her lap and stroked his fur affectionately. "What's the matter, Kles?"

"I feel like we've been swallowed up by a monster," the griffin grumbled. "When I fly, I prefer to use my own two wings and I certainly wouldn't make so much racket when I do."

The propellers grew even louder as they began to back away from the dock, rocking with every motion of the water. Slowly, the Clipper taxied away from the pier and circled in an easy curve. Suddenly they lurched forward, the seaplane rocking up and down as well as sideways as they began to move over the choppy surface of the bay—faster and faster until they were speeding more quickly than Scirye had ever gone in her life.

In the hold, crates shook and rocked, but Mugwort and his compatriots had done their work well. The ropes held the crates in position.

The noise from the engines almost but did not quite drown out the hiss of water against the hull. If it weren't for that sound, Scirye would have thought they were in a cart rolling down a bumpy, rock-strewn hill.

Suddenly, the swaying stopped as they lurched into the air, and then resumed when they splashed back down again with such a hard jar that she almost bit her tongue. They repeated that several times, but each time the lull grew longer and the impact shorter and softer until the clipper tilted upward and they were free of the bay.

As they soared upward, the noise from the propellers lessened.

All of them jumped when a muffled voice greeted them. "Welcome to Pan American Airline's China Clipper en route to Honolulu." From the passenger deck below, the words echoed a fraction of a second later over loudspeakers.

Bayang pointed to the forward bulwark. "Mugwort was right. We have to be careful because the wall is thin."

Leech had been fidgeting all the while. "I can't take being cooped up in the dark. I need light." Taking down a crate, he set it on the floor beneath the patch. Then he stood on it and tried to pry the metal from the window despite the screws holding it on.

"Leave it alone," Bayang ordered.

Leech shrugged. "Who's going to report us? A seagull?"

When Scirye had left the Kushan Empire, she and her mother had gone by sea and then train to Istanbul. Another train had taken them to the next posting in Paris and another combination of boats and railroads had taken them to San Francisco. The only time she'd flown had been on the back of an ambassador's griffin.

She was eager to look out the porthole, too. "I agree with Leech." Setting Kles down on the floor, Scirye unrolled the carpet so she could pick up one of the axes. The boy made way for her as she used the blade to unscrew the metal covering the window. It had been a hasty job so there were only two screws which she had out in no time.

Then she pressed her face against the window. She was looking out just to the rear of the wing, but she could see everything. She thought she had been high up when she had been on the carpet, but that had been nothing compared to now. Below her, the buildings on the hills slid by like rectangular beads scattered over a lumpy rug, and the ships on the bay seemed to be painting white stripes across green glass.

She angled her head, trying to glimpse the Kushan Consulate but she couldn't. "I hope she's all right," she murmured.

"The hospital will be doing everything they can for her," Kles told her from where he sat upon a blanket.

"Second thoughts?" Bayang asked.

Scirye almost tried to bluff, but that would be a lie and she was almost a Pippal now; she had to keep Tumarg. "I still hurt inside about Nishke. I don't know what I'd do if something happened to Mother."

Next to her, Leech nodded. "Same here. I feel bad enough about Primo. It'd be too much if I lost Koko."

Stretched out on a blanket, Koko pillowed the back of his head on his hands. "Don't worry, buddy. I don't intend to let any monster slice and dice either of us."

"When we get to Honolulu, I need to find out about Mother," Scirye said.

"It would be better if fewer people knew what we were doing." Bayang sighed. "But I understand. Do what you have to do."

Scirye watched as they floated over the newly built Golden Gate Bridge and away from land, gliding through wisps of cloud that looked like a torn quilt, its cotton stuffing scattered across the sky.

Would she ever see the city and her mother again?

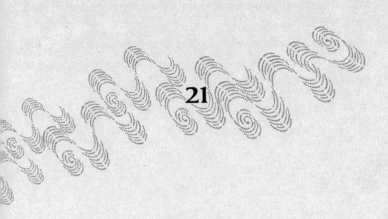

21

Bayang

"Hey, it was my idea. Don't hog the view," Leech said.

"There's not a lot to see now." Scirye shrugged as she slid away.

The boy, though, settled in at the window and stared at the sky as if his eyes were devouring every bit of it. "I'm finally flying," he murmured to no one in particular. "I dream about this all the time, and now here I am."

"Yeah, yeah, you must've been a bird in another life." Koko sounded bored, as if he had heard this fantasy before.

Or you were simply meant to fly, Bayang thought sympathetically.

This was a terrible development because it meant he was one step closer to discovering his true powers. And yet his eagerness reminded her of her own people's hatchlings, so she felt as sorry for him as she would have for one of them if they were denied their birthright to the sky.

And he'd called her a friend. She turned the word over in her mind wonderingly, like a child with a new toy. It was something to be understood and enjoyed.

22

Sciye

Sciye wondered what Bayang was brooding about. The woman had looked somber enough before this, but she had been a bubbling fountain of happiness compared to her face now.

The girl felt her legs cramping, but as she changed position, her foot touched the bundle of axes. When her mind had been clouded by grief and rage, punishing the dragon had seemed like the right thing to do. However, now, aloft over the Pacific Ocean with her enemy perhaps only a few feet away, she was beginning to have her doubts. Her anger was cooling and reason was taking its place, and with its return her task was appearing to be more and more impossible.

Perhaps she should undo the bundle and lead the attack before she completely lost her nerve.

She was glad to postpone the decision when Koko held up a piece of wire that he had found. "Hey, guys and gals, why don't we check the luggage? Roland might have hidden the ring in his suitcase rather than carry it on him. After all, he couldn't be sure that he wouldn't be searched. If it was in a bag, he could always claim it was planted there."

Reluctantly, Leech looked away from the window. "Good thinking, but we just hunt for the ring. Don't take anything else."

Koko gave him an irritated frown. "What's wrong with a guy taking a few souvenirs?"

"It's called theft," Kles said. "We're already in enough trouble for stowing away, not to mention violating a stack of traffic laws back in San Francisco."

"Okay, okay, look but don't touch." Koko cracked his fingers. "Just let me limber up the old digits then."

Bayang took the wire, twisting it back and forth until it broke. "I'll help you."

"Ha!" Koko said skeptically. "Just don't get in my way."

They took down the empty crate and one by one climbed over into the rest of the hold. However, every bag they opened only contained clothes and toiletries. What surprised all of them was how adept Bayang was at picking locks, as well. It turned into a kind of competition with Bayang clearly in the lead, much to Koko's annoyance.

Kles's left hindpaw squeezed Scirye's shoulder and then his right did the same. It was their signal that they needed to talk, so Scirye made a point of searching the hold as far away as she could from the others.

As she started to untie a rope, she whispered to her griffin. "What is it, Kles?"

He leaned his beak close to her ear. "I knew there was something familiar about her smell, but I couldn't put a claw on it until we caught up with the thief back at that seaplane terminal. Her scent's real close to his."

Scirye's eyes widened. "You mean—?"

Kles nodded. "She's a dragon." He clicked a claw against his beak. "I'd trust this anytime over your eyes."

Scirye felt a thrill. She had never expected to meet a dragon in the flesh. Dragons were notorious for avoiding humans, disdaining them in the same manner that humans ignored mayflies who might live just a few days. It certainly explained some of Bayang's arrogance.

So it was odd to have a dragon disguising herself as a human, let alone taking a job that brought her into contact with so many of them—though it was true that the dragon thief worked for Roland and also took human shape.

Scirye studied the elderly woman bent over the steamer trunk, wishing with all her heart that she could see Bayang in her true form at least once.

23

Bayang

Bayang was pondering problems of her own as she rifled through the luggage.

In the short time that she had spent with Leech, she'd come to like him, but even so, that would not have kept her from carrying out her mission if she thought he was a threat to her people. She would regret it later, but their safety came first.

However, Leech was not the heartless monster of the legends. Given his rough life so far, it was amazing that he had grown into a friendly, kind hatchling. There was no point in killing him.

She couldn't help wondering if some of her previous assignments had been just as useless. Perhaps all of them had all been. Suddenly she felt a terrible weariness. Had she wasted her entire life?

If by some miracle she survived the hunt, she would return to the dragon kingdom and try to pull off an even bigger miracle by convincing the elders that Leech was no longer a threat to drag-onkind, and that he had paid the blood price in full after having suffered for his crime many times. And if, as was more likely, she paid the ultimate penalty for disobeying an order—well, so be it.

The decision seemed right to her, and for the first time in a long and troubled life, she felt at peace with herself.

Leech would not die by her paw—or by Badik's, if she could help it. None of the hatchlings would. She would convince them to quit the hunt in Honolulu.

At least if they could find the ring in the luggage, Bayang could argue that it was more important for Scirye to return it to her people than to continue on and battle Badik. That might save the girl's life anyway.

More determined than ever, she went on searching. When they found nothing, she still did not give up hope but suggested trying the other hold. So they restacked the luggage and tied everything down again. Then they opened the door of the port hold and peeked into the corridor. At one end light fell from an observation dome on top of the airplane where, Mugwort had said, the naviga-tor could check the stars for night navigation.

When they were sure no one was around, they crossed the corri-dor and entered the starboard hold, where they had no more luck; they could only conclude that Roland or the dragon thief had kept the ring after all.

Back in their hiding spot, they held a council of war.

"There has to be a stair or ladder leading from this deck down to the passenger deck," Leech said. "I bet it's up front with the crew. I say we rush down it and grab Roland and his buddy."

Taking a breath, Bayang tried once more to get them to abandon the chase. "It would be crazy to attack in midair." She couldn't help smiling at Scirye. "Unless you have another flying carpet up your sleeve."

"Mind your manners before nobility," Kles said, snapping his beak at her indignantly. The griffin was sitting on his mistress's gauntleted hand which, in turn, rested on her lap.

With an amused smile, Bayang dipped her head in an apology. "No disrespect meant. I was merely suggesting that you've tried your best to avenge your loved ones," she added kindly to the children. "There would be no shame attached if you left me in Honolulu. Why don't you leave this to a professional from now on?"

"That makes sense to me." Koko nudged his buddy. "After all, she's a cop. Let her earn her pay."

Leech shook his head. "If it had been you and not Primo who got hurt, what would you expect me to do?"

Koko scratched his head and then stared at his shoes. "I'd want you to get even."

Bayang had to admire the hatchling's courage if not his stubbornness. She turned to Scirye, hoping that she could at least spare her any more danger. "I hope you'll have more sense than these hoodlums. Do you really want your mother to worry about you?"

Scirye stroked her griffin but, in her agitation, her hand moved in a quick, choppy rhythm. "I want to punish that dragon."

For a moment, Bayang felt as if she were talking to her younger self. After what Badik had done to her people, revenge was all she had wanted, too. She'd shed any emotions that she regarded as weak just as steel is plunged into fire to burn away the impurities. She'd forged herself into a weapon strong enough to battle Badik only to find the dragons wielded her against other targets.

"You're choosing a difficult road to travel," she warned. "You'll have to harden your heart and make many sacrifices. And in the end, you may be sorry you did that. Surely the goddess won't hold you to an oath that you took in the heat of battle."

"So you're going to quit?" Leech asked Scirye, sounding sad.

"Because she's smart," Koko snapped, "like we ought to be."

"And because she's got something to lose." Leech shrugged. "Not like us trash."

"Don't let him influence your judgment," Bayang urged the girl. She was aware that perhaps she was pushing too much, and that would be a bad mistake if the hatchling was anything like her. When people insisted she do something, the dragon usually chose the opposite action. The greater the pressure, the greater the contrariness.

And yet she felt an immense need to convince the hatchling to quit the path that Bayang had taken. It only led to a lonely weariness.

"You're too young for this," Bayang argued.

It was the wrong thing to say. Scirye stiffened indignantly. "I've proved I'm tough enough."

"Yes, of course you are," Bayang said, trying to recover. "It's just that I've seen too many lives thrown away for some outmoded code."

Scirye was too annoyed to listen to reason now. "So what code do you live by?" she demanded. "You're going to tackle a dragon and one of the most powerful men in the world all by yourself."

But that is different, Bayang thought. *I have no future. You do.* Out loud she said, "It's all in a day's work for a special operative."

"Especially when that operative is a dragon," Kles sniffed.

Koko and Leech's jaws dropped open, and Bayang sat back, annoyed. The little griffin looked insufferably smug.

Kles was going to say more but his mistress put her free hand over his hindpaws. His beak clacked shut obediently.

Leech stared at Bayang as if he was trying to penetrate her human disguise. "Are you really a dragon?"

"I'm not going to transform myself just to prove your suspicions. But"—Bayang rubbed at a dirt stain on her coveralls—"yes, I am."

"If you were assigned to protect the treasure, then why didn't you change into your true shape back at the museum?" Scirye asked shrewdly. "It would have been dragon against dragon, and you wouldn't have had to bother with the carpet for flying."

Bayang did not want the hatchlings to learn about her original mission, but Scirye was too blasted sharp. Bayang began improvising frantically, knowing that half-truths deceived better than outright lies. "Because the dragon's no ordinary thief. He's called Badik and he once tried to exterminate my people."

Leech nodded thoughtfully. "That's why you scowl when you say his name."

Bayang was surprised at Leech's sympathy. "Do I?"

Kles had taught Scirye enough for her to comprehend Bayang's revelation from a Kushan perspective. "So you're in a blood feud to the death," she said. "I don't think you have anything to do with the Pinkertons. It was the dragons who sent you, didn't they?"

To her dismay, Bayang saw how the lies kept piling up. The more she told, the more likely they were to trip her up eventually. "Yes. My people have been hunting for him all these many years. I stayed in disguise because I needed to see who his accomplices were before I revealed myself. I had no idea it would be Roland."

Scirye straightened. "Then it wouldn't be Tumarg for me to leave when you're about to fight such a dangerous enemy. Kles and I are going with you."

Bayang cursed herself for trying to be too clever as she made one last desperate attempt to spare the girl. "Yes. I think the best aid you can give me is contacting the Kushan embassy in Honolulu once we land."

"I'll do both," Scirye insisted. "I think you're going to need all the help you can get."

Bayang felt as helpless to change things as one of the dragons in the ancient dramas, impaled like a worm upon Fate's hook. "All right then." She sighed. "I suggest that it would be safer to hold off the attack until we've landed. We'll still be able to surprise them."

And at least on that much, they were willing to listen to her. So she settled back against the crates to rest. She'd tried to protect the hatchlings, but there was no helping young humans.

24

Scirye

It was impossible to escape Bayang in the narrow hold, but Scirye scooted as far away as she could into a corner where she could hug Kles. She was still a little shaken by her own decision to go on, but she had resented how Bayang was still treating her like a "little girl." It didn't matter that Bayang's doubts were close to hers. Scirye was determined to prove to the dragon that she was no pampered rich girl.

As she stole a glance at Bayang, she noticed that Leech had gone back to the window.

Leaning on one elbow, Scirye thought she had never seen him look happier. His forehead was smooth and unworried and his smile was broad and open. "You really like flying, don't you?"

"Yeah," he said, fiddling with his iron rings before he asked shyly, "Is . . . is flying always like this?"

"This is my first flight, too," Scirye explained. "Mother and I used trains to travel to her postings in Turkey and Paris, and we took an ocean liner here."

"Ooh," Koko said, rubbing his hands together. "All the food you can eat and people waiting on you hand and paw." He was still nursing a chip on his shoulder. "It must be nice to have someone else taking care of everything."

Scirye shrugged. "It must be nice to be free."

"Sure, it's great never knowing how we're going to get our next meal," he said sarcastically. "We're free to go hungry."

Scirye decided that it had been a mistake to try to sympathize. "I wouldn't like that part," she admitted. "But at least you don't have everyone telling you what to do."

Kles fluttered his feathers, annoyed. "I consider it constructive criticism, Lady."

"Everyone expecting you to live up to your name," Bayang agreed sympathetically.

"Is it that way among dragons, too?" Scirye asked.

Bayang, though, seemed uncomfortable about revealing that much. "I've already said more than I should about my people."

Wrapping a blanket around himself, Koko looked as if he were in a cocoon. "So you got a castle to go with that title?" he asked Scirye.

Kles looked down his beak contemptuously at the boy. "The *Lady's* clan"—he emphasized the second word—"has estates, yes. And they have a castle on each."

Leech smirked. "I knew it. Born with a silver spoon."

His superior attitude annoyed Scirye, but it wouldn't have been Tumarg to lie. "They don't belong to me."

"You *are* in line of succession to the title," Kles reminded her.

"Far down the line, very far." Scirye made a face. "But even if I was next, I don't know that I'd want any of it."

Leech sat back in surprise. "You'd give up a cushy setup like that?"

"Lady Scirye, you shouldn't say any more." Kles fluttered his wings to emphasize his disapproval.

Scirye might have listened, but Koko twirled his index finger in circles by his temple to indicate she was crazy, and that made the girl lose her temper. "That shows what you know. I left home when I was small to be with my mother when she was assigned to the embassy in Istanbul. After that, we kept moving every few years each time Mother got reassigned. So the Kushan Empire is almost as strange to me as it is to you. My father works in the capital, but he always visits us. We never go back there."

"Nonsense," Kles insisted to the others. "The Lady knows an immense amount."

"I only know what you've taught me." Scirye hunched her shoulders. "Face it, Kles. I don't belong to the Empire anymore than I do in the consulate. The staff call me 'The Barbarian' behind my back." She added ruefully, "So do my schoolmates. I'm too Kushan to fit in with them, and too American to fit in with the Kushans. No, I'm not even American. I'm a little bit from a bunch of countries so I'm more like patchwork."

Leech stretched. "Do any of us fit in anywhere?"

"Speak for yourself," Koko warned in a low voice.

Leech stared at his feet as he waggled them from side to side. "That's what I'm doing. All I remember at the orphanage was getting bullied a lot."

Scirye couldn't help smiling. "I guess we have something in common after all."

"At least on this," Leech nodded.

Koko sighed. "Well, I wish we were in one of your castles now," he said to Scirye. "I could use a big steak right now." When his belly began to rumble at such a thought, he patted it. "Down, boy."

Leech reached for the sack and opened it. "Let's see what's on our menu then."

Mugwort had given them several canteens of water, packets of crackers, half a wheel of cheese, and six candy bars.

"How can a guy keep up his strength on just this?" Koko complained. "It's a snack, not a meal."

When a gong sounded below to announce dinner, Scirye instinctively looked down at the floor like the others, but from the corner of her eye she saw Koko palming the extra candy bar.

"On the other hand," Scirye muttered to Kles, "I wouldn't mind owning a dungeon for a little while. I can think of a certain person who might learn something after a week there."

25

Bayang

In the unheated hold, it was growing cold even though they had kept on their other clothes underneath the coveralls. Gratefully, they wrapped themselves in the blankets that Mugwort had provided.

With nothing else to do, they ate and then dozed off and on during the long hours of the flight. Even Leech fell asleep, slumped beneath the window, his head leaning against the wall.

Bayang was grateful to be left alone, surprised by what she had blurted out to the children. Her motives had seemed so clear to her when she was young: protect her people in any way she could. When she had been ordered to become an assassin, she put aside her reluctance and threw herself into her training. She had told herself that she was sacrificing her own life for the sake of her own clan.

Talking with the hatchlings had made Bayang wonder if she

was as much of an outcast among her own kind. Oh, when she went home between assignments her kin were always polite, and yet the compliments were excessive, the service fawning, until it was almost a relief to leave.

Well, she smiled ruefully, *if you were a normal person, would you want to make an assassin angry?*

Long suppressed doubts bubbled up in her mind. She carried out her duties in the shadows, and it was as if her people sensed the darkness that tainted her. They needed her, but they didn't want her. She didn't fit in with the dragons any more than the hatchlings did with humans—*which made them a match for one another*. She shook her head in amazement. It seemed so strange that she had more in common with an enemy than she did with her own people.

She had no hatchlings—there had never been any time for them, assuming that she could have found a mate willing to partner with a killer—but as she watched Leech, she suddenly felt the strangest emotion. It was a tenderness she had never experienced before.

Bayang shrugged off her blanket and then opened her coveralls to the waist so she could take off her coat. Folding it into a pillow, she put it down on the floor next to Leech and eased his head onto it. When she turned, she saw Koko watching her as he lay on his side. He gave her a grudging nod and then closed his eyes again.

Sleep, though, brought Bayang little rest, for she kept having terrible nightmares in which she was a hatchling again and Badik was chasing her. When she woke the next morning, she was sweating, and she found herself staring about wildly for Badik.

"Are you all right?" Leech asked when he heard her stirring. He was already back at his station by the window.

She became aware of her coat, which had been folded up neatly beside her. "Yes," she said shakily as she sat up.

"Sometimes I have bad dreams, too," he said sympathetically. "I'm back in the orphanage again and the bullies are after me."

Strange that she should have something else in common with Leech. "Bullies come in all sizes and shapes," she agreed.

When the others got up, they finished off their remaining food. Koko made a point of grumbling again about the portions.

A few hours later, they heard the pilot's voice dimly through the bulwark. "Aloha, folks. I thought you'd want to know that in just a few minutes, we will be coming up on the newest addition to the Kingdom of Hawaii, the island of Houlani."

By Bayang's watch, it was nearing eleven A.M. by San Francisco time. She thought that would be about nine A.M. by Honolulu time.

Everyone crowded around the window, trying to see. The sky outside was now a vivid blue, lit by the morning sun.

"Up ahead on the starboard side is a diamond in the rough, the island of Houlani. It's the creation of a unique combination of magic and science. Islands are rising from volcanic activity on the sea floor all the time, but most never reach the surface. However, that great visionary, Nathaniel Roland, has sped up the normal geographical process and then shaped the island itself once it broke the surface.

"The western half of the island is the oldest where the new city is rising even as we speak. Mr. Roland is building villas and apartments with every luxury and amenity possible. The eastern half is still being created. Normally you couldn't see it because of the smoke and steam, but the winds are blowing just right today."

They pressed their heads together even more as they gazed down at the large, kidney-shaped island that curled about a harbor facing southwest. The eastern half lay like a black lump of obsidian, but at its heart was a huge crater in which pulsed a bright red and gold oval that was the lava. More red and gold stripes traced their way to the sea, where plumes of steam rose like a feathery fringe.

The pilot continued, "You can see the lake from which the lava is channeled to the edge of the island so Houlani can expand. The crater is about two thousand feet above sea level and measures a half mile in circumference. The lake on the crater floor is just a little under four hundred feet below the rim."

In the center, wharves jutted out into the little harbor and behind them were long rectangular buildings that must have been warehouses and barracks. To their surprise, there was already an abundance of green foliage and blue ponds in the western half, with pink buildings dotting the surface like mushrooms. The structures varied in size from tiny dots that must have been bungalows to sprawling mansions. The morning sun painted the surface with long shadows.

"One of these days, the eastern half will be just as lush and inviting as the western half. Mr. Roland has used the same imaginative blend of the magical arts there to speed up the geological process that converts volcanic rock to rich soil, and then encouraged the trees and gardens to grow. It's truly promising to be a paradise among paradises."

And then the island disappeared behind them and they could feel the plane begin to descend.

Hurriedly, Bayang put the patch back over the porthole by one screw. That left it so it could be tilted slightly to the side so that the outside was still visible. "Koko, you keep watch here. Once we reach the wharf, you tell us. We'll rush out of the hold and down to the passenger deck. The crew will be so busy docking that they won't have time to stop us."

"And then we get the ring back," Scirye said.

"And get even," Leech said grimly.

26

Scirye

The hull rocked as the Clipper's belly slapped against the surface of the water and then leaped into the air again. The seaplane gave a half dozen more bounces, the space between hops growing shorter as the seaplane lost momentum.

And then the loud roar of the propellers lowered to a steady hum as they gently swung the seaplane slightly toward the right. The plane bobbed up and down over the waves as it glided toward the docks of Honolulu's own seaplane port, which bustled with other seaplanes, dirigibles, and boats just as San Francisco's had.

"Welcome to the Kingdom of Hawaii, folks," the pilot announced over the intercom. "The local time here is 9:31 A.M."

Koko gave a jump when he saw the patrol boat glide toward them. From its mast flew the flag of the Kingdom of Hawaii with its red, white, and blue stripes and Union Jack in the upper left-hand corner. And on its deck was a 40mm Bofors cannon swiveling back and forth on its mount as if hunting for a target.

The engines cut entirely so that the seaplane was hardly moving at all against the wind.

"And what do you know, folks," the pilot said with fake cheer. "The queen's sent a ship to welcome us to her islands. She really knows how to say 'Aloha'!"

"Is this for Roland or do they do this for every seaplane?" Leech wondered.

Bayang peered over his head. The gun crew wore platelike helmets and flotation vests and their expressions were grim rather than welcoming. "If this is Hawaiian hospitality, I'd hate to see what they do when they're mad."

Being a diplomat's daughter, Scirye was more aware of the currents of politics. "They're not here to say hello. They're here to protect Roland."

"A big cheese like him has probably made a lot of enemies along the way," Koko said.

Bayang folded her arms thoughtfully. "I read that a lot of the locals, including the queen, didn't want to let Roland create the island in the first place."

"If she didn't want it, why is it getting built?" Leech asked.

"Because it was going to happen anyway," Bayang explained. "Roland said it was in international waters and the United States backed him up. I think the queen's council talked her into it by arguing that if the kingdom participated, they might have a say in how and what things are done."

"From what little we've had to do with Roland," Scirye said, "I can't see him cooperating with anyone."

Bayang chewed her lip. "If the Hawaiian Navy is here, then the army is probably waiting at the pier. We might have to change our plans. So everybody stay put."

Frustrated, Scirye ground a fist into her knee. "We can't just let him walk away. We should tell the police."

"Take it from me, kid," Koko grunted. "We're stowaways. The cops here won't believe us any more than the cops in San Francisco."

"An opportunity always comes up," Bayang said. She sounded as if she were sure it was a fact rather than just a possibility.

Which struck Scirye as a curious attitude to take, but then dragons lived so long that they could afford to wait. Frustrated, the girl rolled up all the axes into a bundle again.

Bayang kept watch by the window as the Clipper slowed. After hours of noise, it was strange when the engines cut back to a dull thumping.

"There's a squad on the dock. No, make that two—blast, it's a whole platoon and armed to the teeth." Bayang slid the cover completely over the window. "The only soldiers without guns are the ones in the brass band."

When the pilot killed the engines completely, the Clipper's momentum kept it gliding forward. It was easier now to hear the tubas and trumpets playing some cheerful marching song, but it failed to lift the stowaways' spirits.

They sat waiting in the gloom among the boxes, listening to the thumps below as the passengers began to disembark. A voice from outside boomed through a megaphone, "Aloha! If you'll follow me, Mr. Roland, there's a little welcoming ceremony in the terminal."

"The ceremony might give us time to set up our ambush," Scirye said, cradling the bundle of axes.

The music dwindled as the band marched away with the soldiers,

Roland, and Badik. It was only a few minutes, but it felt like hours before they heard the sound of a truck pulling up to the Clipper, and another eternity before the hatch opened.

Someone began to whistle but mangled the notes so badly Bayang and the others looked at one another uncertainly, unsure if it was the same tune as Mugwort's.

When they didn't answer, the whistler repeated the torture again. Kles felt like flying up and stopping the butchery of a perfectly innocent song.

A moment later, the empty crate was drawn away, and when a head appeared in the opening, they saw why the signal had been botched so badly. Crocodile lips were never meant to whistle.

The slitted eyes regarded them with a cold, reptilian disdain. "Mugwort didn't tell me about no kids." He gave a snigger. "He must be lowering his standards for smuggling. Are you tone deaf? I gave the signal twice."

Leech was going to make some sassy remark, but Scirye was a diplomat's daughter. "The propellers were so loud, it's still hard to hear now even though they're stopped."

"When I whistle again, come out. And this time, get the cue right." Mugwort's friend disappeared again.

Quickly, Scirye zipped Kles inside her coveralls again and tucked the rolled-up rug fragment with the axes under one arm.

After a moment, from outside, they could hear the crocodile giving orders in a loud voice. "Leave the stuff in the rear to last."

They heard hollow footsteps on the metal deck as baggage handlers worked in front of the wall. After about ten minutes, they heard the strange whistle again.

When they had climbed over the wall of crates, they had a better look at the crocodile. While his head was what Scirye thought a full-grown crocodile would have, it was mounted on a squat, scaled body only three feet high. On top of his head was a hideous black wig that smelled faintly of wet dog. He was so top heavy, it was amazing that he didn't topple over.

Most of the cargo and luggage was gone, but there was still a stack of four suitcases. He motioned to them. "Take those off the plane and put them on one of the carts outside. After that, you're on your own."

"Where is Roland's baggage going?" Bayang asked.

"Do I look like a bulletin board to you?" the crocodile sneered.

Bayang looked ready to shake the little crocodile, but Koko slipped in between them. "Let me handle this," he told her. Then he placed a friendly hand on the crocodile's shoulder. "Sorry, buddy. But she's new to the game so she doesn't know how things work."

"Yeah, well," the crocodile grunted, "nothing's free. You think hippo steaks grow on trees?"

Scirye had no idea where one got hippo meat in Hawaii, but then ships and planes came here from around the world, probably including Africa.

"Help us out and you'll find Mugwort grateful," Koko coaxed. "Him and me go way back."

"He just said to get you off the seaplane." The crocodile tried to shrug off Koko's hand.

Leech grinned and whispered to the others, "No one escapes when Koko puts the touch on someone."

"Literally," Bayang agreed.

"It must have slipped his mind," Koko said, and added conspiratorially, "He's never been quite right in the head since that lead pipe conked him in the bean." Koko wheedled for several minutes until in exasperation the crocodile gave in, sensing that it was the only way to get rid of the pest.

"There's a marina next to the seaplane port. Everything's going to his yacht, the *Sea Breeze*. You can't miss it because it's a white boat big enough to carry a herd of elephants."

"Maybe we should just go with the crates," Koko said over his shoulder to his companions.

"Nix. You wouldn't get past the front gate to the marina," the crocodile said, wagging his large head. "There's been a lot of thefts there lately so security's tighter than a drum. We turn over the cargo and luggage to the marina's personnel, and I can't get you their IDs."

They waited until they had left the Clipper before they talked over what to do.

"Koko, you'll have to distract Roland's escort," Bayang said.

"Why me? Why not you?" Koko demanded.

"Because I'm going to take my true form," Bayang explained. "I only need a minute to zoom in, knock out Roland and Badik, and carry them off to a spot where you"—she nodded to Scirye and Leech—"will be waiting with ropes."

"Like these?" Leech grinned as he snatched up several coils of rope and slipped an arm through them.

"Yes, just like those," Bayang agreed.

They deposited the luggage on one of the carts being drawn by a small tractor and then followed it through the hangars. Though there were fewer buildings than in San Francisco, the ones here had thicker walls of concrete and steel to resist the battering of all the storms that passed through Hawaii.

Certainly there was as much noise and traffic as back in San Francisco, and they had to dodge trucks and carts pulled by teams of giant auks.

The cart entered into a big area at the rear of the passenger terminal and they slipped away then, trying to look as if they were familiar with everything while from the corners of their eyes they hunted for an exit door, eventually finding one that led into the passenger side.

It was like going from night into day. Not only were there more lights, but the walls had been decorated with mosaics of tan-skinned humans in grass skirts or wearing outfits of gaudy cloth.

Coconut and palm trees rose in the background of the pictures and every other square space had been filled with different flowers. But what fascinated Kles the most were the exotic birds that looked as if they stripped all the hues from a rainbow. San Francisco's terminal might have been larger but it was certainly less colorful.

There were lines of passengers at the various airline counters and another crowd standing around the platform where various dignitaries in suits were welcoming Roland. Badik stood behind him. Off to one side was the band and the honor guard, all in tropical white uniforms and enough brass and gilt braid to outfit a temple. On their heads were wide-brimmed pith helmets from which large red plumes rose.

When she felt Kles stirring restlessly, Scirye put a hand on her coveralls over the spot and he grew still. She hoped no one had noticed, but a four-foot-high gecko in a pillbox cap looked at her curiously as he opened the front doors for them.

Outside the sunlight filled Honolulu like warm water in a bowl so that Scirye almost felt as if she were bathing rather than walking. She opened her coveralls immediately and Kles gratefully slipped up to her shoulder, where he began to groom himself.

After the long, cramped trip in the plane hold, they were all grateful to be free and their steps became more lively. Even Bayang felt relaxed enough to play the tour guide. Explaining that she had been here on other assignments, she briefly pointed out the sights.

Waikiki Beach spread out before them in a broad, gleaming crescent of sand. The ocean rolled onto it in bright sapphire waves. And on the crest of the waves men and women were riding on long, wooden boards.

"That looks like fun," Leech said.

"If you like being a shark buffet," Koko said.

"How do they do that?" Scirye said, amazed.

"You have to ride with the waves, and that takes courage as well as balance," Bayang said as she tried to select a place for their ambush. "If you try to fight the waves, you drown."

Several miles in the distance, the Royal Sheraton Hotel rose like a pink palace among the little houses and palm trees, but just six blocks away was the marina where yachts bobbed majestically. There was one large white one big enough to be an ocean liner. In the boulevard next to them, cars, taxis, and buses flowed in both directions while dolphins on wheeled carts playfully darted about the slower-moving vehicles.

While Bayang continued her search, Scirye began one of her own for a pay telephone. If she could find one, perhaps she could borrow enough money to call the consulate. She pivoted slowly, her eyes passing over several peddlers in Hawaiian shirts and shorts on the sidewalk, pestering the passengers as they left the terminal and boarded taxis.

The most persistent was a little elderly lady in a tentlike muumuu that hung loose on her bony frame. The print was of bright red and yellow huge tropical flowers. On her head was a straw hat that looked like an upside-down bowl. Scarlet and saffron feathers adorned the rim and around her neck was a necklace of puka shells and some large pendant, though Scirye could not make out the design.

Like an elderly canary, she hopped about, thrusting a piece of cardboard first at one tourist and then another. Attached to the cardboard were crude earrings. "You buy, eh?" she chanted, her voice rising and falling musically. "I so, so hungry."

"Those are nothing but fishhooks and feathers," a female tourist said, and made shooing motions with her hands. "Go off and catch a fish."

Other tourists made a point of sidestepping around the desperate woman. She turned and held out her trinkets toward Scirye and her companions. "You buy, you buy. Your Auntie, she so, so hungry."

Scirye remembered that she had no money—she couldn't have called home anyway. However, she did have one thing. And that would be Tumarg, too. Pivoting, she jerked her head at Koko. "Give me the candy bar."

"What candy bar, girlie?" Koko asked innocently.

"There were six candy bars and I saw you pocket the extra one," Scirye said, holding out her hand commandingly.

Leech nudged his friend. "Give it to her."

"But—," Koko protested.

"Just do it," Leech said, "or we'll be arguing all day with the junior Amazon."

Grumbling, Koko dug out the candy bar, partly melted from being in his pocket. "A guy's got to stay in practice or he loses his touch."

"Once a thief, always a thief," Kles declared.

"I was going to share it with everybody," Koko insisted, though from the expression on Leech's face, not even his best friend believed him.

Scirye strode over to the old peddler. The girl gave a little bow and presented the candy bar in both hands as if she were an ambassador presenting tribute to an empress. "Here, madam. It's a small enough token, but I hope you'll take it in friendship."

The old lady took it timidly. "T'ank you."

While they were distracted, a voice growled behind them, "Don't move."

Scirye turned her head with a frown.

A huge white shark with stubby legs and short but muscular arms glared at her. His hide glistened like moist sandpaper and his gills made slushing sounds. "You come with us now," he said. "We're going to show you some of the sights."

Behind him were a half dozen smaller gray sharks. One of them snickered, "The last ones you'll ever see."

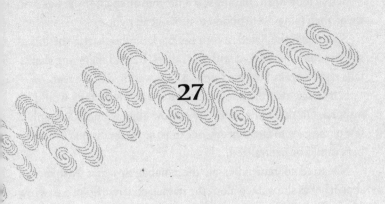

27

Scirye

"Into the alley." The white shark jerked his huge head toward a narrow lane between a T-shirt store and a bar.

"Why should we make killing convenient for you?" Scirye demanded. Before she even had a chance to think, her body responded as Nishke had trained her to do—spreading her legs slightly and shifting her weight so she was balanced on the balls of her feet.

"Fine. We don't care if these other folks get hurt, too." The white shark nodded to the tourists crowding the pavement.

And that would not be Tumarg. Reluctantly, Scirye faced the alley.

Bayang was by her side. "When I give the word," the woman whispered softly to the children, "break into a run and then form a semicircle behind me. If I have to transform, it's better if no one else but them sees me."

Scirye took heart. Bayang was a dragon, after all. If she was with them, then things were bound to turn out all right.

So, though she hated to turn her back on the sharks, she did as she was told and walked with the others. Behind them, the sharks' tails rasped against the pavement as they waddled in the rear.

Scirye saw that the alley ended in a brick wall; they would be trapped. On the other hand, the narrow alley would allow only a few of the gang to attack at any one time, so their advantage in numbers would be neutralized.

She tried to remember all the combat tips that Nishke had shown her as she walked along the stained concrete floor, past a row of smelly garbage cans and over a metal grate, into which dirty brown water trickled from a puddle.

"Now," Bayang said and they ran, stopping and turning at the brick wall. Scirye flung open the bundle so that the axes clattered onto the ground. At the same time, Kles sprang into the air, ready with the claws of four paws and a deadly beak. Leech dropped the rope coils and then raised an axe.

The gang didn't seem the least bit frightened by the threat. Instead, the sharks smiled greedily when they saw the gleam of gold. "A bonus to boot," the white shark said, exposing what seemed to Scirye like rows and rows of fangs.

Scirye placed herself on Bayang's right side just a step behind her, while Leech and Koko took the left.

"Who sent you?" Bayang called to the gang. "Was it Roland?"

"You been making a lotta trouble for him," the white shark said. At a jerk of his hand, two of the gang started forward.

Scirye took her stance and gripped her axe tightly. Overhead, she heard the flapping of wings as Kles gained some height in order to dive faster. Bayang's back tensed as if she were getting ready to change. These thugs were about to get a nasty surprise.

Suddenly the crazy old peddler appeared at the mouth of the alley. "You buy, you buy?" she asked in a high, cracked voice.

Scirye waved at her anxiously. "For your own sake, go."

"Auntie," the old lady corrected her as she shuffled into the alley. "I your Auntie."

"Auntie," Scirye said quickly. "Please leave."

"You good-good girl," Auntie nodded. The feathers on her strange hat fluttered vigorously.

"Yeah, and see what that's going to get her," Koko grumbled.

From a sleeve Auntie took the candy bar Scirye had given her. Flourishing it over her head like a sword, the old woman shuffled forward in her rubber flip-flops, the sandals hitting her heels with each step.

Suss. Slap. Suss. Slap.

The sound reminded Scirye of a giant serpent sliding on its belly. The stunned sharks parted on either side until she was between them and Scirye and her companions.

"Get lost," the white shark said, shoving the little old lady hard. He seemed surprised when she did not fall to the concrete, but remained standing. He pushed even harder, but he might just as well have been pushing against a marble column.

Auntie squinted up at him from under the rim of her hat. "But you"—she frowned—"you bad-bad boy."

"You don't know how bad," the white shark said, and flipped his wrist so that the blade of a gravity knife flicked outward.

"Hey, bad boy." Auntie seemed amused. "What you gonna do with that toothpick?"

"Slice and dice," the white shark said with a wicked grin. "Slice and dice."

"I don't t'ink so," Auntie said with a shake of her head that sent the feathers fluttering. "Bad t'ings, dey happen to bad boys."

Calmly Auntie unwrapped the candy bar. The heat had already made the chocolate mushy so it was easy for her to use the bar like a brush to daub the walls and alley. The white shark watched in astonishment while the gang members murmured nervously to one another.

Sensing he was losing control of the situation, he tried to grab her wrist. "You're dead."

Auntie smiled. "No, you dead." And from her mouth came a series of clicks, rising and falling in tone from bass notes to high ones and then back down again.

For a moment, there was only the sound of traffic in the street, but then Scirye heard a scratching sound like thousands of matches being struck. It wasn't loud, but it seemed to come from all around her as thousands, perhaps millions, of little legs skittered toward them.

The gang looked about uncertainly. Strange brown splotches began to appear on the red bricks and then pulse as the stains spread across the walls.

Scirye gazed in horrified fascination at the nearest one until she realized it wasn't one spot at all but instead was a group of the largest cockroaches she had ever seen. Some were up to three inches long and they kept crawling from the cracks in the mortar between the bricks. More were streaming out of the grate in the alley floor in a steady flood until they were surrounded by the insects. Scirye felt as if she were in the middle of a sea of tentacles with the waves about to crash down upon them.

Auntie folded her arms. "Shame on you, pick on a weak old lady."

Several of the gang were burbling in fear, and the white shark's gill slits flapped open and shut as he stared at the bugs surrounding him. But he tried to tough it out. "I'm not scared."

"Then you should be," Auntie said and snapped her fingers.

From here and there in the alley came a rattling noise like beans in a bowl, and the sound swelled in volume until it filled Scirye's ears. The cockroaches were flapping their wings together.

At another snap of Auntie's fingers, they launched themselves into the air. It was as if the floor and the walls were all collapsing.

A gray shark opened his mouth to scream and a stream of them entered his mouth, choking his cry. Another shark slapped his face and the sides of his head as cockroaches sought to enter his huge mouth and nostrils.

Koko was squatting, holding his hands over his head with his eyes shut. Kles had flown down to Scirye's shoulder so he could spread his wings protectively over her mouth and nose. However, the insects flew past them. Even so, some of the flight paths strayed enough to hit them in their passage. It was like being grazed by bullets.

The insects covered each of the gang in a dark, wriggling skin so that not a hair or wart or an inch of hide could be seen. The white shark flailed his arms, taking a few stiff steps until he fell, and the cockroaches swept over him until he was simply a hump beneath the insect mass. His screams were suddenly muffled as insects filled his mouth. One by one, the rest of the gang plopped on the ground and disappeared under a living brown carpet.

Auntie surveyed her work with a smile that made Scirye shiver despite the heat. Auntie seemed to be enjoying her handiwork.

Scirye shoved Kles's wing away. "Please, Auntie. Stop it."

Auntie screwed her wrinkled face in puzzlement. "Why? Dey try kill you, you know? Dey bad-bad boys. So Auntie fix dem. Den dey no bad-bad no more."

"No one deserves to die like this," Scirye begged. "Not even them."

"You good girl," Auntie said, and tapped a finger against her temple, "but you *lolo*, too." Then, with a shrug, she snapped her fingers again. "But you say please. So 'kay."

The cockroaches swarmed back into the walls or down the grate. Even more rose in a brown cloud upward, toward the rooftops above.

The sharks lay in the alley, flopping and whimpering, with hundreds of little red marks on their tough hides.

Auntie walked over to the white shark and nudged him with her toe. "You bad boy gonna behave?"

The white shark nodded numbly.

"So you listen to your Auntie, eh? Or next time my pets, dey nibble you to . . . da . . . bone." She clicked her teeth together for emphasis.

The white shark nodded his head and then, not sure if that was the proper answer, he shook it vigorously, as well.

"So you go," the strange woman said, jerking her head toward the street. "You don't bodder anybody no more."

The gang did not even try to get to their feet but scrambled on all fours, casting frightened looks over their shoulders at the old woman.

The strange old woman pivoted slowly and swept her index finger along to indicate Scirye and her companions. "And now you," she mused.

"Put down your axes," Scirye said to the others, and squatted down to place her axe on the alley floor. The others quickly copied her and Kles settled back on her shoulder.

Then, bravely, the girl tried to stand up again. As the old woman drew near, Scirye felt the power emanating from the little wizened brown body now, like a thousand-watt bulb. Her comical dress only seemed to add to the menace.

Of all the deadly beings that Scirye had encountered so far, the girl felt that none had been more dangerous than this old lady in her whimsical costume.

Kles growled a warning but because it resonated in his beak, it had a slight echo—like a lion's cub with its head stuck in a hollow tree.

As the old woman's eyes narrowed, the girl pressed a hand anxiously against the griffin's leg to signal him to keep quiet. Kles snapped his beak angrily but fell silent as Auntie leaned forward and took a good whiff of the griffin.

Scirye, in turn, caught the old woman's scent of stale tobacco mixed with sweet coconut milk.

"Birdy pet okay," Auntie declared.

"*I* am not a pet, my good woman," Kles informed her. "I am a servant in this lady's retinue. The first among many, I might add."

"Dat so? Chick-chick tell da fortunes, too?" Auntie asked, amused. When she smiled, the many folds around her eyes crinkled up like paper. "Or you just hoping, eh? Still, I like chick-chick."

It was an impressive sight to see a griffin in full indignation because both his fur and feather bristled. Even more anxious, Scirye squeezed her friend's leg. "Just be grateful, Kles. We saw what happens when she *doesn't* like you."

Auntie's eyes twinkled. "You not just good-good, you smart girl, too." Standing on tiptoe, the old woman sniffed the girl, moving from one cheek and over to the other.

Suddenly Scirye felt dizzy, as if she were standing on one foot on top of a narrow mountain peak and at any moment about to lose her balance. Yes, it was all about balance. This strange old woman was weighing her like someone using scales to tell a genuine coin from a counterfeit.

Trying to keep from shivering in fright, Scirye dropped her eyes and fastened instead on the pendant of Auntie's shell necklace. It was a rectangle of old ivory with a crude but powerful carving of a bearlike man.

"Hmm," the old woman murmured, and then took a particularly loud sniff as if she were a vacuum cleaner and Scirye was a dust bunny. Then Auntie rubbed her nose thoughtfully. "I smell *mana*, big *mana*."

Scirye wrinkled her forehead as she tried to puzzle out what the strange, frightening woman said. "Excuse me?"

The old woman sighed in exasperation. "How come you doan hear? I talk good."

"I . . . uh . . . ," Scirye stammered, even more scared than before.

"Please excuse our ignorance, Madame," Kles intervened, "but we're unfamiliar with your vocabulary and the way you speak."

"Okay, chick-chick," Auntie said. "Den I talk like stupid tourist, too. But I find your brand of English flat and boring. Do you understand me now?"

Kles bowed deeply, ruffling his wings as he did so. "Yes, thank you. We're sorry for the inconvenience." He tapped a claw against Scirye's shoulder to remind her to remember her manners.

"Yes, thank you, Auntie," Scirye said hastily, "and please excuse me, but what is *mana*?"

"Mana is a force that we all share," Auntie explained, still in a musical voice that made the syllables rise and fall like a song. "You, me, the ocean, the sky, the rocks, we all have it. But some have more of it than others. When they have as much as you, they do great things."

Scirye looked up again, blinking in surprise. "Me? But I don't feel any different."

"You can't tell, but I can." Auntie's eyes bored into her. "Somebody marked you for sure." And then she turned to the others, her musical voice now becoming as ominous as the distant rumble of thunder. "But the rest of you. Are you goody-goodies, too? Or"—her eyes narrowed dangerously—"are you baddy-baddies?"

28

Scirye

Koko was shaking openly. "We're . . . goody-goody. We gave you our c-c-candy."

Auntie jerked a thumb at Scirye. "She gave the candy to me. Not you." She stuck her face almost nose-to-nose with the boy and inhaled sharply. "Hmph, a stinking *kupua*! What kind of trouble are you trying to cause here?" was her judgment.

Leech stared puzzled at Koko. "*Kupua*?"

"A *kupua*," Bayang explained, "is a shape-shifting creature."

"Hey." Koko grinned nervously at Auntie. "No hard feelings."

Scirye regarded Koko with new interest. If Koko was in disguise like Bayang, what was his true form? Since Leech didn't show any surprise at the revelation, he must have known his friend's secret already.

"I knew there was something funny about his smell," Kles said.

"I resent that," Koko said, slapping his paunch, which boomed like a drum. "I take baths."

"Oh?" Auntie said skeptically.

"Once a month," Koko mumbled.

Auntie smelled Leech next. Her eyes widened and she bent over, snuffling at his iron bands. Then she held her palms over his armbands as if she were warming her hands. "You've got lots of *mana* here, too. Why did you make Auntie work so hard? Why didn't you fight yourself, eh?"

"I was ready to hit them with an axe," Leech insisted.

Auntie wrinkled her forehead and tapped his hand. "Not with your fists, stupid-stupid." She rapped a knuckle on one of Leech's armbands. "With this."

"What's so special about it?" Leech asked.

"So you don't know." Auntie pursed her mouth and then took another sniff before she held a hand parallel to the ground, twisting her wrist back and forth. "So that makes you a maybe-maybe."

The old woman crooked a finger at Bayang and the dragon bent obediently so that the smaller old woman could stare into her eyes while she sampled Bayang's scent. Then she staggered backward, rubbing her nose vigorously, as if trying to wipe away the smell.

"Hoo, *mo-o*!" Her words came muffled through her hand.

"What's a *mo-o*?" Koko asked.

"The Hawaiian version of a female dragon," Bayang explained.

Auntie nodded at Bayang. "You're bloody-bloody-bloody." She glanced back and forth between Bayang and Koko, eyes narrowing. "*Mo-o. Kupua.* That spells trouble. So maybe I should just get rid of you right now."

Scirye felt her stomach tighten just like it had when the gang leader had forced them into the alley. She was afraid of the old woman and yet she could not stand by and do nothing.

"Please don't harm them," Scirye begged. "They're my . . . friends."

The old woman grinned, revealing her few remaining teeth, all of them stained orange. She flapped a hand to indicate Bayang and the boys. "Why is a smart girl like you with the likes of these, eh?" Despite her smile, the old woman's eyes glittered dangerously, as if Scirye was being weighed on her personal scales once more.

"We . . . we're hunting for the some thieves," the girl said. She felt as if she were babbling from fear. "They're . . . um . . . very bad-bad."

The old woman tilted back her head. "Ah, so am I." She stabbed her thumb against her stomach. "And I would've caught him, you bet. But then you got into that mess. So I came after you. But that meant I missed my thief."

"I'm sorry," Scirye said earnestly. "After we catch Roland, perhaps we can repay you by helping you."

"Roland?" The old woman's head snapped up alertly. "What do you want with him, eh?"

Scirye glanced at the others and Bayang nodded encouragingly. "He killed my sister and hurt a lot of people," the girl said. "And he stole something very valuable from me, too."

"He's a big thief, all right." The old woman's head bobbed up and down in agreement. "He stole something very valuable from me."

"What could he take from someone as powerful as you?" Bayang wondered.

"He knew I wouldn't give permission to build his island," the old woman said. "So he took some of my friends. There are so many of their people scattered around the islands that I couldn't protect them all."

Bayang understood. "They're his hostages so you can't stop him from making his island."

"Even worse," Auntie said angrily, and for a moment Scirye thought that the tips of the old woman's gray hair glowed red, "he's making them build the island itself."

"You mean he's made them his slaves?" Leech asked, horrified.

The old woman grunted in assent. "So I've been trying to catch him. I figure then I can make him let my friends go. But now I've heard a rumor that he intends to take some of them elsewhere and use them on other projects."

Bayang made sure to bow her head politely. "Am I permitted to ask who you are?"

The old woman held up her hand and snapped her fingers mischievously. The next instant there was a tiny flame dancing on her fingertip. "Do you know me now, bloody *mo-o*?"

As Bayang watched the flame waver back and forth, she whispered, "You're the Hawaiian goddess, Lady Pele." The dragon made sure to bend her head even deeper. "You rule the volcanoes."

Scirye bowed her head immediately. Kles, as a veteran of the Kushan court, did it with an elegant flourish of wings and paws. Leech made an awkward copy of Scirye's, but Koko remained defiant. "We don't bow to anyone."

"Show some respect, *kupua*," Pele warned. "Or else." The flame widened upon her fingertip until it hung like a fiery dagger. Then with a casual flip, she sent it an inch deep into the brick wall.

"Right. Gotcha," Koko said, jerking his head up and down like a puppet.

That seemed to satisfy the goddess's pride. "You leave Roland to me, eh?"

"The children should stay behind," Bayang urged, "but let me go with you. There is a dragon called Badik with Roland that I have to catch."

"I've heard of Badik." Pele stroked her chin. "Many centuries ago when there was a great battle beneath the ocean between his clan and another. The fighting churned the water so much that the surface seemed to boil and turned it red with blood for miles and miles."

"Many of my people died that day," Bayang nodded, "but we destroyed his armies."

Pele let out her breath in a little puff that pushed out her lips. "Hoo, another victory like that would have destroyed the rest of your people."

"True," Bayang said, "which is why I have to stop him before he can try again. My people have always valued their relationship to you and will be very grateful if you help me."

"Your kind and me, we go way, way back," Pele agreed, waving a hand to indicate a great distance. "Sometimes we've been on the same side and sometimes not. But oh, yes, you'll pay someday. I'll come to you like this." She held out her palm. "And you'll fill it with whatever I want." The tiny leathery palm seemed to stretch until it was as wide as a baseball mitt. "If you don't," she warned, "you'll be sorry."

Bayang breathed a sigh of relief. "We'll honor that debt."

Pele nodded to the children. "So you'll stay here, eh? On his island, Roland has got guards. He's got wizards. He's got lots of monsters with teeth, who'll gobble up bitty things like you. Even *I* didn't want to go there. That's why I was trying to nab him here."

Scirye remembered how, back in the museum—that seemed like an eternity ago—she had mentioned casually to Kles that it might be fun to meet a goddess. She now realized that her friend had been right. A being so powerful and dangerous was most definitely not amusing—especially when her moods could change so quickly and her temper could erupt just like her volcanoes.

However, as terrifying and whimsical a creature as she might be, Pele was also honorable. It had been Tumarg to save Scirye and her companions and it was Tumarg to rescue her friends. Pele was a goddess worthy of respect, perhaps even admiration.

Scirye bowed reverently to the little old spirit again. "I swore an oath to my goddess when Roland's creatures killed my sister. I can't break it, even for you, Lady Pele. If you try to leave me behind, I'll ... I'll follow you even if I have to swim all the way." She tried not to cringe as she waited for Pele to throw a dagger of fire at her.

The goddess, though, folded her arms in amusement. "Are you that good a swimmer? It's a long way from here." Pele patted the girl's head with a hot palm. "But I think you would. So who is this goddess, eh?"

"N-Nanaia," Scirye stammered.

"I can't say I ever met her, but I've certainly heard about her." Pele shrugged one shoulder as if it couldn't be helped. "And from those tales, I think it's better if I don't cross her. So if she told you to go, then you need to go. Because," she intoned solemnly, "blood is blood." The words rang with a dreadful finality like the last blows of a hammer upon a newly forged sword.

So Nanaia's name brings respect even in this faraway place, Scirye thought. *I guess that it's just as well I didn't break my vow and quit.*

No matter what Pele had said, Scirye felt like the same girl she had always been. Leech and Koko, though, had taken a step away from her and were examining her curiously as if looking for some special sign like a third eye.

"So it was Nanaia that made you take down the carpet?" Leech asked.

"No, I did it on my own," Scirye insisted and then scratched her head, her fingers surreptitiously feeling for a halo. "At least, I think so."

Leech turned to Pele and his hand motioned to Koko and then himself. "Well, we don't know Nanaia, but our friend got killed at the same time."

Pele clasped her hands behind her back. "Blood is blood," she repeated reverently as if it were part of a ritual.

Or a curse.

With yet another typical sudden shift of emotion, Pele went

from being solemn to being cheerful. With a deep laugh like gas bubbling out of mud, she said, "Well, if you come with me, you'll have to make yourself useful and carry my treasures."

As they followed her out of the alley, Scirye whispered to Kles, "Do I smell any different to you?"

"No, or I would have said something," her griffin replied in a low voice.

Self-consciously, Scirye felt her forehead for some other mark left by Nanaia. "What about my face?"

"Just more dirt than usual," Kles answered. Licking his paw, he wiped vigorously at her cheek.

Scirye knew it was useless to resist so she submitted with a sigh. "I don't feel any different, though."

"Neither do I," Leech said, and tapped his armbands. "And I certainly don't see what's so special about these, either."

Kles fluttered in the air, circling around Scirye so he could inspect for more dirt. "You can't judge someone or something by their appearance," he said as he settled back on her shoulder.

"Maybe that's something else we have in common." Scirye smiled at Leech.

Leech grunted in agreement. "It's funny, though."

Out on the sidewalk, Pele squatted by the cardboard with her cheap earrings. She tapped one with a fingertip. "Why do you think no one bought my lovely earrings, eh?" she asked in a hurt voice.

Scirye had assumed the jewelry was merely part of Pele's disguise, but apparently she was serious about selling them. It seemed odd that a goddess would be concerned with trinkets instead of divine matters, but then Pele seemed like a very odd deity. *I guess her hobbies are just as whimsical as her moods.*

The girl thought they were too gaudy but now was no time to tell the blunt truth. On the other hand, to lie would not be Tumarg. *What would my mother the diplomat do?* Scirye wondered to herself and then said, "Everybody has different tastes." Which was true enough and kept to the spirit of Tumarg, if not the letter.

Pele pursed her lips thoughtfully. "Maybe the earrings need something more, eh?" She glanced up at Scirye and Bayang. "What you think?"

Scirye and Bayang looked at one another. Neither one of them kept up with the latest fashions. On the other hand, the goddess seemed to be expecting some sort of help and it wouldn't be wise to annoy her. "A lot of the passengers in the terminal were wearing orange," she suggested.

"Ah, there you go." Pele's head bobbed cheerfully. "Then I'll add some orange feathers next time." Now in a happy frame of mind, the goddess handed the card to Leech. "Don't break anything."

Scirye had expected to head toward the harbor so it puzzled her when Pele led them inland instead.

The goddess strolled across the busy boulevard as if the speeding vehicles were as harmless as chickens. Scirye twitched every time she heard brakes screech and horns honk but she stayed with Pele. When they reached the sidewalk on the opposite side, her shoulders sagged in relief.

"That was as scary a trip as our flight through San Francisco," Kles panted. His fur was all sweaty.

Scirye couldn't help noticing that after the announcement of her bond to Nanaia, Leech and Koko were being careful to keep Bayang between them and her. That made Scirye feel a little sad.

"Aren't we going to take a boat?" Leech asked.

"You think Roland only pay those fishy boys to protect him?" Pele asked, jerking a thumb in the direction the sharks had taken.

"So there are guards on the sea?" Bayang asked.

"And under it and above it." Pele nodded and then explained that not only did Roland have human guards patrolling in boats, but monsters keeping watch beneath the surface, as well as in the air. "People who go without an invitation, they don't come back."

"So how are we getting there?" Koko asked.

"First we walk," Pele said, and shuffled away.

"On water?" Leech protested. He flinched when Pele's bony hand patted his cheek.

"I got my ways, maybe-maybe boy," the goddess said confidently.

It was a hot sunny day in Honolulu and the tourists were out in droves, reeking of suntan lotion as they strolled from one store with paper leis and T-shirts to another. Pele, though, shuffled on steadily. Anyone in the crowd who blocked Pele's way suddenly found themselves brushed to the side by invisible hands. And one tourist who made the mistake of commenting on the crazy old native suddenly had his belt break.

Pele smiled slyly as she passed the man struggling to hold up his pants. "You're too big for your britches," she said—just as a pigeon landed on his head. They left him still trying to mop up the mess with his handkerchief.

"Neat trick," Leech said admiringly. "Could you teach me how to do that?"

"I think you know enough tricks," Pele said.

"That man"—Bayang chuckled—"doesn't realize how lucky he is to get off with just that punishment."

"I'm saving all my meanness for Roland," Pele promised with a look that made them all glad she wasn't directing her anger at them.

A stream of taxis was pulling into a huge hotel, emptying out passengers, luggage, and steamer trunks. "Some ocean liner must have arrived in port," Bayang hazarded and glanced at Pele. "I'm surprised that you put up with all this development."

"Children have to play, you know? Or they get bored. And then

I get bored." Pele stopped by an overflowing trash can and rummaged around. She pulled out a broken backscratcher, but after trying to satisfy an itch unsuccessfully, she tossed it back in. "Pah! This thing is boring."

"So people are your hobby?" Leech asked.

"But maybe one day everybody gets too big for their britches like that tourist. Then I show them just who's the boss still." She swept her arm in a wide circle to indicate all the stores, hotels, and crowds. "This is all very pretty. This is fun. But this is also all fake."

At a snap of her fingers, the asphalt of the street began to bubble and melt as cars changed into crystal-sided tortoises that nosed into the blackness and disappeared except for their colored backs. Traffic lights became trees with flowers decorating their leaves. The white pavement became as brittle as bone and cracked as shrubs began to wriggle upward like green, leafy serpents. Brightly colored shirts in a store window suddenly dissolved into a flock of parrots that flapped about.

Pele gave her bubbly laugh, dancing in delighted circles like a small child. "This is the truth."

Faster and faster grew the vines as they overran the buildings, until they were hills and mountains of green, and the neon signs became dense mats of lianas with huge scented flowers. The trees multiplied, branches hiding the sky, leaves devouring the sunlight.

Scirye and her friends stood dazed as the city disappeared like cheap watercolors dissolving in the rain and revealing the real surface beneath.

It was as if the mural in the plane terminal had come to life—or something beyond even that. After all, the mural had been some human's interpretation of a jungle so the artist had made it comfortable for humans. But that was just a friendly mask hiding the true face.

Everywhere they were surrounded by green—a green so lush that Scirye could taste it, chew on it, swallow it. But the green kept darkening, absorbing the light like a sponge so that it grew dimmer and dimmer around them. Scirye began to feel as if they were imprisoned inside a dark emerald box.

"Duck!" Koko yelled, crouching as a mosquito the size of a sparrow zoomed past. The boy stayed low, glancing overhead nervously. "Did you see the schnozola on that thing? It was the size of a knitting needle."

"She's gone!" Leech gasped.

It was true. There was no sign of Pele. She had left them alone in the middle of that gloomy green cavern. Had they made her mad somehow? Had the goddess become bored with them already? Or was she simply playing a prank?

As Scirye frantically searched for the goddess, she became aware of larger, deadlier things prowling about in the shadows. Hungry things. She pressed a hand against Kles for reassurance and felt him trembling, as well.

Scirye drew closer to Bayang, realizing as she did so how much she had already come to rely upon the dragon. Leech did the same and so did Koko, despite his misgivings about her.

The next moment a nearby tree started to shake and there came angry squawks. Then Pele appeared, sliding down a vine-wrapped trunk and holding one fist over her head. "Quit complaining!" she yelled above her. "You won't miss a few of these." Then, oblivious of their frightened faces, Pele held a fistful of orange feathers above her head and announced triumphantly to Scirye and Bayang, "I got them. Now those tourists are bound to buy my pretty things."

"Ah . . . um . . . I'm glad," Scirye said, glancing about uneasily, for the shadowy creatures had not gone away. In fact, there seemed to be more of them—as if they were being drawn to Pele.

"What?" the goddess asked, finally noticing how nervous Scirye and the others were. She followed the direction of their eyes. "Oh, them." She turned to the trees. "Not today," she called to the shadows. "We'll play some other time. Maybe I'll bring you a millionaire as a toy."

Then the goddess snapped her fingers again and they were standing in modern Honolulu with tourists bumping into them and cars honking in the street.

Pele handed the pile of feathers to Leech. "Don't lose these," she warned, "because you only mess with Pele once."

Leech carefully stowed them away in his pocket. "I'll guard them with my life."

Scirye couldn't help shivering. She had never heard of a spirit so powerful that she could remake the world. That was far more dangerous than one who threw thunderbolts.

"Don't worry. I'm not fed up with the city." Pele winked. "Yet."

"H-how did you do that?" Scirye stammered.

"I know who I am." Pele clenched her fingers into a fist. "That's my power." She opened her hand again to reveal the empty palm. "If you don't know who you are, you're really nothing."

"Well, how do you...uh...discover who you are?" Scirye asked.

Pele put a hand on her shoulder and her palm felt hot but reassuring. "I think you'll find out when you carry out Nanaia's plan."

As they walked on, following the elderly goddess, Leech worked up enough nerve to speak to Scirye directly. "Are you scared about your mission from Nanaia?"

"Who wouldn't be?" Scirye admitted.

Leech scuffed his heels against the sidewalk thoughtfully. "There's her and there's Pele and this Roland guy. They wouldn't get involved if they weren't all playing for high stakes. Usually a guy like me wouldn't even be allowed in the door, let alone sit at the poker table."

Scirye thought she saw a traffic light's shape flicker and change for a moment into the shape of a tree with strange red and green fruit before it transformed back again. "I wish I knew why she chose me. I don't feel special."

"Well, you look normal"—he grinned reassuringly—"for someone walking around in a funny costume and a sweatshirt under her coveralls."

Despite the warm air, Scirye hugged herself. "For now, I think we ought to try real hard not to cross either Pele or Nanaia."

"A wise strategy with any goddess," Kles agreed.

29

Scirye

The goddess's path wandered away from Waikiki, the hotels and big stores giving way to smaller buildings and houses where the locals lived in trim little houses with palm trees instead of oak or pine and fragrant plumeria instead of roses in the well-tended gardens. The more traditional kept *ti*-leaf bushes at the corners of their boundaries for good luck. Even here the little bungalows flickered between wooden boards and woven grass walls.

Some braver souls called out polite greetings but most simply bowed to the goddess.

Once Pele left the sidewalk and climbed the front steps of a house where a man was eating a plate of rice and pork as he sat on his porch. Without a word, she helped herself to a handful and stuffed it into her mouth, chewing as she wiped the grease on her muumuu.

The man made no complaint but presented his lunch to her as reverently as if the plate had been heaped with gold. She shook her head, though, and went back to the street, resuming her stroll but pausing every now and then to take whatever she wanted with all the assurance of a goddess accepting offerings from her worshippers. It might be a flower from a window box or prying a polished hub cap from a Studebaker. She might have the imperious attitude of a divinity but she had the taste of a magpie attracted by shiny or brightly colored objects.

Still Pele shuffled on, taking them down seedier streets where pawn shops and pool halls began to replace the grocery stores. Here both businesses and homes had bars on the windows and the people dressed more shabbily. However, even here they treated Pele with respect and did not object when she helped herself to a scarf, a pair of red plastic chopsticks, and various other things that had caught her eye.

By the time they reached the edge of Chinatown, they were all carrying some of her loot. Here awnings shaded the pavement from one end of each block to the other. In the cool shadows, restaurants and souvenir shops jostled one another for their attention. On the second story, above the awnings, were verandas where people sat fanning themselves.

Pele stopped by a beaten-up little café with a sign on which was painted a seagull and the words, "The Salty Bird." It was hard to tell whether the seagull had always been gray or if years of dirt had collected on its white feathers. On the window were fading letters proclaiming it the home of the "Hot Barbecue."

Leech followed her inside and a grumbling Koko shortly after him. Scirye stepped to the side to make room for them and Bayang. The café was even dimmer than the jungle had been, and Scirye blinked instinctively as her eyes tried to adjust.

On one side, stools rose in front of a counter like tall, immovable toadstools, and on the other side, worn tables and chairs squatted in wooden stalls like strange beasts. A man sat in a corner strumming a ukulele, and though Scirye did not know what the Hawaiian meant, the melancholy tune suggested it was about someone very, very lonely.

Sizzling sounds were coming from the kitchen, and when a man in a dirty apron opened the door to peek out at them, the smoke from the oven rolled into the restaurant itself.

Pele simply waved a hand at them. "They're with me," she said.

The man rolled his eyes as if this was the weirdest thing that Pele had done in a lifetime full of odd behavior.

That was when Scirye's eyes made out the telephone sitting on the counter. Suddenly she felt a pang of guilt. Screwing up her courage, she asked the goddess, "May I call San Francisco? My mother's in the hospital."

"There's a pay phone near the restrooms," the man croaked in a voice like a giant frog.

"I . . . I don't have any money," Scirye said.

"No long-distance calls," the man snapped, but when Pele stared at him, he shoved it toward Scirye. "Go on. But don't take too long," he said sullenly.

Sulking, the man disappeared into the kitchen again, returning to the process of turning food into lumps of charcoal.

Anxiously, Scirye picked up the cone-shaped receiver and put it against her ear. When she had dialed, she spoke to the operator. It took a few minutes but she got through to the consulate, where she learned her mother had returned from the hospital, having just been released two hours ago.

"Hello?" Lady Sudarshane asked and Scirye suddenly wished she were safe in her mother's arms that instant.

"This is Scirye," the girl said eagerly. "Are you all right?"

"Thank Nanaia that you're alive!" Lady Sudarshane exclaimed, relieved. "The police have been turning San Francisco upside down looking for you, and then there was this absurd phone call from the airport that made no sense. Where are you?"

"Uh, well, in Honolulu," Scirye said awkwardly.

"This is no time for one of your fibs, young lady," her mother said anxiously. "You've had everyone worried."

"Honest, Mother," Scirye said. For a moment she held the receiver toward the musician, who had kept playing his ukulele. Then she spoke into the telephone again. "Hear that?" she asked, feeling foolish that her proof was so weak. "You have to believe me. I'm in Hawaii."

"But how—?" Lady Sudarshane began and then caught herself. "No, never mind. You can tell me all about it when you get home, dear." She was relaxing now. "Just tell me where you are and I'll contact our consulate in Honolulu to pick you up."

Scirye didn't know where to begin talking about what happened. She had felt the terrible deep sorrow of seeing Nishke die, and the fear and anger and relief of having survived three battles. And how many people could say they had given fashion tips to a goddess?

She certainly didn't feel like the girl whose head had once been filled with all those ridiculously romantic notions about heroism. And the rude people at home, who had once seemed so significant and hurtful, now seemed silly compared to the monsters she had encountered.

With a heavy heart, Scirye said, "I'm sorry, but first I have to find the ring."

Kles, who had his ear pressed to the receiver, heard everything her mother had said. "You should listen to your mother," the griffin scolded.

"Are you there too, Klestetstse?" Lady Sudarshane asked. "Oh, of course you would be. I think you're a better mother to Scirye than me."

"That's not true," Scirye said, trying to protect her mother's feelings.

"Thank you for fibbing, dear." Lady Sudarshane sighed. "I'm sorry for getting so involved in my duties that I neglected you. The Princess Maimantstse sent Klestetstse so you wouldn't be so lonely. But we'll start over again. You and I will spend more time together from now on, all right?"

Scirye fiddled with the phone cord uncomfortably. "I'd like that. It's just that I . . . I made a promise to Nanaia if she would help me get even for Nishke and find the ring."

"Nanaia would never expect someone as young as you to keep a vow as major as that," Lady Sudarshane argued urgently.

The Scirye of a week ago would have been glad of an excuse to get out of some unpleasant chore, but not the Scirye of today. How to explain that to her mother? "I wish I could," she said, feeling as if she were stumbling about in the dark, "but I think the theft is part of something very important. That rich Mr. Roland is behind it all."

Her mother paused as if she were finally sensing the change in her daughter. "I don't care how big you think the plot is. Come home."

The concern in her mother's voice touched Scirye, but she glanced at Kles, then Bayang, Leech, and Koko. They had fought beside her. She was responsible to them as well as her mother. "It wouldn't be Tumarg to leave it to someone else to do."

"As a Kushan, I understand Tumarg but"—her mother's voice almost broke into a sob—"as a mother, I don't care. I'm scared for you, darling."

I'm frightened, too, Scirye thought, *but I can't hide from it, either*. And that made her sad because she knew she had to refuse her mother's pleas. "I'll be home just as soon as I can."

Her mother's voice rose with anxiety. "Please, Scirye," she begged. "Listen to me."

The same proud warrior who had defied monsters and a dragon

had been reduced to pleading with her. Miserable, Scirye clutched the receiver, unable to speak.

Her mother managed to choke out, "We're ... we're burying Nishke tomorrow."

If Scirye caught a Clipper back, perhaps she would be able to make it. Tears streaked down her cheeks.

Pele perched upon a stool next to her. "Take a minute. Think," she suggested kindly as she held up a hand. A package of peanuts detached itself from a rack against the wall and floated into her palm. Ripping it open, she shook some peanuts into her brown palm and held out the package, giving it a little shake so that the peanuts rattled inside the paper. "Here. Don't make a decision on an empty belly."

The last thing she wanted was peanuts, but it wasn't wise to turn down a gift from Pele.

Kles fluttered down from her shoulder and fetched two peanuts. "My lady thanks you." With slow beats of his wings, he rose to the level of Scirye's mouth and fed her like a newly hatched chick before he returned to shoulder, where he tried to dry her face.

Scirye chewed automatically as she felt the ache in her soul.

"What do you really want to do?" Pele asked. "Go home where it's nice and safe? Or go with me and maybe die." She began to crunch the peanuts between her few orange-stained teeth.

Scirye couldn't help staring. Up until now, she had always thought every goddess was a serious, elegant lady like Nanaia. A goddess would have a nimbus of divine fire about her head and shoulders, not a tangled bird's nest of gray hair. And Scirye had certainly never expected to be sharing a bag of peanuts with one in a rattrap of a café.

As the girl rubbed her fingertips together, Scirye thought that of all the odd creatures she had met so far, Pele was the strangest and the most terrifying—and yet sitting beside Pele right at this moment, Scirye had also never felt more alive, never more Tumarg.

This had to be what it meant to brush up against the divine: to feel like you were part of the magic itself.

Accompanying Pele was doing the right thing and scuttling back home like some frightened kitten was all wrong.

The girl spoke into the receiver again. "I don't want to hurt you, Mother, but I think if I went home now, I'd be a coward." Scirye's voice caught. "Good-bye, Mother. I love you and Father." She started to hang up before she could change her mind.

Before she did, though, Kles's head darted toward the mouthpiece. "I'll watch over her, Lady."

Lady Sudarshane's tearful voice sounded tinny in the receiver. "I'm . . . I'm counting on you."

A new wave of homesickness and guilt washed over Scirye as she finished hanging the receiver on the holder.

Pele patted her hand sympathetically. "You're growing up. It's what all mamas want and what they also hate."

"I don't like it much, either," Scirye admitted ruefully.

Leech was watching her curiously. "I always felt sorry for myself because I was an orphan, but if it hurts this much, maybe I was better off not knowing mine."

Bayang was more practical. "Your mother will have the Honolulu police searching for you," she warned.

Pele gave a bubbly chuckle. "They'll never follow where we're going."

"That's just what I'm afraid of," Koko groaned.

30

Scirye

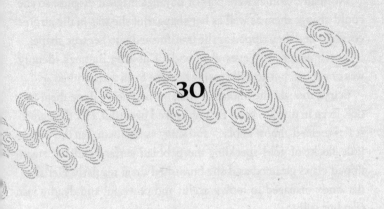

Pele led them through another doorway into a basement. As they descended the rickety steps, the wood and plaster walls gave way to dirt, and the air was warmer. With a snap of her fingers, a small flame danced once again upon Pele's fingertip.

In the flickering light, they saw they were in a basement with a floor that sloped downward at a slight angle. Against one wall was a table and an old boiler with assorted boxes and crates stacked haphazardly. But most of the cellar was lost in shadow.

"Leave my stuff there." She used her free hand to point to an old card table. "And don't forget my feathers."

Obediently, Leech deposited the cardboard and the new feathers on top of the table as Pele nodded to Bayang. "You change now, *mo-o*. Maybe no time later, eh?"

Normally, clothes were part of Bayang's magical disguise so she could change them as well as her shape. But she was in the airport coveralls and they ripped as she transformed into her true shape.

Leech and Koko's eyes went wide. Knowing Bayang's identity was one thing, but actually seeing her true form was another.

Scirye thought the photos of dragons had never done them justice. Even in the dim light, Bayang looked beautiful. Her dark green scales seemed almost as black and shiny as obsidian, but there were little flecks of gold speckling the pebbled surface and her steel-tipped claws gleamed as if she burnished them regularly. Her slender body managed to look graceful and powerful and deadly just standing still.

Scirye found herself wishing that she could be a dragon, too.

Pele glanced shrewdly between the new deadly Bayang and the small human boy called Leech. Then she shuffled over toward him as he watched her uneasily. Pursing her lips, the goddess flicked a fingernail against an iron armband.

Ting.

The sound reverberated like a bell.

"Yes," she said, a broad smile spreading across her face. But she struck it again to be sure. "Yes, it is."

Remembering how Pele liked to extract tribute, Leech covered up the ring and stepped back. "Please don't take them, Your High Auntie-ness. I've had these since I was born."

Pele held up her palm. "I wouldn't think of it," she said and glanced at Bayang. "And neither should anyone else." Then she faced the boy again. "This," she said, tapping the armband a third time, "is a powerful weapon." She pointed to the disks decorating the top. "And these will let you fly."

"Really?" Leech asked in amazement.

Putting her hands on her hips, Pele jerked her head at Bayang. "Isn't that so, *mo-o*? Don't lie. True facts should go with a true shape."

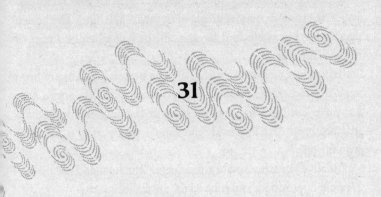

31

Bayang

"I'm not sure what you mean," Bayang said reluctantly. She wasn't afraid of helping Leech find his true powers because she was sure he wasn't a threat to dragonkind. Rather, she didn't want him to discover her original mission.

Though Pele only came up to Bayang's chin, suddenly the goddess seemed to loom over her. "We might need him for the battle," Pele said.

"Need who?" Leech asked, puzzled.

Pele pointed a dirty finger at the iron armband. "We need that."

"They're just something I've always had," Leech said, fingering them. "It was with me when I was found as a baby and brought to the orphanage."

Pele shook her head. "You still got no luck with your family, do you?" She turned commandingly to Bayang. "Tell him." The brown eyes seemed to swell until Bayang felt she had fallen into cups of molten chocolate.

Bayang was unable to resist. "When a person dies, they're born again in another life. Thousands of years ago, you were once a hero known as Lee No Cha." Against her will, the dragon indicated the iron armband. "As Pele said, you can fly with part of it and fight with the rest."

"Really?" Leech asked in amazement. "But how do I use them?" He poked, prodded, and rubbed the armband.

Aware of Pele's stern eyes upon her, Bayang directed him. "Take the flying disks off the armband and then spit on them."

Leech looked skeptical, as if he suspected them of playing a practical joke on him. But when he pulled at the disks, he was surprised when they came off in his hand. "So what am I supposed to do now? Am I supposed to clean them?"

"Spit on them!" Pele commanded. Her voice resonated in the cellar; the sound seemed to fill the boy's head.

Feeling foolish, Leech spat on one of the bracelets.

"Now say, 'Change!'" Bayang said.

"Change," Leech mumbled sheepishly. Instantly the disks rose from his palm and expanded to eighteen inches in diameter.

"Whoa," Leech said as his jaw dropped open. The disks hovered only inches away.

"Give them a gentle push from above," Bayang instructed.

Cautiously, the boy tapped one with a fingertip. It spiraled downward where it waited a few inches above the floor. When Leech nudged the other one, it, too descended until it was next to the other.

"Now step onto them," Bayang said.

Puzzled, the boy set his right foot on one. "It's sticking like glue to me," he said in surprise as it clung to the sole of his shoe.

"Now the second disk," Bayang said.

As soon as his left shoe touched the other disk, Leech began to rise into the air.

32

Leech

Leech's feet felt so light that it almost seemed as if they had turned into balloons as he began to rise unsteadily. "Hey!" He spread his arms to keep his balance.

"Whoa," Koko said as his mouth dropped open.

Leech had always been shorter than his friend but suddenly he was gaping down at the top of Koko's head. And then everyone was looking up at him as he floated eight feet in the air.

Suddenly his legs crossed and he began to spin madly like a top. "What's...what's happening?" he yelled as the cellar seemed to whip round and round.

"Oops. The disks must be on the wrong ankles," Bayang said. "They're like shoes with a left one and a right one." She gripped his ankles so that he stopped whirling.

"I feel sort of dizzy," the boy said, feeling almost at the point of throwing up.

She pulled him down until she could hold him by the shoulders. "Lift your legs against your chest," Bayang told him. He obeyed, feeling like a human beach ball. With Koko and Scirye's help, he made the switch.

"Ready?" Bayang asked.

When he nodded, she let go. This time he shot up into the air until he almost bumped against the ceiling, ten feet up. It was scary being that high without a ladder or anything, but also thrilling. He gave a whoop.

Inside his head, he heard a voice exult, *Yes!*

As the fierce joy washed through him, he did not stop to wonder where that came from.

With a kick, he sent himself zooming across the cellar into the darkness. It was like skating on an invisible rubber sheet because he felt how the air bounced beneath his feet occasionally, making him dip a few inches or rise up a foot. It didn't matter. He knew his body would adjust and keep him upright—knew with every fiber of his being, knew as certainly as the sun rising in the east—because this was where he was meant to be: flying through the air.

The next moment, he whizzed back toward his friends, outstretched, hair flying behind him. He let out a joyous yell for the sheer pleasure of being alive.

The boy's delight was so infectious that Kles rose into the air and darted beside him. Boy and griffin looked at one another and laughed at the ecstasy of it all.

"Race you!" Leech challenged.

"You're on!" Kles brought his wings down in a sudden slap and shot forward, but not for long.

With another kick, Leech shot after him. Bending his knees, he crouched in a more aerodynamic shape. He caught up with the griffin. "Bye-bye." He grinned, and with another kick left Kles behind.

Leech almost ran into disaster as he reached the far wall. He tilted so that he could bank to the right, but at that speed he found himself capsizing. As he swung upside down, he saw the cellar's right side looming ahead.

Somehow he managed to get himself turned, and as he headed back, the chagrined boy thought, *I guess I'm not automatically going to stay upright after all.*

"How do I stop?" he shouted as he flailed his arms at the air.

Bayang ran forward on her hind legs to meet him, her forelegs raised. "Say 'change' again," she ordered. "But wait until you start to slow—"

But Leech was so panicky that he misjudged the timing. The landing was abrupt but not particularly violent except for a few bruises. As the boy lay on his stomach, the flying disks shrank and hovered over him.

Bayang stopped in mid-stride and lowered her forelegs. "Oops. Sorry."

Koko was almost immediately by his side. "You okay, buddy?"

"My body felt so light, like I was the wind," Leech enthused as his friend helped him to sit up. "I bet you could ride on my back."

"You were flying as if you were made for that." Scirye beamed.

Leech's face was pure joy as he took the flying disks and attached them to his armbands again. "I was, wasn't I? I knew it. I just knew it. This is better than wings."

"I wouldn't say that," Kles said indignantly as he settled on his mistress's shoulder. "I won, after all."

Leech conceded defeat with a dip of his head, but that didn't lessen his pleasure any. "I never thought I could do anything like that! I can fly anywhere!"

"Don't get a swelled head, boy. You need more practice or you could wind up diving right into the sea." Pele tapped Leech's forehead in warning and then jerked her chin at Bayang. "Now will you tell him the rest, *mo-o*, or I will I have to? You weren't hunting Badik originally. You had another target in mind."

"What else are you hiding?" Koko asked the dragon suspiciously.

33

Bayang

Bayang realized that she had no choice and was surprised at how that saddened her. Her career hadn't allowed friendships so she'd come to treasure the hatchlings' companionship—yes, and even that pompous little griffin. She'd barely had time to savor the experience before she had to alienate them with the truth. But ever since that day when Badik had invaded, she had vowed to face trouble head-on.

"When the original No Cha was just a child," Bayang said reluctantly, "he killed a dragon prince and used his hide to make a belt."

Leech went pale. "I did?"

Koko sprang to his friend's defense. "You're crazy. He wouldn't do a thing like that."

"Not Leech here and now." Bayang was quick to make that distinction. "That was the first No Cha." She could see how horrified the boy still was and tried to comfort him quickly. "I don't believe you're that way now. And perhaps not even then. I've heard that Lee No Cha wanted a gift for his father. So perhaps his intentions were good. But he was a hatchling with powers so immense that even an adult would have had trouble handling them."

"I see," Kles said. "If you dragons are anything like the Kushans, the prince's death would have started a blood feud between the dragons and No Cha."

Scirye looked as if Bayang had just kicked her. "So all the time you were keeping the truth from us. How could you?"

Bayang wanted to defend herself but by now she knew a bit of how the girl thought: What Bayang had done was not Tumarg. There was no denying it and no defending such a great deception. "I'm not proud of what I did," she said lamely.

Pele poked a bony finger into Bayang's side. "Go on. Tell them the rest."

Bayang felt as if she were caught in an avalanche that was sweeping her along relentlessly. With her eyes, she pleaded with the children for understanding.

"The dragons demanded that you . . ." Bayang corrected herself. "I mean, *he* be killed. And his own family agreed that would be the end of the matter."

Koko placed an arm protectively around his friend. "So if that ended the feud, what are you doing here?"

Pele nudged Bayang once more and the dragon went on. "No, your . . . his mother was able to use magic to bring him back to life." Another nudge from Pele and Bayang felt now as if the avalanche of truth had begun. "Because of his mother's disobedience, the dragon king demanded that the Lees track down No Cha themselves and carry out the sentence."

Leech's face scrunched up as if he were in pain. "My family?"

Bayang almost thought it would have been kinder to have killed the boy while he was still blissfully ignorant of his past rather than reveal the terrible truth. "Your father and brothers," she explained. "They all had powerful magical weapons but none of them could beat you."

"How could their heart be in that fight?" Scirye asked, as sickened as the others.

"They fought as hard as they could," Bayang said, "or the dragon king would have declared war on their entire clan."

"So my own family killed me again?" Leech asked in a small voice.

"What does it matter, buddy," Koko said, trying to console him. "After all, you're alive here and now."

Leech looked ready to cry. "It was bad enough when I thought my mother had dumped me at the orphanage. But it's even worse to hear that my family tried to murder me."

"In another life, not this one," Koko said, but Leech still remained crushed.

Dragons did not encourage physical contact as much as humans did, and Bayang's kin had been more extreme than most. Yet at that moment she wanted to hug Leech. Instead all she could do was go on battering his fragile soul. "Even though you were a child, they couldn't stop you. Heaven itself intervened and the battle was stopped."

"Otherwise, my own family would have kept on trying to kill me," Leech said miserably.

Kles folded his forelegs. "But you dragons never forgot," he said to Bayang.

"Or forgave," Bayang admitted. For the first time in her life, she felt ashamed of her kind.

"So the blood feud went on not just for one life but for all the other lifetimes." Even Kles, who knew of Kushana blood feuds that went on for centuries, was stunned by the vast scale of time.

It was time for the big confession. "Dragons live far longer than humans," Bayang said. "We have tracked Lee No Cha in his subsequent lives and each time . . ."

"Your kind 'stopped' me before I could kill another dragon," Leech said, full of hurt and anger at her betrayal.

Koko touched an axe in his belt. "I think it's more personal than that. It sounds like the 'lady' here fought some of those other No Chas. And the fact that she's still alive means she won."

"I could never beat No Cha with his full power and knowledge." Bayang spread her forelegs helplessly. "I'm sorry for what I did."

Leech stared at her as he realized what she was leaving unsaid. "Is that why you were in the museum? You were tracking me so you could . . ."

Bayang felt as helpless as she had the day Badik had attacked her home. There were no excuses she could give for what she had done to his other selves. Truly, she was the monster and not him. "Yes."

Leech lifted up his chin in brave defiance. "So when were you going to kill me?"

Bayang had served her people as well as she could, but no longer. She had spent most of her life on missions away from the dragon kingdoms, alone like some abandoned waif. In the brief time they had been together, Leech, Scirye, Koko—and yes, even the pesky griffin—had given her more companionship than any dragon had in centuries. They were her clan now. It was time to quit being an assassin.

"I'm not going to obey my orders anymore," Bayang insisted vehemently. Scirye and Kles both sucked in their breath. At least they understood what Bayang was doing. Unfortunately, the boy didn't, so all the dragon could do was go on. "You saved my life. You're my friend. Or"—she sighed sadly—"you were."

Still keeping his eyes on Bayang, Leech tapped the armband and asked Pele, "Goddess Pele, is this really a weapon?"

"Yes, but I don't know more than that," Pele said and then jerked her head at Bayang. "*She* would."

Bayang hesitated, but she owed it to the boy to prepare him for those future assassins. Knowing that she was adding treachery to her list of crimes, Bayang explained, "It expands, and yet in your hand it will be as light as a feather. You'll be able to throw it at a target and have it return to your hand."

"Why should I trust anything you say?" Leech shot back.

Bayang was surprised when Scirye jumped in to defend her, but the girl had balled her hands into fists, ready to stop an injustice. And Bayang was glad that Tumarg drove her to speak the truth as she saw fit.

"Think about it," Scirye argued earnestly. "Bayang's turning her back on the other dragons. That will make her an outlaw."

Leech leaned to the side to gaze around Scirye at Bayang. "Is this true?"

"Yes," Bayang said uncomfortably. "But then my profession has accustomed me to being alone anyway. If we're successful, I'll return to the kingdom to tell them what I've seen—that you're no longer a threat to my people."

"What will they do to you after that?" Leech demanded, suddenly sounding worried.

Bayang shrugged a shoulder fatalistically. "I'll be placed under a sentence of death, too. But again, my career has made me used to that risk, as well."

Leech scratched his head. "You'd do that for me?"

Bayang bent her head with great dignity. "It's the least I can do."

Leech studied Bayang intently and then spoke slowly. "I'm still not sure I can trust you." He extended his hand. "But I'd like to try."

"Yes," Bayang said, pleased as she took it. "So would I."

After they had shaken hands, Koko tilted his head back. "But will the other dragons hold off, too?"

"Unfortunately, no," Bayang said. "Someone else will be sent to carry out the task. So let me teach you how to defend yourself."

Leech pulled the iron band from his arm and held it up. "Okay, what do I do with it?"

"Spit on it and then say 'change' again," Bayang instructed, and sketched another flaming sign in the air. Again the boy found it easy to copy.

The iron chimed melodically, and he felt the armband shiver in his fingers until he felt as if his whole body had turned into a tuning fork. But the vibrations didn't make him feel sick at all. Instead, they filled him with a strange, powerful energy. The armband expanded in his hand and the open ends fused together to form a solid ring about twenty inches across, and yet it felt light as hollow bone.

Yes! Yes! the inner voice said again, and he felt strangely complete.

When he swung it experimentally, the air made a whooshing sound and the wind nearly knocked the others down. "Sorry," he called, and then beamed at Pele. "This is amazing."

When he tapped the ring experimentally against the concrete, small cracks appeared.

Koko whistled. "That's harder than iron now."

"It can shatter armor and sword blades like they were eggshells," Bayang said.

Koko was stroking his chin speculatively. "What about a bank vault?"

"I don't know about that but it would certainly dent your skull." Bayang's hand shot out to stop Leech when he lifted it to throw. "Be careful where you aim that."

Leech nodded at the wisdom of that and shifted so that he could aim at a crate. With a flick of his wrist, he sent the ring spinning across the room. Boards splintered and bottles shattered, spilling catsup everywhere in a tomato massacre. The next moment the ring was back in his hand.

"It can do many other things," Pele said, and turned to Bayang. "You say the feud's over for you, so will you teach him?"

"You can also use the ring for defense," Bayang explained. "You can parry blows and if you time it right, you can disarm an opponent. But it means catching a sword or spear thrust inside the ring. Then with a twist of the wrist, you'll either break the blade or take the weapon away. But you'll need a very strong wrist and a lot of training."

Leech's eyes grew big. "Wow."

Pele nudged the boy. "You need a lot more practice. Don't be reckless when you use it."

"Sure," Leech said, only half listening as he ran his fingers admiringly around the rim.

Pele pursed her lips skeptically and then nudged Scirye. "Keep an eye on him, eh? You don't want him knocking down any skyscrapers."

"May I?" Scirye asked Leech as she extended a hand.

Leech handed the ring to her. "It's funny, but it seems just like the plain old ring I always had."

"And how do you feel?" Scirye asked.

"Not any different than before," Leech admitted.

Scirye gave him a small smile. "It's funny, isn't it?"

He gave a nervous little laugh. "And a little scary, too. Is that what it's like for you?"

"Yes," she admitted.

Leech turned to Bayang as a new thought occurred to him. "Bayang, if you catch Badik, maybe your people will forgive you for letting me go."

"If I can kill Badik, I wouldn't care what happened to me," Bayang said.

"Your enemy is still our enemy, too," Scirye said, and glanced at Leech.

"That's right," Leech agreed.

All of Bayang's adult life, she had operated alone. It was strange to have allies now—and not even her own kind at that. Her voice caught. "Thank you."

Koko sidled over to Leech. "Well, partner, when you're done playing cops and robbers, that nifty armband'll open up all sorts of opportunities for two enterprising gents like us. When you're on the tenth floor, who worries about thieves coming in an unlocked window? And if we found a wall safe, one tap and bing! We crack it like a walnut."

Leech knew his friend too well. "Planning a big crime spree?" he asked as he slipped the armband back on.

Koko corrected him indignantly. "More like redistributing the wealth."

Pele shuffled up beside them and put her arms around their shoulders. "Before you do that, bad-bad boys, we stop Roland, eh? And to do that, we might need your power too, *kupua*."

Koko pulled free in alarm, "What, hey, no?"

Pele let go of Leech so she could put her nose almost against Koko's. "You don't want me to get mad, do you?"

"Go on, Koko," Leech urged. "She knows what she's doing. Besides, the cat's out of the bag now."

"Geez, have a heart," Koko whined. "Do you know how uncomfortable fur is in this kind of heat? And anyway, I'm stronger as a human."

"But my transformation magic is stronger in my true form than as a human. Isn't it the same way for you?" Bayang asked.

Leech glanced at the goddess, whose frown had deepened. "Do like she says, Koko," he urged, "before she gets mad."

"I thought you were on my side," Koko said, but he turned and with a muttered spell and a quick sign, the pear-shaped human disappeared to be replaced by a furry creature four feet high. Koko's clothes hung on him except around the hips, which seemed wider than his human form's. His fuzzy jowls made his small head seem round. Most of the fur about his face and throat was white but there were black patches around his eyes and cheeks. He had a short, sharp nose tipped by a black muzzle.

Taking off his coveralls, Koko began scratching furiously. "I'd forgotten how itchy this shape was." His chest was thinner than his waist and stumpy legs so that he resembled a hairy striped pear.

Bayang couldn't help making spluttering noises as she tried to control her laughter.

Kles wasn't even bothering to be polite. "What are you?" The griffin chuckled.

It was Leech's turn to defend his friend. "He happens to be a very fine example of a *tanuki*, a Japanese raccoon dog."

"Otherwise known as a badger." Bayang smirked. "But raccoon or badger, a *tanuki* is a pest pure and simple."

"What's a Japanese badger doing in San Francisco?" Kles asked.

"What's a griffin doing there?" Koko shot back.

"We were there because of my mother," Scirye explained as she unrolled the carpet and tucked two axes into her belt.

Leech refused to take any of the axes from the remnant of the carpet as it hovered in the air. He seemed to be trusting to his arm rings.

Koko started to take one of the axes, but then realized there was no place to stow it in his fur so he put it back. "Well, girlie, I wound up in 'Frisco because of five aces."

"Ahem, it's Lady Scirye to you," Kles was quick to correct him.

"Yeah, well." Koko shrugged indifferently. "I was in this poker game in this Yokohama dive with these guys that suddenly got all fussy about the rules."

"Let me guess," Bayang said, folding her forelegs. "They thought there should only be fifty-two cards in a deck instead of fifty-three."

"More like fifty-five." Koko waved a paw airily. "But who's counting? Anyhow, the next thing I knew I woke up on a tramp freighter bound for the States."

"Where the Americans wouldn't have heard about your kind or know how to protect themselves," Bayang said. "I bet you were licking your chops like a fox in a henhouse."

Kles still wasn't about to forgive the *tanuki* for being so familiar with his mistress. "If you ask me, Koko's had one too many chickens."

Self-consciously, Koko pressed his forepaws on his ample hips as if he were trying to reduce their size. "My fur does seem a little tight since I last wore it. Do you think I put on weight?"

Lies were forbidden by Tumarg, but Scirye felt sorry enough for Koko to bend the rules a bit. "If I were a *tanuki*, I'd find you, um, very fetching."

"Hmph, you never had someone try to turn you into a coat." Koko sniffed, but he turned to inspect himself in a broken mirror on the wall. "But you really think so, girlie?"

Somehow the girl managed to keep a straight face. "Would I lie?"

Koko started to preen. "Well, if you say so, girlie."

"How many times do I have to tell you?" Kles snapped. "It's Lady Scirye."

Koko flung up a paw. "Right, right. I finally get it. From now on, it's Lady Scirye. After all, only a classy broad could appreciate a chassis as special as mine."

Scirye

Pele crooked a finger at them. "This way." She shuffled toward the far end of the cellar though it was so dark that Scirye could not see the actual wall, and they kept walking through the blackness. Scirye was sure they had passed beyond the boundaries of The Salty Bird and must be under some other building, though she could no longer see anything. She stumbled on, following the distinctive sound of Pele's sandals.

The floor itself began to slant until it was as steep as a hillside, and the air grew warmer. The dirt became gravel that rattled away in small cascades with each footstep, and then gave way to rock that rippled downward like layers of dark cake batter but crunched crisply beneath their feet. When Scirye slipped and put her hand down, she understood why. The rough surface was whiskered with fine, sharp needles that pierced her hand in a dozen places.

As a precaution against further falls, she pulled the gauntlet over her hand, wondering how long the soles of her boots would last as the floor rasped at them. Without any light, it was as if the night itself had swallowed them up, and Scirye lost all sense of up and down. And yet she felt she had to keep up with Pele or be lost in the darkness for forever.

Though she still wasn't quite sure what to think about Bayang, her eyes searched instinctively for the dragon. Though the girl had felt physically sick when Bayang had revealed her deceit, Scirye still turned to her when she was in trouble.

Scirye desperately wanted to believe that someone so beautiful and noble looking wouldn't lie when she said she was going to disobey her orders. Was Scirye just fooling herself? Did she have a choice anymore? Like Leech, Scirye was going to try to trust Bayang.

The girl felt a little twinge of panic when she could not find Bayang in the darkness. That didn't last for long, though, for at the core of Scirye's soul was the same stubbornness that had kept her ancestors journeying through hostile lands and across mountains and deserts until they found a home. And that determination was stronger than any fear.

She forced her legs to keep moving forward, taking a little comfort from Kles's reassuring weight upon her shoulder.

She felt rather than saw the steam that began to puff from crevices. The vapor carried a faint whiff of sulfur and curled itself about her arms and legs like warm tentacles, as if trying to hold her, but she always managed to pull free.

By now, she had lost all sense of time and distance. It might have been fifteen minutes or hours, and it might have been a few hundred yards or miles.

Leech's voice came panicked from the dark. "I . . . I don't like being cooped up like this."

"It's okay, buddy. I'm here," Koko said. "You're not alone."

"So are we." Scirye groped around blindly until she could find a hand. "Is that you, Leech?"

"Y-yeah," came his shaky voice. He gripped hers as tight as a vise.

"I got your other hand, buddy," Koko assured him.

Hand in hand, the three children continued on. The air had become so hot that Scirye was sweating all over as if she were inside a furnace. Finally, though, ahead of her she heard a puffing noise like a steam locomotive.

The noise grew louder until it was a steady rumbling and the air was so sulfurous that she almost gagged. Scirye was grateful to see a red glow ahead of her, and she and the others staggered toward the light—and then almost immediately retreated as a rope of liquid fire lashed at them.

It took a moment for the girl's eyes to adjust, but she saw a huge cavern of black stone in front of them. In the center was a huge pool of lava as bright as the sun. It churned like a pot of boiling water so that the yellows, whites, and reds swirled and changed into interesting shapes like creatures in a witch's cauldron.

Every now and then a huge bubble of gas broke the surface, flinging strands of burning, sticky mush about the cavern. Where it hit the walls or the pool's ledge, it formed lumps like broken pots with many sharp points. As soon as it began to cool, it changed from white to yellow to scarlet. Other lumps, thrown out earlier, had already cooled to stone. They looked like pillows bristling with black needles.

Pele shuffled out onto the uneven surface, oblivious to the flames and the heat, and knelt by the pool's edge. When she dipped her hand into the molten rock, Scirye held her breath. How could even a goddess survive that fiery pit?

However, Pele acted as if the lava were cold clay, splashing it for a moment with a playful smile, before she gathered some up in a cupped palm. Her lips moved as she alternated between murmuring a spell and blowing on the mud to cool it, her other hand nimbly shaped the viscous material into petals until the lump had become a lovely little jet-black flower. She did not stop until she had fashioned five of them, one smaller than the rest.

Then she gathered them into her lap and, holding up her long dress slightly to make a basket, she brought them over to the companions. "Each of you, take one of my charms. They'll protect you from the heat and the fire and let you breathe. But whatever you do, don't lose them. Or you'll be in big trouble."

When Scirye took one, she was no longer able to smell the sulfur. Or perhaps it was just that it seemed natural to take in the mineral. Nor did it feel hot.

On her shoulder, Kles was panting uncomfortably, a wing shielding his beak against the stench and heat.

Hastily, Scirye tore off a sleeve from her coveralls and used a strip from that to fashion a collar so she could hang the tiniest stone blossom about Kles's neck.

The griffin took a deep breath and spread his wings slightly in delight. "Ah, that's better."

The others seemed more comfortable, as well, but the moment that Scirye had stopped touching the original flower, the stench and the heat returned so she was glad to take the last one from Pele's outstretched palm. Quickly she made a necklace for herself.

Next to her, Leech was doing the same with one of his sleeves, using part of it to make a collar for Koko and the rest for Bayang.

"Now we'll go to Roland's," Pele declared.

Leech looked around the cave. "Where? This is a dead end."

"Volcanoes rise from an undersea ridge of mountains," Pele explained, "so they're all connected like the tunnels in an ant colony."

Bayang nodded in comprehension. "You're going to use the lava tubes like they were streets in a city."

"Go into that?" Scirye asked. Tumarg spoke of how fire purified the soul—but only in a figurative sense. She'd never expected to have to do it literally.

Returning to the pool's edge, Pele slipped two fingers into her mouth and let out a piercing whistle that the cavern amplified until it seemed as loud as a siren.

Immediately, the pool began to seethe until a column started to rise. At first, Scirye thought it must be a giant bubble of gas, but the column continued to grow taller instead of bursting. When the column was about twenty feet high, Pele chopped at its base with the edge of her palm, toppling the column like a tree.

When it splashed against the surface, it sent more ropes of lava lashing at the cavern. The column did not sink but floated.

Pele calmly stepped out onto the molten surface as she shaped the column, trimming here and flattening there until it had become a long, oval board with fins. It bobbed up and down on the whirling lava pool. Putting a fist on her hip, Pele surveyed her handiwork critically and then made minor adjustments.

Finally, though, she seemed satisfied. "Hop on," she said.

Though the board was still in contact with the pool's lava, it had already cooled until it was almost black.

"There's nothing to hold onto," Koko said skeptically.

"Mainlanders," Pele snorted. She fussed over the board some more, grumbling to herself about sissy tourists. Then she stepped back. "There. I've made handholds and toeholds." She gestured to the indentations she had made in the stone board. "Satisfied?"

"Can't you do better than that?" Koko wheedled. "After all, you're a goddess."

"If you don't like it, you can leave." Pele pointed at the way they had come.

Koko glanced anxiously back at the dark tunnel. "I guess it's worth a try." Leaning in close to Leech, he added in a whisper, "But sue the old bat for everything she's got if I fall off."

Unfortunately for Koko, Pele's hearing was sharper than he had thought, for she motioned him to very front of the board. "You take the seat of honor."

Koko held up his forepaws. "Naw, I couldn't."

As Pele squinted at Koko, her voice took on a dangerous edge. "But *I* insist."

"Well, sure, ha, ha." Koko laughed nervously. "Can't disappoint a goddess, can I?"

He waddled forward, keeping one eye on the explosive lava pool and the other on Pele. Gingerly he set a hind paw onto the board, which rocked dangerously. "Whoa, can't you steady this thing?"

"Don't be such a baby," Pele said, and shoved Koko onto the board with such force, he slid across it until his head and shoulders plunged into the lava itself.

"Koko!" Leech raced to help his friend.

However, Pele was already hauling Koko out of the lava by his hind paws. "Oof. This is no time to play, *kupua.*"

When Koko turned over on his back upon the board, a small fountain of lava rose from his lips. Afterward, he lay panting on the board for a moment and then sat up in amazement, staring at his forepaws and then feeling his shoulders and head. "Hey, I'm not burnt."

"As long as you have my flower, you'll be okay," Pele assured him. At her urging, he put his paws to the holes that she designated. "And hold on tight, *kupua.* Or whoosh"—Pele's hand pantomimed something flying off—"the lava will sweep you away and you could wind up in the middle of the earth."

Leech climbed onto the board behind Koko, nearly falling into the lava himself as the slab of stone rocked under his weight. He and Koko held on for dear life when Scirye got on. She managed it without mishap, and as she sat down, she was relieved to see that

Pele had made smaller holes for Kles. Her griffin scrambled down from her shoulder and took his place beside her.

The largest ones were for Bayang, whose balance was so expert that they hardly noticed when she joined them.

"Where are your handholds?" Bayang asked Pele.

"Only you tourists need sissy things like that," Pele scoffed, leaping nimbly onto the rear of the board.

Even Bayang cried out as the front of the board rose out of the lava and then slapped back down.

Pele was laughing. "Now you get the ride of your life." Thrusting her hands in front of her, she began to sing. Sometimes the syllables bubbled like the lava around them and sometimes were as harsh as stone grinding on stone, but Scirye thought she could pick out a strange melody the longer she listened to it—as if the song measured itself not in speedy human time but by the slow, patient time of the earth itself.

The lava began to foam about them until the board was bucking up and down. When Scirye glanced behind her, she saw that Pele's gray hair was flowing about her shoulders and her hands were now making intricate signs in time to her song, sometimes as graceful as a dancer and sometimes as violent as a battling warrior.

The lava roiled all around them, exploding now in big gouts of flame and gas that splattered even the ceiling. The molten rock splashed over them as harmless as ocean surf but the boiling surface seemed to rise all around them.

Frightened, Scirye looked back at Pele again, but she was smiling, holding her hands extended from her sides now for balance. The girl fought against her own sense of panic, telling herself that the goddess would not let them suffocate. She almost screamed as a wave of lava washed over them so that they were surrounded in the bright mudlike stuff. Now she knew how an insect must feel when it was trapped in sap and became amber.

She waited for the lava to drop away but it clung to them, hiding the black cavern walls and entombing them in an incandescent cocoon, as if they had been swallowed by a giant fiery coal. Pele let out a gurgling sound that might have been a whoop as they began to sink.

Scirye held onto the board as they shot downward. The lava roared around her ears as if she were trying to swim in boiling honey. The molten rock was thick enough to cling and resist but not enough to slow down their passage very much.

The board veered sharply to the right, then the left. Though Scirye could not see the goddess, she was sure Pele must be steering them through the currents by shifting her weight like a surfer on her board.

Every now and then through the curtain of lava, Scirye thought she glimpsed the rock wall of a tunnel. But mostly it was just the fluid rock that filled her eyes with an intense light.

They seemed to descend for a long time before they leveled off and suddenly burst into a chamber vast enough to swallow all of San Francisco and Honolulu combined. The lava became like a sea over which they glided. The rumbling noise was even louder now, as if they were near some great engine at the center of the earth.

The board sped up, the nose rising out of the lava. Poor Koko looked miserable. He twisted his head so he could look at his friend. "Okay, I've been triple-dipped in lava. You want to swap places with me?"

Scirye realized that even if the lava wasn't burning him, he was getting the brunt of its force at the front of the board.

"Sure," the loyal Leech said.

"You stay put, you two," Pele commanded, and she laughed. "And, *kupua*, maybe next time, you'll think twice before you call me 'old bat.'"

"Me and my big mouth," Koko groaned.

There were dozens of exits from the chamber but Pele guided them confidently to an exit on the right. Once again, the wild ride began as lava engulfed them and the currents swept them along.

Scirye's arms ached and the trip became even more violent, requiring all of Pele's skill to maneuver them. She even sent them in a spiral as if they were traveling through a tunnel shaped like a corkscrew.

Finally, though, they seemed to be rising, moving even faster now until they suddenly shot out of the lava and into the air with a gray ugly sky overhead.

35

Scirye

Scirye exhaled slowly, hardly believing she had survived the wild ride.

Kles's head turned from examining himself to his mistress. "I think your hair's singed. Yikes!" he yelped as Pele stamped
her foot angrily, making the slab rock up and down like a teeter-totter.

"My charms work good," the goddess declared.

"Of course, of course," Kles agreed hastily.

They were floating in a huge lake of lava in the center of the crater
that they had seen from the air in the eastern half of Roland's island.
Smoke and steam rose up in streamers, soaring up into the ball overhead so that it was possible to see across the crater. Surrounding them
were the crater's black walls, about a quarter mile away on all sides.

The lava on the shore of the lake had partly cooled and solidified, forming a crust of twisted, jagged stone. But there were plenty

of holes through which smoke and lava oozed in ribbons, mixing with other streams so that the lake's rim was framed in a flaming net.

About ten yards beyond the lake's rim rose a ring of cones, some twenty or thirty feet high, from which lava fountained in a brilliant spray of light. It was, thought Scirye, like being surrounded by fireworks or dazzling flowers that were forever changing their shapes.

The lake itself was rougher than anything they'd been on so far. The molten rock churned about them like the waves of a storm-tossed sea. Patches of dark, half-solidified lava rode the surface like crumbling rafts. A constant low, bubbling rumble filled the air, punctuated every now and then by the ugly gurgle of gas exploding, scattering flaming rocks the size of footballs and gobs of lava about.

The group might have been in serious trouble if Pele had not slapped her foot against the surface. "Behave!" Instantly the lava calmed down. "Roland's wizards are controlling the lava with such a powerful system of spells that even I'm having trouble making the lava do what I want. I'm trying to keep it quiet"—the goddess's face wrinkled with strain, as if she were wrestling with an invisible opponent—"but the lava keeps wanting to move."

"We've got company," Bayang said, pointing to the east at a giant woman some twenty feet tall with yellow skin and red hair that had been twisted into braids. On her head was a horned helmet, and she was dressed in coveralls with a leather apron and boots. Fortunately, she had her back to them.

"*Muspeli,*" Bayang whispered to her companions. "They're fire giants from the north. I once had a mission at Muspelheim, their home. Roland must have hired them and brought them here."

The female fire giant certainly seemed at ease in the midst of the volcano. She swung her huge sledgehammer with quiet efficiency, shattering some lava that had begun to cool and solidify along the sides of a channel. Lava flowed along the huge trench from the lake and out through a gap where the crater wall had been shattered and the debris heaped on either side. A rolling sheet of steam rose in the distance where the lava met the sea, hardening and widening the island.

In between blows, the giant yelled instructions to a half dozen fire elementals. Larger and more intelligent than the elementals that resided in lanterns, these generally resembled globes with tentacles, though their shape changed for what the task required and they could even take on human shapes if their employer demanded it. Fortunately the entire crew was too absorbed with their tasks to notice the intruders.

Near the fire giant was a fifty-foot fire salamander with black and yellow stripes nosing among the rocks as it looked for some tidbit. *It's grazing*, Scirye thought, *just like some ox*. Around its great head was a halter of some iridescent metal and slung over its back were panniers of the same material to guard against the smoking debris from the channel.

Bayang reached out cautiously. Scooping up a pawful of the hot mud, she shaped it into a globe. Then, drawing back her arm, she whipped it at the salamander's rump.

The lava ball didn't burn the tough hide, but it startled the creature so that with a loud bellow it bolted across the rocks away from them, scattering boulders in her wake like pebbles.

Throwing down her sledgehammer, the fire giant gave chase, calling for the salamander in some foreign tongue while the fire elementals trailed after her.

"Good. That will keep them busy," Pele said, still laboring to keep the lake flat. With another motion of her hand, a lava current picked up the board obediently and carried it toward the shore.

At the last moment, Pele swung the board broadside so that its side bumped against the lake's edge. "Be careful. Sometimes the rock crust is thin. If you break through in the wrong place, you can fall into lava." Crouching, she held the slab steady against the stony shore. "Get off now."

Koko tested the surface gingerly before he finally clambered off the board and the others quickly followed. As she climbed onto solid ground, Scirye felt the stone crunch under her feet and saw the hundreds of tiny needles along its surface.

Pele was the last on board the slab and as she got off, she gave it a kick that sent it spinning out onto the lake, which had already begun to boil again. Without Pele's protective power, their board began to crumble along the edges, its rocky sides melting to join the lava already in the lake.

Pele jabbed a finger at Koko and commanded, "*Kupua*, change into a fire giant."

Koko turned so that they could not read his lips as he said the spell. His outline blurred and then became a creature like the giant, widening quickly but no taller than he had been as a human boy.

"Is that as big as you can grow?" Pele giggled as she looked down at Koko.

"I can't grow any larger because I can't change my mass," Koko said, irritated.

"It's a question of taking what you need from your surroundings and adding it," Bayang said. Her own outline waved and then expanded upward twenty feet. The next moment it grew sharp again and a female fire giant was standing before them. "In this case, there's plenty of fire to use for padding."

"Show-off," Koko grumbled.

Pele patted Koko on the top of his head. "What's the matter, *kupua*? Did you flunk your transformation lessons?" In the blink of an eye, she had swelled thirty feet high, becoming a fire giant herself. Then, after squinting up at the sun, she nodded to their left. "This way west."

Lava fountained from a nearby cone, spraying dabs of lava on them, but so powerful were Pele's charms that they might just as well have been raindrops.

Fine gray strands drifted through the air and Leech tried to catch one. "What's that?"

"They look like something from a giant spiderweb," Koko said nervously.

"They call that my hair." Pele tugged at the strands on her own head.

"Some of the lava is like molten glass," Bayang added. "When it falls apart in the air, it stretches out into fine threads."

With the goddess leading, they began to trudge across the lava slowly, toward the crater wall a quarter mile away. The lava here had solidified in wrinkled lumps that would made walking difficult, and jets of steam and gas hissed from fissures so that it sounded to Scirye like they were inside a giant tea kettle.

Pele scanned the rolling, lumpy surface, and listened intently to the noises around them. Every now and then, they detoured when she told them the crust was too thin ahead of them.

They came to another section of cones some thirty feet high that rose around them like giant tents. Fortunately, these cones didn't seem to be active so perhaps they belonged to an earlier stage of the lake.

As they rounded one of the cones, they suddenly came upon a man on a platform. His robes were covered with magical symbols that must have protected him from the fire, the heat, and the gases. Apparently they didn't work against falling rocks because he was also wearing a dented football helmet on his head.

The platform was covered with a complex pentagram with various devices at the points. One looked like a star constructed out of animal bones and feathers. Another was a pyramid constructed with bubbling tubes. At a third point was a crystal globe in which a shadowy blob writhed and twisted.

In the center, the man looked very harassed as he tried to monitor the devices and at the same time stir a cauldron filled with a bubbling white fluid like melted marshmallows. With a twist of his paddle he sent the fluid surging to one side.

A fire giant some forty feet tall stood next to the platform, providing excellent shade. "First you stop the lava. And then you send it too fast, wizard." So the wizard was working the spells that made the lava flow so furiously on the lake.

"I told you that I don't know what happened before. Suddenly the stuff in the cauldron went all stiff. We've got to make up for lost time, Surtrson. We're already way behind Mr. Roland's schedule," the wizard argued. "We're supposed to add ten feet a day to the island."

"Do we backtrack?" Bayang asked Pele softly.

The goddess shook her head. "No, we have to hurry. What if Roland's only here a short while? We could miss him. Let's see how good our disguises really are."

"Perhaps you should let me do the talking then," Bayang whispered to Pele. "I don't think there are many Norse giants with Hawaiian accents." Pele nodded.

Surtrson tugged at his belt, which was ringed with a variety of hammers. "The plan was made up by wizards who never left their homes. It never took into account that the more the island grows, the farther the lava has to travel."

"Go ahead and tell Mr. Roland that," the wizard dared him, swirling the fluid even harder. "As for me, I try to do what I'm told."

Surtrson scratched his cheek. "Maybe we should open up another chan—" He stopped when he caught sight of Scirye and Leech. "What are human children doing here?"

With the pleasantest smile she could manage, Bayang said, "A sorceress's family came here to buy one of the homes on the west side, but these children wandered off and got lost. We're just taking them back, sir. Lucky their mother gave them such powerful charms or they'd be charcoal by now."

The wizard squinted at Koko. "Hey, aren't you a little small for a fire giant?"

Koko dipped his head respectfully and then added several more bows for good measure. "I've been a little sick—the Shrinking Influenza." Koko gave a cough in illustration and then tried to look pathetic. "I'll get bigger as I get better."

Surtrson scratched under his horned helmet. "I never heard of that." He stared at Bayang and then Pele. "And how come I've never seen you two before?"

"We just got hired," Bayang said, trying to look like an eager new employee.

That was when Pele drew back a huge foot, and with a kick demolished one leg of the platform. Instantly, the magical apparatus tumbled off the platform and smashed onto the crater floor.

"Are you crazy?" the terrified wizard screeched from the middle of the debris.

Instantly, the crater floor began to tremble. Scirye couldn't help looking behind her and gave a yelp herself when she saw the lava flooding out of the lake so that the shore was crumbling like thin pie crust.

"What're you doing?" Scirye asked, shocked.

"Running," Pele said. She had already scampered ten yards away.

Bayang smiled weakly. "My friend's always playing practical jokes. What a card, huh? She's the life of the party." She would have started after her but Surtrson blocked her way.

"Who are you?" the fire giant demanded, taking a hammer in either hand.

"We don't have time for this," the wizard shouted. "Let's get the fire salamander. Maybe we can get it to plow a trench to stop the lava from flooding in this direction."

Surtrson, however, stayed where he was. Looking suspiciously at Bayang, he waved a hammer toward the oncoming tide of lava that washed toward them. "That would just be a hot bath for real fire giants, but fake ones might burn their tootsies. Let's see what happens."

Bayang, though, trusted to the charm that Pele had given them. "That's fine with me. Frankly, that one"—she jerked a thumb at Koko—"could use a good wash." She nodded down to Scirye and Leech, who were still in her arms. "But I think Mr. Roland wants more than their ashes."

Squatting, Bayang grabbed a broad rock and nodded for the children to get on. Then she raised it to the level of a huge boulder, where they slipped off.

"What're you doing?" Scirye asked in a low voice.

"Just watch," Bayang said, and strode toward the surging lava. "Could a fake fire giant do this?" she inquired. Stooping, she made another lava ball and flung it straight at Surtrson. "Or this?"

With a laugh, he ducked, and the missile splattered over the rocks behind him. "Hey, no fair. I haven't got any ammunition."

"Too bad," Bayang said, sending another lava ball his way.

Surtrson tried to dodge, but stumbled over the uneven rocks and caught the fireball squarely on his belly. The force knocked him backward and he broke through a patch of thin crust so that steam and gases shot upward around him. Surtrson tried to rise but couldn't. "I'm stuck. Help me up." He stretched out a hand as big as a wheelbarrow.

There was a ripping sound as Bayang hauled the giant to his feet.

He twisted his head around and looked behind him. "Whoops. Excuse me while I make some temporary repairs." The fire giant unbuttoned his coveralls so that the top half hung down like a skirt. By now, he was laughing so hard that little amber tears were falling from his eyes. "I haven't had this much fun since I left Muspelheim. What's your name?"

"Sigrid," Bayang said. "Sigrid Eriksdotter."

"Well, Sigrid Eriksdotter," he said, picking up the hammers that he had dropped when he had fallen, "I like a prank as much as the next guy. But I'm afraid our boss doesn't have any sense of humor. I'll have to report your friend."

"Ingeborg Bjornsdotter," Bayang supplied quickly.

The giant nodded. "Maybe I'll see you in the cafeteria later. The cooks make sure the meals are hot enough for us, but the flaming venison loaf is a little too peppery for my taste." He marched toward the widening lake as the wizard ran to keep up with his strides. "But for now I've got an island to save."

Bayang got the flat rock again and held it so Scirye could get on again.

As Leech joined her, he said, "That wizard didn't seem too powerful to me."

"No, he's probably just an average one," Bayang said, "but he's using a set of spells and charms and devices created by a legion of the best wizards. All he has to do is operate the setup—just like someone driving a car that's built by someone else."

Next to them, Koko hopped up and down on the steaming rocks. "Hey, hey, how about giving me a lift, too?"

"Don't you want to stay behind and help Surtrson?" Bayang grinned as she added him to her armload.

"No, thanks. I'm allergic to work," Koko insisted.

Leech asked, "Why did Pele knock over the cauldron?"

A siren began sounding an urgent call. "To make such a big mess that most of Roland's employees are going to have to come here. It wouldn't surprise me if she turned on the alarm herself."

"She's using us as part of the distraction," Koko groused. "She really made patsies out of us, all right. She might as well have painted targets on our backs."

As she balanced on the rock in Bayang's hands, Scirye shook her head in hurt puzzlement. "Why did Pele desert us like that?"

Bayang started to walk west again. "She never promised to stay with us."

Scirye frowned in disappointment. "But she seemed so honorable."

"Just because she's done us some favors doesn't mean she's our friend," Bayang explained. "Tumarg is for humans. Goddesses live by their own rules. You might keep that in mind about your Nanaia, as well."

Scirye had never been a particularly devout person but she thought she should defend her goddess. "She's just as angry about the museum as we are."

"I'm just warning you against blind faith," Bayang said. "I trusted the dragon elders and look where it's gotten me. Whatever Nanaia wants you to do may not be in your best interests."

Scirye had thought Kles would side with her, but the griffin conceded, "True, but as I see it, we have no choice now but to go on."

Scirye was still reluctant to think the worst. "You don't really doubt Nanaia, do you, Kles?"

"I just wish you had asked my opinion before you made that rash vow," her griffin replied. He relented a little when he saw how uneasy he and Bayang had made his mistress. "But since you've given your promise to Nanaia, I'm here to help you keep it."

"It may all work out for the best," Bayang said, "but it would be wise to watch out for any nasty surprises along the way."

As if in answer, the smoke and vapor suddenly stopped rising to the ball above and began to swirl across the crater floor, blurring everything.

"Pele must have gotten to the wizard controlling the smoke," Bayang said. "She's trying to sabotage all the magic holding this island together. But that would create a catastrophe for all of Hawaii."

"Well, that does it," Koko huffed. "As of today, she's off *my* Christmas card list."

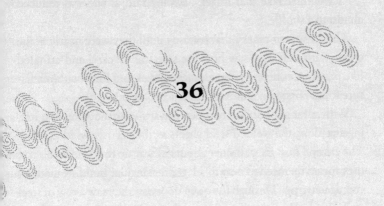

36

Bayang

As the smoke and gas swirled around the crater floor instead of rising into the air, their pace became even slower. And without Pele to show them where there was solid footing, their progress slowed still more because one or the other of Bayang's feet sometimes broke through a thin spot in the crust and she would have to stop to extricate it from the hole. Most of the time it was only empty air beneath but once there was lava that burned the sole of her boot. And both of her legs were gashed by the sharp edges of the breaks in the crust.

Leech glanced overhead to see that the volcano's vapors no longer gathered into a ball overhead but were spreading outward in a roiling black cloud. "More of Pele's sabotage, I'll bet," he said, pointing above them.

"I wouldn't take that wager," Bayang said as she was reduced almost to a shuffle.

The air was so murky that it wasn't until they were nearly at the crater walls that they saw how the side was cracked and crinkled like paper. A concrete ramp zigzagged back and forth within a fissure for the first two hundred feet to a broad ledge.

With surer support for her feet, Bayang took the ramp at a run, jogging along the welded steel sheets as they crisscrossed upward. The gas and dust grew thinner about halfway up the crater wall, and they found themselves next to a large rectangular building made of corrugated iron. Through the open doorway, they saw a row of steel stalls inside. Within one of them, a fire salamander was idly chewing from a trough of coal.

"That must be the stables," Scirye said.

Below them, the crater floor looked as if it were hidden behind a thin gray veil of smoke and gas. Even so, the fiery lace of lines seemed to be spreading and increasing as if the crust everywhere was breaking down. Pele had seen to it that Roland's crews would have their hands and paws full.

A metal staircase rose the last two hundred feet to the rim. It was painted black so that it nearly blended in with the volcanic rock.

Koko eyed the steps nervously. "Maybe you ought to change back to a human," he said to Bayang. "I don't think that thing's going to take your weight."

"I assume that's how all the workers get to the crater, including the fire giants, so it has to be strong," Bayang reasoned. "And if I transform to something lighter, lazybones, it'll take longer and you'll have to get out of the volcano under your own power."

"Well, when you put it that way, I guess there are advantages to being carried like a baby." Koko covered his eyes with a hand. "Just tell me when we're on top."

Despite her assurances to Koko, Bayang tested the first step anyway. It was a reinforced steel platform big enough to take even her fire giant's foot, and it seemed as solid as the rocks around them. Reassured, she began to mount the staircase, but she couldn't go as fast as she liked. The steps were a compromise for both its human and giant pedestrians, with broad steps for the giants but set at a height for short human legs rather a giant's long ones.

The result was that Bayang climbed in a series of fast but dainty steps as if she were dancing up the crater wall, following each set of zigzagging stairs and pausing only when a trembling in the crater made footing hazardous.

She was puffing by the time they reached the top. She tapped Koko on the head. "You can open your eyes now. It's all downhill from here." She panted, nodding to the roadway that led down the outer slope of the crater. "Everybody off." She set them down on their feet.

Near them the siren on top of a metal tower was still wailing urgently. A platform leaned against the ground, one of its legs broken. More magical devices lay broken upon the rocks, including a huge crystal globe. Smoke wriggled up from the crack in its sides, and Bayang assumed this was how Roland had been controlling the ash and smoke from the volcano.

In the middle of the debris lay another wizard with the same protective symbols on his robes they had seen on the first one's. Bayang took his limp wrist delicately between her thumb and index finger. "I can feel a pulse."

Suddenly smoke and gas jetted upward from the crater floor, and there was a chugging sound like a hundred locomotives speeding down the track. Then there was the sound of a huge explosion.

Immediately Bayang thought of the wizard's dented helmet and what it might mean for them. Setting the carrying rock down, she got down on all fours. "Get underneath me," she told the children. "Pele's charm might work against fire but not against falling rocks."

Scirye and Kles scooted beneath her but Leech and Koko hesitated. Scirye seized one wrist of each. "Either you trust Bayang or have your brains knocked out!"

A stone hit the ground nearby, shattering into dozens of sharp bits. Koko needed no more urging and he hopped beneath Bayang. Leech slipped in a moment later.

Bayang grunted whenever a rock smashed against her, but she maintained her position as a living shield. As the crouching children saw how she shivered and heard the meaty smack of each impact, they could guess at the pain it cost her.

Scirye looked at Leech. "She's trying to make up for what she did in the past."

As another falling rock thumped Bayang overhead, Leech could see how her arms and legs were trembling. "I figure she is."

Koko tugged at his ear. "Yeah, I guess I could be wrong. That happens every few years."

As quickly as it had begun, the rain of stones ended. Scirye risked poking her head out from underneath Bayang to check. "I think the rocks have stopped falling," she said.

As Leech got up, he extended a hand to Bayang. "I'm sorry I doubted you."

"I don't blame you," Bayang said. "But I promise you, I won't make the same mistakes that I did in the past."

"Neither will I," Leech said. "But you'll have to tell me more about what I did."

"Let's stroll down memory lane later and get away from here," Koko said as he skipped out of the way of a rolling rock the size of a watermelon. "My mother didn't raise me to be roadkill."

Suddenly a dark column, as huge as a hill, began twisting out of the crater floor as if the smoke, ash, and gases were escaping. However, instead of collecting into a ball overhead, they began to flow over the crater's lip like a nest of twisting serpents.

Bayang waved a hand toward the west. "If I remember right, there were buildings that looked like barracks there. If that's what they are, I bet there's also an infirmary there. I'll take the wizard to it, and Leech, you lean on Scirye and Koko and pretend like you're going there, too."

She gestured to Koko. "And since we don't want Roland's workers wondering how a fire giant can touch humans, we'll have to change back into humans." Since she couldn't be sure that Roland had hired human women as well as female fire giants, she transformed into a man in coveralls with protective symbols like the wizards'. The air sparkled briefly as she released the elements she had taken in for the change.

Koko imitated her without the glow, since he was still the same size. "I thought fur was hot enough but skin on fire tops that any day." He scratched luxuriously.

Bayang was about to tell Scirye to try to disguise herself as a boy and noted with approval that the hatchling had already figured out what she had to do just from seeing Bayang metamorphose. With her griffin's help, she was pulling her hair back into a tight bun.

Koko's coveralls had the correct signs but Scirye's and Leech's were plain. Still, that couldn't be helped.

"Whoa!" Koko said in awe as a huge pillar of smoke and gas shot heavenward. Fires on the crater floor outlined the billowing folds so that the pillar seemed to glow with a life all of its own.

"Hurry," Bayang said, and hefted the wizard onto her back. "Oof, if I have carry passengers, I ought to charge fares like a bus."

When Leech had taken his place between Scirye and Koko, his arms slung over their shoulders, Bayang led the way down the path.

Halfway down the paved road, the crater wall began to sway, making it hard to keep their balance. Stray rocks rattled down the slope so that they sometimes had to jump out of the way. Bayang kept an eye on the hatchlings, steadying them when necessary and even shielding them with her body against the larger missiles, but they all took some bruises. By the time they reached the foot of the volcano they were all aching.

"We've got company," Koko said, and pointed.

A convoy snaked its way along the path toward the emergency in the crater. Fire elementals were rolling along the asphalt while fire giants jogged alongside the trucks. In the back of the vehicles were humans in coveralls and pith helmets, as well as piles of picks, shovels, cauldrons, and other wizards' paraphernalia.

With a jerk of her head, Bayang gestured them to step off the roadway, but they continued on over the hard mounds covered with black veins.

The first truck was forty feet away when all four of it tires popped and then shredded into ribbons of rubber. Its wheels screeched along the road for thirty feet, sending up sparks, and then it fishtailed about, blocking the road. A human in coveralls and pith helmet got out of the passenger side. The cloth was covered with magical symbols.

"Are you all right?" Bayang asked as they trudged up to him.

"Yeah, but that was quite a ride." Turning, he motioned to the workers who were pulling themselves up straight in the back of the truck. "Everybody out. We've got to drag this heap out of the way so the rest of the convoy can go on." As the workers obediently piled out of the truck, he examined one of the tires. "What the . . . ?" He yanked something from the rubber and held up the cluster of iron spikes. "Where did this come from?"

The next moment, the air was filled with whirring sounds.

"Down!" Bayang shouted, dropping the wizard so she could stretch out her arms and knock the hatchlings down.

The rough rock scraped their hands and faces as ropes weighted at the ends with heavy wooden sticks spun past overhead. By the truck, though, Roland's employees were hollering as the ropes wrapped themselves around legs and torsos, tossing their trapped victims to the ground.

Cries from all along the convoy suggested that there were more workers being trapped.

"It's an ambush," Bayang said.

Leech struggled out from under her. "But who did it?"

As if in answer, little men popped up from crevices like gophers. They were only about a foot high and were dressed in everything from skirts made out of what looked like tree bark to torn pieces of human coveralls that hung on them like long coats. Somewhere on each's clothing were some of Roland's magical symbols to protect them from the volcano's effects. Their hair was done up in topknots, and despite their large bellies, they quickly swarmed over the fallen prisoners, trussing them tightly with more ropes. On the bare backs of some, Bayang saw the stripes scarring their skin and realized they'd been whipped.

But then she had worries of her own as one little man swiveled to glare at her.

Hastily, Bayang held up the flower charm. "We came with Pele."

The little man nodded. "The Lady told us to keep an eye out for you because you might be delayed."

"I bet she didn't tell him she caused the delay," Koko muttered to the others.

At that moment, a man only about four feet high stood up in the back of the truck. A pith helmet covered his head and enormous dark glasses covered a quarter of his face. From his belt, he pulled a whip. Raising it over his head, he brought it down sharply with a loud cracking noise.

"Watch out," Bayang said. Springing to her feet, she knocked the little man to the side as she raised her arm, wincing as the lash wrapped itself around her wrist.

With a jerk, she yanked the little man from the truck onto the road. His pith helmet fell off, revealing a head of brown tufted feathers instead of hair. His giant sunglasses dropped down at the same time. His huge eyes, which seemed to fill his face, squinted at the little man. "Lice, vermin."

Then he disappeared under a pile of little men. There was a scuffle and then the first little man shouted, "Don't kill him. Lady Pele says we will have justice. But only later." Despite the ominous words, there was a musical lilt to his words.

Reluctantly, the other little men began to tie up the man with huge eyes as the little man unwrapped the lash from Bayang's arm.

"Thank you, friend," he said. "I am Eleu of the Menehune."

"Menehune?" Scirye asked Bayang as Bayang helped her up.

Eleu slapped his chest proudly. "We are the cleverest of peoples and the quickest with our hands. We can build bridges and houses overnight."

"That's why Roland kidnapped you," Scirye said sympathetically.

Eleu spat on the creature with big eyes. "And set our mortal enemies, the Owl folk, to torment us."

"But no more," Bayang said, and then introduced herself and the others.

Koko scratched his head. "If that bum's one of the Owl folk, why didn't he fly away from here?"

Eleu pointed up at the sky, which was growing darker with pollution by the minute. "Would you?" Then he threw away the whip. "We had been planning this revolt ever since our captivity began, but when Lady Pele came to rescue us, we put our scheme into motion."

Scirye pointed behind her at the volcano. "There's at least one human, two fire giants, and some elementals in the crater."

Eleu nodded. "They're already being taken care of."

Bayang let the flower charm dangle beneath her throat again. "Could any of you fine gentlemen tell us where Lady Pele is?"

"I know where's she going," Eleu said, "and she told me to take you there."

As little men stepped forward to tend to the unconscious wizard, Bayang glanced over at Koko. "I think we'd better transform back to our true shapes," she said. "We might not always get a chance to show our little gifts from Pele before we get mobbed."

"Right," Koko said, and changed back into the tubby, furry badger.

Bayang sighed and stretched with satisfaction after she had changed herself into a dragon again. "Much better." Then she bent one leg. "Climb up on my shoulder, Eleu," she said to the little man.

Eleu scrutinized Bayang's fangs suspiciously. "First, tell me if you've already had lunch, *mo-o*."

"I've had to cut Menehune out of my diet," Bayang said. "Doctor's orders—though you do look very appetizing."

"I've always wanted to ride a dragon," Scirye said, practically shoving Eleu up onto Bayang.

"I don't remember inviting you," Bayang complained, but it was already too late as Scirye got up behind Eleu, and Koko and Leech scrambled up a moment later.

"Aw, have a heart," Koko wheedled. "We'll go faster on those stilts of yours."

"Well, don't sue me if you fall off," Bayang warned. She would have liked to have galloped but could only manage a slow walk on the undeveloped ground to the side of the road.

As they went along, they saw that the entire convoy had been taken prisoner, even the fire giants and elementals who were being bound with chains of an iridescent metal similar to the bridle of the salamander back in the crater. While they were being taken prisoner, little men stood by with heavy odd-shaped balloons.

"What're those?" Leech asked Eleu.

"They're the organs from the cattle that get shipped here," the little man explained. Now that he was on the dragon, he seemed to be enjoying himself so he was willing to chat. "Roland used some of us in the kitchen and made the mistake of having us doing the butchering. We've been saving these."

"But what's in them?" Leech asked.

"Water," Eleu explained. "It hurts their skin."

There were brown patches on the giants and elementals as if they had been burned—not by fire but by the water.

When they reached the rear of the convoy, they saw that the last truck had also been wrecked to prevent the other vehicles from retreating. Little men were dragging it off the road now.

When they were past the roadblock, Bayang stepped back onto the asphalt and began to gallop, but here the crust had cooled in uneven layers so that the pavement undulated up and down, jolting her passengers.

"Y-y-yikes," Koko gurgled. "It's l-l-like sitting on a runaway leather sofa."

The road angled down to the harborside of the island where it followed the shoreline. The complex of barracks and warehouses looked deserted. And the wharves were empty of both people and ships.

Just a little past the piers, they saw tufts of hardy grass springing from cracks and even a few determined tree sprigs, all of them growing from seeds blown here by the wind. After the devastation of the crater, even these signs of life were welcome.

When they reached the border of the western half, though, the ground suddenly began to grow flatter where the violent land was being tamed. Areas of rough, bumpy stone lay like islands in smooth black dirt, and in the rich soil grew patches of weeds, shrubs, and even saplings.

Several hundred yards on, they saw a broad, shallow pit surrounded by young palm trees. Flats filled with young flowers sat ready to be planted. Rocks had been piled into artificial hills and a track cut down the face as if for a waterfall that would pour into the pit, which, Eleu explained, was going to be a lagoon. "We were breaking up the rock here like we did in the first half of the island. And the wizards would use magic to make all the trees and plants grow faster."

"So they chop down the real jungle to make a fake one," Leech said with a shake of his head.

Scirye remembered Pele's jungle. "But a safer one."

Leech grunted the truth of that while Koko said, "Personally, I've never trusted any plant—even with blue cheese dressing."

When Bayang saw the whips lying scattered about like brown snakes, she could guess what the incentive had been.

"What happened to the owners of those?" Scirye asked Eleu.

"They're our captives, too," Eleu said with satisfaction.

Farther along, they saw their first developed areas. Little bungalows encircled a glistening blue lagoon and transplanted flowers bloomed everywhere in a riot of color. Here the palm trees were some thirty feet high. Crews of Menehune surrounded them as they chopped industriously at the wooden trunks. They were smiling and chanting as if they were truly enjoying their work.

"Okay, the owl guys I understand, but what did those trees ever do to you?" Koko asked.

"We need to make rafts for us and our prisoners," Eleu said.

They sped by luxury villas that were in different stages of completion, from simple wooden frames to a few finished homes with tiled roofs and pleasant, spacious verandas and shady palm trees. The villas were so large they would have made up ten of the cottages.

Finally, they reached the city itself. Pink buildings of two or three stories lined the spacious boulevards. The shops and apartments all stared with empty windows as they passed.

The streets had once been lined with palm trees some forty feet high, but they were being cut down by more small squat men with axes, while others were already trimming and then lashing fallen logs together.

Ahead of them lay a park with spacious lawns and fountains with borders of flowers and trees; past that was a beach of black sand and blue ocean. Bayang could only guess at the pain and suffering that it had cost the Menehune to create that lovely vision.

"Turn left," Eleu instructed, and Bayang wheeled onto a broad avenue that led toward the tip of the western half. Directly across the harbor, the volcano seemed to watch them with fiery eyes.

The street itself ended in a circular park where a mansion stood. It was a tall, stately building with marble columns rising from a porch. Most of the windows had been shattered, and there were smudge marks on some of the sills. The double doors hung from the hinges in pieces, as if they had been battered down.

In front of it stood a giant bronze statue of Roland—which a team of Menehune were industriously sawing off its base. More teams, ready to pull it down, waited by ropes that had been hung about its neck. Scattered around were what Scirye thought were colored sacks until she realized they were humans and owl folk trussed up and gagged, also waiting for Pele's justice. They wriggled on the pavement like colored worms. Broken guns lay like firewood all around.

The Menehune froze when gunfire sounded from within the mansion.

Instantly, the Menehune picked up the shovels and pickaxes that had been neatly stacked together. In the wink of an eye, they disappeared up the steps and into the mansion.

"You're so quick. I can see how you beat the guards," Bayang complimented Eleu.

Their guide sprang from her back, landing neatly on a captive. "We're not as quick as a bullet, but we're quicker than the eye of the person pulling the trigger. What you can't track, you can't shoot."

As Eleu walked forward, he tugged a sledgehammer from his belt. The shaft had been cut down for him to handle. Though the iron head was huge and heavy, he hefted it as if it were only cardboard to point at the mansion. "Pele is in there."

"Can you—?" Scirye began when a tommy gun poked its barrel out of an upper window, spraying bullets at the paving slabs. Sharp-edged chips showered from the spot where Eleu had been. Even as she began to duck, she saw the little man already up the steps and rushing through the door. The next moment there was a cry from inside.

Bayang sharpened her claws upon the slab. "Well," Bayang said, "shall we help the goddess dispense her justice?"

"I think she's doing just fine without us," Koko said. "Maybe we should hang back. You know, be the bench for the team on the floor."

"Off," Leech said, shoving his friend over the side. "We've got an appointment to keep."

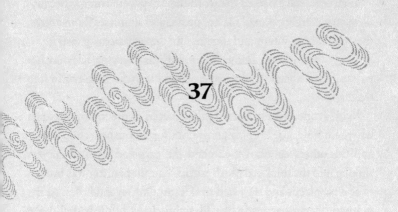

37

Scirye

Bayang led the way up the granite steps and through the broken doors. The smell of gunsmoke was thick, but not so heavy that they couldn't also smell the stink from the erupting volcano. Scirye had accompanied her mother to mansions on diplomatic functions before this so she had seen quality before. Roland had spared no expense when building his home.

The floor of the foyer featured intricate marquetry designs and the walls were paneled with mahogany polished to a deep, reddish brown. It must have been impressive before all the bullet holes pockmarked everything.

An antique grandfather clock lay on its side, chairs had been reduced to kindling, and several man-high vases had been shattered like eggs. About a dozen humans and owl folk lay tied up with a skirted Menehune standing guard over them with an axe.

Eleu must have passed the word that they were coming because the guard merely pointed his axe up a grand staircase. From above, they could hear shouts and thumps and the occasional gunshot.

Scirye had put on her gauntlet and was carrying Kles on her wrist. "Scout ahead," she whispered, and launched the griffin into the air.

With gentle beats of his wings, he darted to the top of the stairs where he hovered, keeping an eye out for ambushes while Scirye and the others cautiously climbed the carpeted steps, their feet sinking into the thick red plush fabric. The gilt banister was broken in several places and they had to skirt around several holes. At the top had been a barricade of tables and chairs but it had all been smashed in the Menehunes' anger.

They walked down the central hallway. The doors had been shattered in the rooms on either side, revealing broken beds, tables, statues, paintings, and cabinets. The little men's fury was as powerful and destructive as a hurricane. The only decorations left were the plaster medallions on the otherwise smooth ceilings.

Koko's eyes darted everywhere for something of value. Finally, he put his paws on his wide hips. "Geez," he said in exasperation, "all this stuff is worthless now."

"You try being whipped," Leech snapped, "and then see how patient you'll be."

"No thanks," Koko said, and then a sly expression crossed his face. "You know, maybe one of us should check out the kitchen."

Leech knew his friend too well and grabbed Koko's foreleg before he could leave. "You mean you want to check out the silverware."

Koko shrugged. "Well, it's not like Roland's going to need it anymore."

"We're not here to loot," Leech said, dragging his friend along.

"Says you," Koko said sullenly.

Halfway down the hallway a doorway opened onto the grand ballroom. A massive chandelier had fallen so that hundreds of shards glittered like gems across the floor. About twenty guards were being tied up by Menehune. A dozen more of the little men were methodically smashing the giant mirrors that covered one wall.

"Don't they know that's bad luck?" Koko murmured.

"Bad luck for Roland, you mean," Kles said. "If they have their way, they'll probably turn this mansion into a hill of rubble."

Koko shot a worried look below. "All the more reason to get to the kitchen. Ow! I'm coming, I'm coming," he added as Leech pulled him along.

When they reached the rooms at the end of the hallway, they found Eleu supervising squads of Menehune. They had gone beyond vandalizing the contents and were zipping about and destroying the rooms, beginning with the mansion's walls.

Eleu recognized them and swung his hammer to point, smashing a small table in the motion. "The Lady is in there," he said, indicating a room across the way.

"Kles," Scirye called, holding up her gauntlet, and her griffin, who had been scouting overhead, landed on her wrist. Then they crossed the hallway, pausing on the threshold. The room was huge, almost a quarter the size of the grand ballroom, with fabulous views of the ocean. The bed and furnishings were heavy, and the expensive antiques and molding were even more ornate than the other rooms. The only thing that marred the perfection of the room were the rows of black sprinklers that marched across the ceiling.

There were about a dozen Menehune inside but instead of zipping around at their usual frenetic pace, they were moving about with their faces pressed against the walls and floor like bloodhounds.

Pele had taken on her human form and was sitting on a huge bed in the center, with her knees crossed and a foot swinging impatiently. "Ah, there you are. It took you long enough." She grinned when she saw them and beckoned them inside. "Come in, come in."

"There's something odd about this room," Bayang muttered as she decreased her size to fit through the doorway.

"What? You mean every bedroom doesn't come equipped with a goddess?" Koko joked.

Scirye marched straight toward the goddess and asked the question that had been burning in her mind as hot as the lava of the crater. "Why did you desert us?"

Kles pinched her arm to remind her to mind her manners and Scirye added hurriedly, "Lady."

Pele folded her hands on top of her knee. "You didn't need my help. You got here on your own, right?"

"No thanks to you," Koko murmured.

Pele lifted her head like a cobra getting ready to strike. "What was that, *kupua*?"

Koko slipped hastily behind Leech. "No banks for you," he lied frantically. "There ain't a place where we were going to cash a check. I was going to make a donation to your favorite charity."

"But where was your honor?" Scirye didn't want to believe that the goddess could be so calculating. "Did you just bring us along to be a distraction?"

A concerned Kles began hopping from one foot to another on top of her wrist. "For Nanaia's sake," he hissed, "be quiet."

The goddess's eyes bore into Scirye until the girl felt the room drop away and all that was left was her reflection in the goddess's pupils. Then Scirye was plunging down into those eyes themselves as if into a warm lake, and the goddess's whisper was like a breeze inside her head. "Nanaia could have picked any hero, but she put her mark on you. And you've just proved that she made a good choice."

Then the goddess blinked and Scirye was back in the room,

feeling a little scared and overwhelmed. She shook her head in disbelief. "I didn't do much by myself. We did it together." She motioned to her companions.

The goddess clapped her hands together in approval. "A hero has to be smart, too, and choose the right friends to help her on her quest."

Kles spoke in a low, urgent voice to his mistress. "From what little I know, it's not like Pele to explain her actions. I suspect that she's being very patient with you."

There was no keeping secrets from the goddess. "You listen to the chick-chick, smart girl," she agreed. "I've taught you a bitty-bit right now because you have the mark. You can do more than you think."

Still dissatisfied, Scirye scratched her shoulder. "You keep talking about how I'm special. But I'm just ordinary. I don't even have magical gadgets like Leech."

Pele pointed her index finger at Scirye and emphasized each word with a tap against the girl's forehead. "So you don't have magic toys. Maybe your magic's all up here, eh?"

Scirye stepped back, rubbing the spot, which felt hot from Pele's touch. "If I'm so smart, how come Roland keeps getting away?"

Pele's nostrils widened as she sniffed the air. "Patience. We saw him go in here. We'll find him."

Bayang inspected her surroundings carefully. "There must be a hidden safe room."

Pele nodded her agreement. "This is the one part of the mansion that my friends didn't build."

"Because Roland didn't want you to know about it," Bayang said, joining her friends.

Pele pointed to the little men inspecting the room. "They'll find the door."

Koko, though, still had looting on his mind rather than revenge.

Waddling over to the bed, he pulled his plump body up on top of the coverlet and headed straight toward one of the gilt eagles decorating the teak headboard. "I wonder if it's really gold," he mused, and pulled at it. Suddenly gears began to grind in the wall behind the bed.

"It's not my fault," he shouted as he plopped back on to the floor.

Pele got to her feet as the bed began to swing up so that the foot of the bed rose into the air, revealing a flight of stairs. At the bottom was a steel door as solid as a bank vault's.

"Ha!" Pele cried. "Got you!" Her voice was deep and resonant, like footsteps echoing in a cave.

Suddenly her shape began to shimmer, and when it solidified, she was no longer the tiny old lady but a woman eight feet high, towering over everyone. Her hair had deepened from gray to black that drifted about like smoky vapor. Within the floating strands tiny red and yellow stars sparkled. Her high cheekbones gave her a proud and haughty look but her eyes twinkled with mischief. Her tan skin glowed with a soft iridescence like pearls before a fire. Scirye thought that she had never seen anyone so lovely, or so dangerous.

Bayang threw up a warning paw. "No, wait," she said. "I finally figured out what's been bothering me—this is the only room with sprinklers."

The warning came too late as a lance of flame shot from Pele's hands and splashed across the door.

Then, from up above, Scirye heard an ominous click. The next moment water began to shower down like miniature waterfalls, drenching them all.

Pele staggered and would have fallen if Scirye and Leech hadn't caught her. "Water," she panted, "makes me weak."

"Get her out of here," Bayang ordered, but too late. A sheet of steel slammed down from the doorway. Etched across its face were runes and mystic signs. When a Menehune struck it with his hammer, there was a flash of blue light. With a cry, he leaped back. A Menehune aimed a crushing blow at the nearest wall with the same stunning effect.

"There are wards on this room," Bayang said. "They were set to activate when the sprinklers went off."

Grabbing a hammer from a Menehune, Koko scrambled up Bayang's back. "Okay, the door's not going to work. So it's out through the penthouse."

"Hey!" the dragon complained as he perched on top of her head like a furry hat.

"You're the nearest thing we got to a ladder," Koko said, and swung as hard as he could at the ceiling. Blue light exploded from the hammer head and over him.

"Argh," he cried in pain, and would have toppled backward if Bayang hadn't caught him in her forepaws. His dropped hammer would have hit her hind paw if she hadn't pulled it back in time. Instead of smashing Bayang, it bounced off the wet boards with blue light shining along its bulky surface until its owner reclaimed it.

"Koko, you okay?" Leech asked, worried.

Koko opened one eye groggily. "Oog. Now I know how the electric chair feels. I don't recommend it."

The door at the bottom of the stairs swung open silently on its well-oiled hinges. Badik appeared in his dragon form, though he had shrunk down to the size of a human. The sprinklers had turned the staircase into a waterfall, and with the help of a cane Roland slogged up the steps behind him. He was in a raincoat and hat, down which the water dripped. On his left hand was the Jade Lady's ring.

"It's no use trying to break out," Roland announced when he reached the head of the stairs. "I had my wizards place powerful charms on this room."

Then he noticed the children, badger, and dragon beside Pele. "Ah, how delightful. You brought an entourage, goddess." He pressed the jeweled head of his cane against his lips. "Oops. Pardon me. Could they be your menagerie instead?"

Despite the dripping water, Badik swelled up his chest and unfurled his wings as if he were trying to appear even more imposing. "I am Badik of the Fire Rings," he called in formal challenge, "where the volcanoes are as many as the scales of my skin. Who are you, dragon?"

"I am Bayang," Bayang announced, "of the Moonglow, where the waters shine brighter than the moon." Her home had been named after the luminescent plankton that made the sea glow at night.

Badik's eyes narrowed. "You curs have been hounding me for centuries, but there'll soon be one less of you. And the world will be a far better place for it."

With a growl, Bayang crouched, getting ready to spring. However, Pele held up a hand. "Wait! He's mine!"

Twirling his cane, Roland sauntered the few steps over toward Pele while Badik walked by his side. "I knew you were a sporting goddess."

"I don't need fire, just my bare hands," Pele growled, shrugging off the children. The wet strands of her hair hung like dank strings, and she swayed slightly on her feet.

"My associate might have something to say about that," Roland said, using the cane to indicate Badik. "And do you really have time for a wrestling match? You know as well as I do how unstable this island is"—he pretended to admire the cane's jeweled top—"don't you, goddess?"

Pele raised her hands. "Of course I do. If you hadn't been holding my friends hostage, I would have sent this place to the bottom of the sea a long time ago."

"Well, allow me to help," Roland said, and swung his cane against the wooden frame of the upturned bed. The jewel at the top exploded in a yellow and red fireball.

"There," Roland said with satisfaction, "that should send my home tumbling back to the sea floor. Satisfied?"

The next instant, the windows rattled as the volcano across the harbor thundered. Through the glass panes, they could see flames shoot upward from the crater, rising like a fiery tower.

Pele smiled when she saw the spectacle. "Fool! Even at this distance, that fire will make me stronger."

Roland's hand shot out and seized the pendant of her necklace. At the same time, Badik grabbed the rich man by his waist and then bounded backward toward the staircase with Roland in his arms. The necklace's cord snapped, and as Badik and Roland disappeared down the staircase, they left a trail of puka shells behind them.

For a moment, though, Scirye glimpsed the trailing ends of the necklace's broken cord and thought it seemed to sparkle with a life all of its own.

As Roland stepped back inside his safe room, he tipped his hat. "But not before this place tumbles back to the sea floor. And you along with it. *Adieu*, goddess."

Shocked, Pele tried to send fire at him, but managed only some sparks that disappeared in puffs of steam from the cascading sprinkler water.

"Get that back!" the goddess ordered the Menehune.

Even as the little men sprang down the staircase, the door slammed shut again. A Menehune struck at the door as soon as it was in reach. However, by now Roland had put wards on the door, too. The Menehune bounced backward only to spring to his feet again and renew the attack. The other little men joined him, rising up each time they were knocked down to hammer at the door. The effect of the group blows created an almost constant glow of flashing blue light.

The goddess was angrily rapping her knuckle against her forehead, each time sending off fiery sparks that the sprinklers quickly turned into wisps of steam. "I'm stupid, stupid, stupid. He built this whole island just so he could trap me."

"To capture you?" Leech wondered.

Pele pressed her hand beneath her throat mournfully. "No, to steal my necklace." She pressed her lips together in a thin, grim line. "And now that he's got it, he'll finish me off by drowning me in the ocean."

To Leech, it had looked like other cheap necklaces he had seen on sale at the souvenir shops they had passed by. "That must be some piece of jewelry."

"Yü the emperor made it for me," Pele said ruefully.

"He owned the archer's ring," Scirye gasped.

Pele's head whipped around. "Is that what you're trying to get back from Roland?"

Koko scratched his damp head. "Hold on a moment. I thought this Yü guy lived a long time ago. How did he get from China to here?"

"He was a powerful wizard after all," Bayang said.

"Some kings, they want gold. Some kings, they want power. But Yü, he wanted knowledge. He was curious about everything," Pele explained with a little smile as she remembered him. "Even though he had a bad leg and limped, he refused to let that stop him. He traveled around the world, and wherever he went, he aided people."

Scirye helped the soggy Kles take refuge within her coveralls. "We think the ring might be magical, but we're not sure. What about your necklace?"

"The puka shells and the pendant were souvenirs of his visit, but it was the cord that was very special," Pele said. "It was the string from Yi's bow."

"Who's Yi?" Scirye asked.

Bayang gave a shiver, but not from the cold water sprinkling down—she was used to far colder temperatures within the depths of the ocean. "I only know him by reputation. He's an archer in China who saved the world many times with his bow. He killed monsters. For its time, it was a sort of super weapon."

Kles had left his head poking out of Scirye's coveralls. "Maybe the archer's ring belonged to Yi first," he suggested. "Now that Roland has the ring and the bow string, all he needs next is Yi's bow and the arrows."

"And he'll have the super weapon again," Leech said.

"Whatever he's got planned for Yi's weapon, it must be something awful," Pele said, shaking her head.

"Maybe Yü had another reason to travel around the earth," Scirye said, working out the possibilities. "He kept the ring, but he was scattering the other parts of that super weapon just so someone like Roland couldn't get hold of it."

Kles finished her thought. "With some powerful person to protect each one piece."

"And I failed." Pele began to berate herself again. "Stupid, stupid, stupid."

From the hidden room came the roar of a generator; the walls and ceiling vibrated with the sound of secret machinery.

"What's Roland up to?" Koko demanded.

The rest of his words were drowned out by a gigantic explosion that shook the whole mansion. They turned in horror to watch a whole side of the crater crumble in a cloud of smoke and fire, and the shoreline on the eastern half of the island began to disintegrate, throwing up sheets of water.

38

Leech

Outside, as ash from the explosion began to fall like gray snowflakes, Badik fluttered down into view, his flapping wings sending the ash whirling about. He'd grown to his regular size so he could carry Roland on his back.

"Where are my manners? I forgot to thank you, goddess, for delivering Yi's necklace to me. Be assured that I'll use it for more than ornamentation," Roland declared, his voice muffled by the scarf he wore against the falling ash. He shook his cane at Scirye, Kles, Leech, and Koko as they glared at him through the window. "And I hope you four have learned your lesson and won't get involved in adult games anymore. Ah, but that's right. You'll never have a chance to do it again anyway."

"You're lucky, Bayang, that you're going to die so quick," Badik called. "If it was up to me, you would die slowly and painfully."

"We'll get out of this," Bayang shouted back defiantly. "And then there'll be no place you can hide from me. I'll follow you to the ends of the earth."

"We all will," Leech yelled.

Roland kicked a heel against Badik's flank commandingly. "I'm sorry, Badik, but I'm afraid we don't have any more time for you to chat with your surly little friends," he said. "We really must keep that appointment in Nova Hafnia now. So we mustn't miss our ship." Roland gave them a cheerful salute. "Ta-ta forever." Then he rose out of sight, borne away by the mighty dragon.

Bayang spread her talons and slashed at the air in frustration. "Roland must have had a secret passage out of the mansion."

Leech stared at the sky through the window but there was no sign of Roland anymore, only more and more ash drifting down. "Where's Nova Hafnia?" he asked.

"It's the capital of the former Nu Danmark," Bayang said, "near the Arctic Circle. Nova Hafnia means New Copenhagen in Latin. I'll bet another part of Yi's bow is there."

"First fire and now snow," Kles said thoughtfully. "I wonder who's guarding the next part? And what it is?"

Despite all the hardships that Leech had been through, he had remained an optimist at heart. He had always known he would escape the orphanage. He had always felt he would find friends. And he had done both. "We'll find that out when we get there," he predicted.

Scirye nodded solemnly. "Whatever it is, it's Tumarg to help the guardian keep it away from Roland. It's a lot bigger now than getting back a priceless treasure."

"Or revenge," Leech agreed.

Bayang clenched her paws, her talons clacking together. "It's about saving the world."

"If we ever live long enough to get out of here," Koko said, looking mournfully out the window.

Leech elbowed his friend. "Come on, Koko. We've already been attacked by monsters and dunked in a volcano, and we survived, didn't we?"

Pele's eyes crinkled up as she grinned. "Hey, *kapua*. Try to think like maybe-maybe boy."

The ash was making it harder to see outside so Bayang had to squint. And what she saw made her spine go to ice. "The sea's going out."

Through the glass panes, they could see the ocean retreating from the harbor, leaving behind a few fish flopping on the exposed rocky shore.

Pele looked frightened for the first time. Cupping her hands, she shouted into the hallway beyond the steel door. "Eleu, get out! A tidal wave, it's coming soon!" And then she barked orders at the Menehune by the safe room.

Despite the water beginning to pool around their ankles, some continued to attack the door. But others scampered back up into the room to join the others in striking the walls and floor—all with the same electrifying effect. That did not stop the tough little men, however, who kept on striking with their tools. Though they kept getting knocked down by the shock, they kept bouncing back to try again.

Leech looked overhead. "Maybe *I* can do something about this." Pulling off the disks from his armband, he put them in his pocket.

Then he took off the armband and spat on it. "Change!" he shouted, and drew the sign in the air. Instantly, the armband expanded and the ends fused into a solid ring.

Koko grabbed him. "I tried hitting the ceiling already, buddy. I wouldn't recommend it."

"With a hammer, not with this. I've got my own super weapon." Pulling away, he struck the plaster wall. There was a dazzling burst of light and then he was tossed backward. His shocked hand was unable to hold onto the armband and it spun away.

Bayang caught him neatly in her forelegs. "That was a good try, but Roland could hire the best wizards. I don't think even your ring can break their wards."

Koko splashed over to him. "You all right, buddy?"

Leech felt the tips of his hair, which were singed. "Yeah, but I don't think we're going to batter our way out of the room."

Scirye stared at the ring, which seemed to float in a blue halo. The film of water had retreated from beneath it to form a hollow circle as the floor continued to repel the metal.

"Kles," she wondered to her friend, "why doesn't the floor shock us when we walk on it? Does the magic only work against metal?"

The griffin lifted his head excitedly. "Yes, that must be it. The wards would have to defend against everything, and that's beyond the skill of even the greatest human wizards, the Arch-mages."

"They would have to be as strong as those that guard the Dragon King's vaults," Bayang agreed. "It took several generations of the finest magical minds to create those spells."

Kles nodded. "Roland assumed the tidal wave would get us long before we figured it out or fists and feet could make a hole."

Pele smiled weakly at Scirye. "He didn't count on smart-smart girl. See? You've just shown why Nanaia picked you. You've got brains."

"And he didn't count on having another dragon either," Bayang said, setting Leech down while Koko picked up the armband.

Leech nudged Scirye. "I was wrong. You've got what it takes to live on the streets."

"Yeah," Koko agreed. "When this is done, you can come with us."

Scirye took it as a compliment, coming from them. "Thanks."

Pele pointed at the ceiling. "Go up toward the roof."

Bayang nodded. "Then step back and give me room."

Scirye and others ducked out of the way by scrambling down the staircase until they were packed shoulder to shoulder.

In the room above them, Bayang ballooned in size. Glancing

about to make sure there was no one in the way, the dragon crouched on all fours as she swung her tail at the ceiling. The thick column of bone and hide thumped like a steel club. Twice, three times, and the plaster crinkled and boards cracked as the ceiling broke.

Instantly, some of the Menehune zipped back into the room, scooting up Bayang's back to attack the jagged opening with dozens of small hands. In the next instant, plaster and broken boards began raining down until they had created a small hole wide enough for a Menehune. Seconds later, the first group slipped through and began working from the other side while the next team left the staircase to continue widening it from below.

Bayang squirmed slightly. "You know, your feet tickle," she called to the little men.

On the staircase, Scirye was helping to support Pele. Wet, the goddess really did seem like a frail old woman. Pele's skin seemed to be growing cooler, and when the girl tried to feel for a pulse, it was weak and sporadic. "I think we have to get Pele away from the sprinklers real soon," she called up to Bayang.

"I'll finish the opening in the ceiling," the dragon ordered the Menehune laboring above her. "You see if you can make an opening through the roof."

The little men vanished in a blink of the eye. With a new sense of urgency, Bayang crouched on all fours so she could thrust her tail up through the hole, and with several blows widened it.

"All right, I think it's big enough," Bayang said as she slid her tail back out. The plaster dust mixing with the water made it look as if the tip had been whitewashed. She rose, curling her tail about her hind legs as she sat upright with her head near the hole.

Dozens of Menehune took Pele from Scirye and reverently carried the goddess back up the steps on a raft of small hands. Scirye followed, and then Koko and Leech stormed up after her along with the little men.

Leech shrank his armband and put it back on as Bayang took the goddess into her forepaws and lifted her up through the hole to the next room.

"The sea's coming back," Koko yelped, and pointed at the window.

Through the murky swirl of ash, Leech saw the horizon rippling. Was that the tidal wave that Pele had predicted would come?

Bayang frowned. "That's maybe eighty, a hundred feet high," she estimated, and then looked down at her friends. "The ocean's my natural home, but it's not yours. We have to get you away from here."

Grabbing Scirye by the waist, the dragon hoisted her and the bedraggled griffin through the ceiling. Leech was next, while Koko, climbing up her back again, scrambled over her head and away.

When the last of the Menehune had left the trap, Bayang told the children, "Get ready to pull me up."

Then, clapping a paw on either side of the hole, she shrank herself until she was small enough to fit. Above her, Scirye and Leech pulled at one foreleg while Koko pulled at the other. Even Kles tried to lend a claw.

Finally the five of them lay panting on what was the floor of a large attic. There were a few crates and pieces of discarded furniture lying across the broad space. But, Leech guessed, in about the spot where Roland's hiding place had been, was a small platform.

Bayang rolled over onto all fours and got up, sprinkling water about as she shook it from her hide. "Roland had a lift. That made the humming noise we heard."

Ash was falling through a huge opening in the roof and through the attic. Hinged doors hung down on either side. It was just perfect for a large dragon to fly through.

"He thought of everything," Scirye said, shivering in her damp clothes. Her griffin solicitously began to rub her arms with his wings.

"Except us," Leech grunted. "Though I don't know what good we really did."

"You'll do plenty." Pele coughed. "I'll make sure of that." The goddess was sitting up, steam rising from her as she murmured a spell and made passes with her hands.

Eleu padded over and bowed. "Take the Lady and your friends," he said. "The rest of us will be fine." He indicated the ropes that had begun to drop from the roof into the attic. "Our kin are already out there with rafts."

"That they carried up to the roof?" Koko gasped.

The little man said smugly, "There's nothing we can't do. We knew we were going to have to leave so we used the chopped-down trees to make the rafts. When the word went out about the tidal wave, our kin brought some of them up to the roof when we got out. We built other rafts out of broken doors and furniture."

"How could you be so sure we'd get free?" Leech asked.

"You were with Lady Pele." Eleu laughed and zipped away.

With a flap of his wings, Kles fluttered into the air and over to a pile of discarded window curtains that lay folded up on the floor. "We'll need some sort of masks. We'd better tear these up." Catching the hem of the top one, he flew upward so he could stretch it out.

As the little men scrambled up the ropes to the roof, Scirye, Leech, and Koko tore strips from the expensive cloth. In the meantime, Bayang had retreated far enough into another part of the attic so she could grow to as large a size as she could.

From outside, the tidal wave's roar grew louder and louder, like a locomotive thundering toward them. When the children had tied strips of fabric around their mouths, Bayang crouched on her belly to let Scirye scramble up onto her shoulder with a large cloth patch in her hand.

Kles took one corner in his beak and flew in front of the great head, around to the other side, and back to his mistress, who finished tying the cloth in front of Bayang's muzzle. Then she tied a small one around her griffin.

As the others scurried up behind her, Leech couldn't help thinking that the masks made them all look like stagecoach robbers. "I could use my flying disks." He was eager to try them out.

Bayang shook her head. "The winds will toss even a dragon around like a kite. It's no place for an inexperienced flier." Reluctantly, the boy joined the others.

Pele had disdained a mask since the gases were like perfume to her, so as she sat astride Bayang's back, they could see her smiling as happily as a girl at Christmas. "I've never ridden a *mo-o* before," she declared as she climbed up and sat in the rearmost place.

The dragon moved toward the hole just as the little men disappeared up the ropes. "Hang tight, everyone, and keep your heads low," Bayang instructed, her voice muffled by the mask.

Trotting over to the opening, the dragon crawled out onto the roof. The air was murky with gray ash that pattered against their faces.

The hole had been designed for a dragon who only needed to carry one passenger. Bayang was carrying several, so she needed to increase her size.

"Whoa," Koko said. "Warn us when you do that."

Then, with a downward swing of her wings that sent the ash whirling about, she launched herself through the hole and into the air.

Before them, the tidal wave towered like some huge crystalline beast.

39

Leech

Leech clung with the others to Bayang's back as she soared away from the roof. Beneath him, he felt the tremendous muscles that powered her great wings. They rippled rhythmically against his chest. She was such a wonderful combination of strength and beauty, and his admiration quickly changed to shame when he thought of how he had once made a dragon into a belt.

Below them, cracks had opened in the streets and flames were stabbing skyward as lava bubbled upward. The walls of buildings were beginning to crumble and the roofs to collapse. Everywhere the city had begun to blaze with fire.

However, his enjoyment dulled when he began to gag. The material of the mask could not screen out the finer particles in the polluted air, and they were all choking, except for Pele.

As Bayang's muscles moved more sporadically and violently and her wings began to jerk up and down in a ragged series of beats, Leech knew that she must be having the most difficulty of all of them. Because she had to take in such great gusts of air in order to carry so many passengers, she was having the hardest time breathing. They actually began to descend.

Leech twisted around to look at Koko, who had his eyes closed.

"It doesn't look good, buddy," Leech said to Koko, his voice muffled by the mask.

"You're telling me," Koko moaned. "I left my water wings at home."

Leech had said those words to Koko, but he could have spoken about his worries to anyone. They were all friends—even the goddess, after a fashion. He couldn't let them die. Not like Primo.

He pulled the disks from his pocket and slipped his mask down long enough to spit on it. "Change!" he said, and then pulled the mask back to cover his mouth right away.

Instantly, the disks expanded and hovered nearby.

"What are you doing?" Scirye asked.

"Maybe Bayang can fly higher if I lighten her load by two people," Leech said as he stepped carefully onto the flying disks.

"You little idiot," Bayang panted. "You can't handle these air currents. You'll just get yourself killed."

Leech could feel how the air tugged and pulled at them unpredictably, coming first from one direction and then the other. Bayang was probably right, but at least the others would have a better chance with her.

"I'm going to die anyway if I don't make it easier for you," Leech said. "Come on, Koko. You're coming with me."

Koko, though, had already figured out the odds. "Uh, no, no, goddesses first. Take Pele. I'll stay here."

"Once we get off, Lady Pele's safer with Bayang," Leech said.

"We're friends to the end, right?" He pulled Koko's forepaws tight around his waist and then swung his legs around so he could step onto the disks. Immediately, they jerked upward away from Bayang's back.

"I'm complaining to the management about the takeoffs," Koko protested, wrapping his hind legs around Leech's middle, as well.

The winds tumbled them about as if they were inside a barrel rolling down a hill. Koko was still screaming shrilly when the winds calmed enough for Leech to right them somehow. He was glad that the disks seemed stuck to his feet as if glued there.

Koko squeezed his limbs around Leech in protest. "You know how I hate roller coasters."

"Sorry," Leech said absently as he checked on the oncoming tidal wave and then Bayang. She'd managed to rise only a bit more without them—and not enough to get above the wave's top.

"If you can escape, then save yourself," Bayang gasped.

"You don't want Roland to win, do you?" Leech urged.

"Of course not," Bayang snapped in irritation. Leech noticed how Bayang managed to stroke her wings harder in just that moment.

With a momentary pang, Leech thought of Primo again, remembering a long training session. Leech had grown tired by the second hour and had become sloppy and careless. Primo, though, had not let him use that as an excuse. "If you're in a life-and-death battle, you can't ask for a time-out from your opponent. You have to find something that gets your juices going—your adrenaline. It might be encouraging words. Or it might be something that makes you mad."

In that one instant, Bayang's annoyance had given her just a little extra juice. What she needed now was a much bigger, stronger dose.

It was only a short distance to Bayang, but between Leech's inexperience as a flier and the turbulent air, their flight path was more of a crazy zigzag. The winds had picked up, and bucked and twisted like wild snakes who took cruel delight in flipping the boy and badger about like rag dolls.

Leech twisted and wriggled, wrestled and squirmed, until he was finally in front of Bayang.

The dragon was exhausted, her eyes filled with sorrow. "Save yourselves," she puffed.

As Leech struggled to keep his place, he purposely curled his lip up in a sneer. "Ha, I thought dragons were such great fliers. But look at you. You're too pudgy and too old. A sparrow could beat you any day."

"Old?" Bayang spluttered. "Fat?" For a moment, her wings beat furiously, sending her upward.

Leech's strategy was working. "And stupid to boot."

In his fear, Koko was practically choking Leech. "Ix-nay on the easing-tay. Don't you see the size of those fangs?"

Bayang's fangs did, indeed, seem as large and as sharp as swords, but Leech had to risk them.

Bayang found enough breath to roar, "How dare you say those things to me!" She rose still higher through the outraged strokes of her wings.

"Lee No Cha does," Leech said, fighting to get above her. "I've come to gloat."

"You lying little cheat!" Bayang shouted. In her anger, she forgot how tired she was and swept her wings frantically.

"Ha, ha, can't catch me," he taunted.

Mindless with rage, with only one thought on her mind, Bayang flapped her wings, trying to reach her tormentor. The noise from the tidal wave was thundering in Leech's ear and he was sure the dragon could not hear him. So he set his thumb against his nose and then, with his palm open, he wagged his fingers at the dragon.

Bayang jerked farther upward.

The next moment, the wave hit them. Leech and Koko were a couple of yards above its top, but the sheets of spray drenched them and the air became even more violent. They spun about crazily.

As they whirled around, Leech caught a glimpse of Bayang. To his horror, he saw that despite his efforts, she wasn't going to clear the tidal wave. Its sudsy white crest smashed against the dragon's legs and belly and then carried her along as white foam surged all around her.

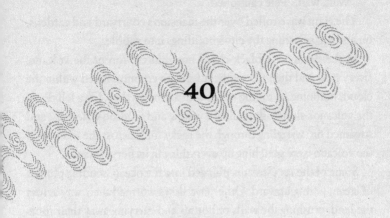

40

Bayang

Bayang knew the ocean well, from the depths where no light ever reached to the sunny surface, but she had never ridden a tidal wave.

It swept her along as if on a giant, sudsy hand.

"Remember what you told me about the surfers," Scirye yelled.

Yes, Bayang said to herself. *Don't fight the waves. Ride with them.*

Roland's huge mansion lay far beneath them. On the roof the Menehune were waiting, tied to the makeshift rafts. From this distance, they looked like ants on discarded crackers.

Then the little men and the mansion disappeared as the bottom of the wave engulfed them.

Bayang got ready even though her wings were so drenched now that they felt as heavy as stone.

"Wait, wait," Pele cautioned.

The giant wave rolled over the mansion's courtyard and gardens, on and on, smashing the city's buildings into rubble.

In the distance, a black cloud now hid the top of the volcano. Every now and then the red light from an eruption flared within the cloud, outlining its rolling edges with a bloody glow. Lava fell down the volcano's slopes like brilliant yellow and crimson waterfalls, and streamed on, wriggling through the rocky folds across the island as if the volcano were snatching up everything in its fiery tentacles.

Some of the lava streams plunged into the ocean, sending plumes of steam jetting upward. Other lava flows wormed their way across the land, crushing the walls of houses and carrying away their roofs until the timbers caught fire, creating beds of flaming flowers. Cinders blown from the volcano had rained all over the island so that trees and other buildings were already burning. The whole city had caught fire; it looked like chains of bright, glowing beads.

Beneath her, Bayang felt the sea crest begin to drop. The tidal wave was coming down.

"Now, fly!" Pele commanded.

Bayang brought her wings down on top of the tidal wave with loud splashes. She hadn't been able to get a full beat so she moved forward rather than up. And now that insufferable little pest, Leech, was nearby again, but this time he was shouting encouragement rather than insults.

Scirye and Kles joined him in urging her on, and soon Koko and Pele were doing the same. As Bayang flapped her wings determinedly, they seemed to rise with agonizing slowness.

She felt the ocean make one last grab at her tail as if trying to yank her downward into the wave, but still she fought on. And then her tail was free, and the noise was growing softer as the tidal wave finally reached its end and began to crash down.

She watched the sea wave smash against the land, covering the burning buildings and then flooding on in a dozen streams through the streets and leaving behind steaming blackened frames. On and on the sea charged until it collided head-to-head with the lava.

There was a huge, hissing explosion like a thousand boilers rupturing. Steam tumbled upward like a misty hill springing from the ground. And from out of the white cloud sailed lumps and slabs of burning rock as the lava cooled and then burst like bombs.

"Well done, *mo-o*," Pele crowed excitedly. "I'll go surfing with you anytime."

Leech flew in front of Bayang again. On his back was a very sick badger.

"I'm sorry that I said the things that I did," the hatchling said as he struggled against the winds to stay in place.

"Yes, well, I've been called worse things. And I realize you were just trying to motivate me." Bayang clashed her fangs together. "But even so, never, never do *that* again."

Koko was so dizzy that he was resting his head on Leech's shoulder. "Yeah, buddy. That goes double for me."

"Why didn't you listen to me when I told you to leave us?" Bayang demanded, puzzlement now replacing her anger.

"And leave you behind?" Leech asked, surprised. "What kind of person do you think I . . . ?" He paused. "Oh, that's right. I do know."

"You've just proved how wrong the dragons were all those centuries," Bayang said gently.

Leech smiled shyly. "So we made a good start at trusting one another?"

"I'd like to think so," she said, hooking a talon toward her back. "So hop on board."

The boy laughed. "Does that invitation include one airsick badger?"

Bayang rolled her eyes in mock resignation. "Even him."

Scirye reached out to clasp his forearm. "Welcome home."

"There's no place like it." Leech grinned as he eased in behind her.

As the boy took off his flight disks, Bayang surveyed the sea. She was glad to notice there were several makeshift rafts filled with Menehune bobbing up and down on the surface where the mansion had once been. A little farther away were dozens more. On these were more of the little men, as well as their prisoners. There were even large platforms with metal sheets on which the fire giants sat, looking seasick and miserable. Already, the industrious Menehune had gotten their tools and were improving their vessels.

Bayang tried to hold herself steady in the increasingly turbulent air. The air, heated by the inferno below, rose in strong, twisting winds. When she glanced up, she saw that they were shoving the huge black cloud westward toward the other Hawaiian islands. In those clouds were enough ash and gases to smother and suffocate thousands.

And if that didn't kill the poor islanders, there was more trouble. The ocean below was churning like a boiling pot as the island's edges began to crumble and fall. New tidal waves would soon be smashing through towns and cities.

"What do we do?" Leech gulped.

"I'll fix it," Pele shrugged. "What else?"

Throwing back her head, the goddess began to sing a series of deep clacking notes, like polished stones tumbling against one another. The music was lovely in its own way, like the streaks of black in a sheet of white marble that seemed to make a picture but never quite did.

It was impossible not to listen to it. The song swept the mind along as irresistibly as a tide of lava carried huge boulders swiftly toward the sea.

And then she stopped and folded her arms, tapping her heel anxiously against Bayang's side.

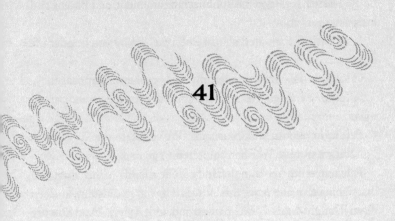

41

Scirye

Suddenly sheets of water fountained upward on the horizon as a gigantic torpedo zoomed toward them. As it neared, they saw a huge dark shape as large as an automobile racing toward them through the choppy sea.

Koko patted Bayang's side. "Take us up higher! It's another bad guy."

"Well, sometimes he's bad-bad, all right," Pele admitted affectionately, "but he's also my husband, too."

As water rilled downward from his bony fins, the huge fish surfaced like a submarine. Yellow and black stripes streaked diagonally across his silvery sides. For such a giant fish, though, he had a tiny mouth, but small tusks stuck out from either side. His eyes, which were set high up on his head, also seemed puny in comparison to his body. The fish regarded the bobbing rafts around it, and Bayang and her passengers above it.

"You," the fish grunted almost like a pig. "Why you bodder me fo'?"

"Howzit?" Pele waved cheerfully. "Long time, Kamapuaa, eh?"

"Not long enough," Kamapuaa snorted, blowing up showers of water.

Pele indicated the sinking island. "We've got trouble."

"*You* got trouble," the fish corrected. "I go nap."

Pele jutted out her chin defiantly. "The island's falling apart and that's going to make more tidal waves. How are you going to sleep through all that noise?" She paused and added slyly, "And how are you going to eat, eh? Those waves are bound to wreck the reefs. If they don't kill the fish, they'll drive them away."

The water bubbled as the fish moaned. "You make mess, I clean up. Like always, yeah?"

"I didn't do this for fun," Pele argued, and waved a hand below at the Menehune. "I did it for my friends. That bad man Roland stole them so I came to get them back."

"Hmph," Kamapuaa said, making waves with every swish of his great tail. "Dat Roland make big island and big noise. Hard sleep. You fix him?"

Leech assumed that eating and napping were the fish's main interests.

"Not yet," Pele said, "but soon."

Eleu was floating on a nearby raft. Cupping his hands around his mouth like a megaphone, he shouted, "We could build a trap that would catch lots of fish for you."

"See, you could have a luau," Pele coaxed.

Kamapuaa spread the fins on his sides and back so that they looked like large dark sails. He jerked his snout at Kles. "Maybe chicken, too? I like drumsticks." He smacked his lips in anticipation.

Kles drew himself up, all eight inches. "I beg your pardon? I am not and have never been a chicken."

Scirye put a hand protectively on the griffin. "He's a friend."

"And besides, he'd be too stringy," Koko contributed.

Pele put up her hands and patted the air soothingly. "You want chicken. We'll get you chicken."

"Yeah, yeah. I help dem." The great fish fluttered a fin at the Menehune and then at her. "But not you."

"And I'll dance, too," Pele offered slyly. "Just for you."

Kamapuaa waggled his tail, churning up the water white. "Yeah, yeah. Like old times."

"So you'll stop the waves?" Pele asked.

"Yeah, yeah." The last word ended in a burbling sound as Kamapuaa sank beneath the surface again.

Scirye couldn't contain her curiosity anymore. "You were married to a fish?"

"Sometime he takes human form, too. But human, fish, we always fight a lot. Still"—Pele sighed, brushing her hand through hair so that the strands curled around her fingers like smoky vapor—"how does he stay *so* cute?"

In Scirye's many encounters with other cultures, her mother had often informed her that there was no accounting for taste. It just seemed that a goddess's were much broader than a human's.

Whatever Scirye's opinion of Kamapuaa's looks, the spirit was certainly powerful enough. Even as they hovered in midair, the surface of the sea seemed to be growing calmer by the moment.

"That takes care of the sea," Pele said smugly, and turned her attention to the sky. "And now the air."

Streamers of white mist were rolling toward them, and it was almost as if the black cloud cringed, shrinking away and creating a space high overhead. More and more pale ribbons streaked across the sky until they began to wheel about in a circle like the snowy threads of a giant skein of yarn. Quickly the strands tightened into an opaque, milky ball.

Suddenly ivory creatures began to drop out of the milky globe. They descended so gracefully that at first Scirye thought they were angels. But instead of flying with wings, each stood with one foot in front of the other upon lemon-colored rods, riding them as easily as the surfers had ridden their boards at Waikiki.

Their sweet voices blended with notes played on flutes of bone bleached ivory by the sun, creating a melody as gentle and welcome as a summer breeze on a hot summer day. Like dancers, they wove their way down through the air in time to their song.

The men and women all had dark hair and pale skin and were dressed alike in white tunics and kirtles. In the arms of many were children as lovely as their parents.

Scirye felt her shoulders relax for the first time that day, feeling sure that no creature would go into battle with their children. And the closer the fliers came, the more the winds calmed, until they died altogether and Bayang was able to hold them in one spot with gentle strokes of her wings.

Soon the playful beings were wheeling through the air all about them so that Scirye and the others were at the center of a living, ever-spinning globe.

Pele greeted them politely. "*Heahea*, welcome Cloud Folk. You follow the paths of the sky. You know the secrets of sun and wind."

All the Cloud Folk bowed low to the goddess, and one man descended lower on what Scirye now realized was a giant yellow stalk of some grasslike plant.

The man's eyes were as deep and bright a blue as a sky on the clearest day, and flecked with golden sunshine. Around his throat was a necklace of golden disks that were rayed like the sun. "Thank you, my lady, ever-changing and yet ever the same, who knows the heart of the earth. You summoned us?"

"The air's poisonous." Pele wrinkled her nose as she pointed at the black clouds. "Will you fix it, Chief?"

The chief glanced at the sky. "It's not good to have such a thing fouling the air. We can take care of that, but there's more coming from beneath us."

"I'll fix below," Pele said, indicating the island, "if you'll fix above?"

"Then consider it done," the man with the sun necklace said, and raised a hand.

The Cloud Folk shot upward like arrows aimed at the dark clouds, somehow staying on top of their strange craft as easily as if they were standing on solid ground. Faster and faster they sped until they were a blur, but as they neared the clouds, a group spun away at the last moment and Scirye saw they were the ones with children. The rest plunged straight into the polluted mist before the vapor had a chance to draw away.

Soon, white threads began to intertwine with the dark smoke until stripes of white and black wrestled one another like snakes fighting to the death. No sooner did the Cloud Folk seem to be gaining the upper hand than the blackness was reinforced with more poisonous gases and ash spewing from the erupting volcano.

"I'm going to use my *pu* voice now," Pele warned Scirye and the others, "so cover your ears." When they obeyed her, Pele began to sing.

Even with her hands over her ears, Scirye could hear the harsh notes explode from Pele like rocks ejected from a spouting crater. At the same time the goddess moved her hands like agile sparrows. There was a sharp contrast between the ugly sounds and the graceful gestures. Scirye barely had time to think about it before the island cracked beneath them and lava spewed upward, falling again in thick, glowing droplets that covered the surrounding black stones with bright red polka dots.

The crevices spread like the threads of a spiderweb, racing across the crust. As lava oozed out of the fissures, the whole island seemed caught in a fiery net. Rifts widened into chasms into which the remaining buildings tumbled in bursts of flame. Suddenly there came a loud, rumbling crash that sent the sea heaving beneath the rafts, and they looked down to see that a huge chunk of the island had fallen into the sea.

The island began to break up like a dry, brittle pie crust. More and more sections splashed into the ocean as the lava fountained upward in gooey, fiery curtains and steam rolled toward the sky with the hiss of thousands of serpents. The earth was reclaiming its own.

The war was being fought simultaneously in the air, the sea, and on the land. Beads of perspiration formed on Pele's face as she struggled to destroy the island quickly while Kamapuaa tried to stop the destructive tidal waves created as the island broke up. Up above, the Cloud Folk did their best to cleanse the sky.

Finally, all that was left of the black smoke was a bank of fluffy white clouds and all that remained of the island was a great column of steam rising from the spot where the island had once stood to mix with the white clouds overhead.

The sea beneath them sparkled in the late afternoon sun with gilded scales, and the Menehune were already paddling the rafts across the placid surface toward the other islands.

"That's that then," Pele said, slapping her palms together in satisfaction.

Bayang swung her head around on her long neck. "Excuse me, Lady, but it's not finished until we catch Roland," she reminded the goddess politely.

"True, true," Pele agreed. "You're going to Nova Hafnia?"

"I'm afraid my wings would tire before I reach there," Bayang explained. "Roland said he was going on a ship. He probably had one anchored nearby so all the dragon had to do was get him there and then sail off safely."

Pele scratched her cheek thoughtfully. "That figures."

Despite her desire to catch Roland, Scirye couldn't help tilting her head back to watch the Cloud Folk's graceful descent and listen to their contented tune; it filled her heart with ease and delight. Her happiness only increased as the Cloud Folk gathered around Pele once more.

"It was a hard fight, but our homes are safe now," declared the man with the necklace.

The goddess bowed deeply. "Thank you. But I need to ask one more favor now." She nodded to Scirye and her companions. "These friends need to go faraway to the ice and snow." She motioned to the north. "Can you help them get there?"

The chief regarded Scirye and the others. "You have the most peculiar friends, Lady."

"They will catch the man who made the island and then broke it." Pele gestured toward the place where the island had been.

"That man did something very evil," the chief said gravely, "so we will gladly help them." With a twirl of his wrist, he held a dozen yellow stalks. Soon others were also holding up more so that they seemed surrounded by golden whiskers.

"Now," the chief said, and threw his stalks into the air. The others copied him until the sky was full of them.

Then the Cloud Folk began to sing a different tune, busy and happy as birds building a nest, as bees gathering nectar from a field. The stalks swirled about, darting toward one another, dipping and bobbing, almost as if in some complex dance.

When Scirye saw the triangle start to appear, she realized the Cloud Folk were weaving the stalks together. The triangle grew in size until it was a huge delta-shaped mat some thirty feet along at its base. Smaller triangles rose perpendicular from the tail and its belly like fins. Across the top was a large boxlike frame woven from more stalks.

As the notes of their song died away, the Cloud Folk clapped their hands together in delight at their creation. Their applause was enough to shove the air raft about until several men and women caught the sides to anchor it.

The chief gestured for Bayang to rise above the triangle, and when she had done so, he pointed to the air raft's middle where there were loops to hold onto. "The wind will carry you where you want to go, but you must stay in the center and not go near the edges." He indicated the frame. "While you are inside here, you will be as cozy as if you are in a hut." Then he floated over the largest loop. "Use this to steer."

Then he drifted over to the edge of the wing so he could grip it in his two hands. "Remember this word," he said, and spoke a string of syllables. Instantly the mat began to fold itself a portion at a time until it was a little triangular box resting on his palms. "This package is very small but very heavy. Whatever you do, never say the folding word while you're still flying on it." Finally he pronounced another group of syllables and the wing unfolded itself until it was as large as ever. The Cloud Folk came in to hold it in place again.

A dozen of the Cloud Folk left straw baskets on the wing, taking care not to overload one spot and tip the wing over. "Food for your journey," the man explained.

"Thank you," Bayang said.

Pele bent over Scirye so that the girl was engulfed in the drifting smoky strands of the goddess's hair. "Hey, Smart Girl," she said, hugging Scirye. "You come visit Auntie, okay? We have more fun again, eh?"

Scirye wasn't sure it was wise to want to see such a powerful but whimsical spirit again, but it was probably even more dangerous to refuse her invitation. "Yes, um, Auntie."

Pele kissed Scirye on the cheek. "Bring da bad boys, too."

"Hey, thanks, Auntie," Koko said. "Any chance you could take your nephews to some diamonds? Ow!" he cried as the tip of his ear caught fire. As he and Leech patted it out, Koko yelped, "I thought we were friends."

"But not that friendly, *kupua*." Pele laughed.

Two large men floated alongside Bayang and gripped each other's wrists to form a cradle. Pele slid down the dragon's side and into the living sling where she kicked her legs like a child on a swing.

Other Cloud Folk picked up the hatchlings from Bayang's back, but the man who tried to take Koko was having trouble.

Kles circled nearby. "You've got a bit too much ballast," he said to the wide-hipped creature.

"At least I won't get blown away by the next breeze," Koko grunted, "like a certain feather duster I know."

The chief gestured to another of his people, a man with huge arms who swung down to help the other. Each took one of Koko's forepaws and hauled him through the air like a sack of potatoes.

The cloud man carrying Scirye in his arms glided over the wing. Scirye hesitated, seeing how flimsy the straw mat looked. *You've been afraid this whole trip and managed.* So she hopped onto the wing, half expecting to rip a hole in the fabric and plunge into the ocean. She was surprised and relieved to find there was only a slight springiness to it; stepping on it was like walking across a blanket on a sandy beach.

"Come on," she said, motioning to Leech. He dropped down a moment later.

"Bombs *away!*" Koko said, and plopped next to them. The wing swayed only slightly.

"Careful, you idiot," Kles scolded as he perched upon Scirye's shoulder. "You could tilt this wing too much. And what would happen to Lady Scirye?"

Scirye tried to keep the peace. "Easy, Kles. Someone would catch me. We've gotten this far only because everyone's worked together."

"Yes, that's right. We're a team," Leech agreed, and glanced at Bayang. The dragon had shrunk to about the height of the hatchlings and was landing light and graceful as a leaf on the wing near him. "Even old enemies."

"Who are new friends," Bayang agreed, furling her wings.

As she looked at the others, Scirye felt a glow inside that grew steadily warmer. They had shared their tears and laughter and even risked death for one another. They were like family now, a brave family. "Nothing can stop us when we're together."

Koko clapped his paws together. "Ha! When we catch Roland, he won't know what hit him."

"Hmph," Kles said, folding his forelegs across his chest. "I still wouldn't loan any money to a certain 'teammate.'"

Insults rolled right off of Koko. "I guess you're out of luck, teammate," he called up to Bayang.

"It's no use, you know," Bayang advised Kles. "He's too dense to know when you're trying to annoy him."

"Maybe a well-chosen rock then," Kles said thoughtfully.

"Kles!" Scirye ordered. "Be quiet."

Pele pulled out five strands of her long, curly hair, muttering a spell over them and then handing them to the five friends. "Keep these. They'll help keep you warm when you reach the north."

More Cloud Folk clustered around the wing, gripping its sides. At a command from their chief, they began to guide the wing upward until they reached a point where columns of hot steam still rose from the sea. The wing billowed in the mist, as if trying to tug itself free from the grip of the Cloud Folk.

"Good-bye," Scirye called down to Pele. "And thank you."

"Good-bye, good-bye. Don't forget your Auntie!" Pele shouted, blowing them a kiss and then waving both her hands enthusiastically.

Surrounded by Cloud Folk, they rose steadily toward the white clouds that stretched from horizon to horizon as if someone had torn a covering from a giant cotton mattress. And then they were plunging upward into it, mist brushing their faces like wet washcloths. For a long time, it was impossible to see, so they were all grateful when they broke through the clouds at last and the sun could bathe their faces in its golden glory. Wisps of mist trailed behind the friends' ankles like white ribbons.

Somewhere, one of the Cloud Folk broke into song, and the others joined in as if welcoming the sun. None of the companions could understand the lyrics, but the Cloud Folk's joy was unmistakable.

As the sun touched the upturned faces of the Cloud Folk, they began to glow as if they were filling with sunlight and their clothes shimmered as they rippled in the air. Every eyelash seemed sharp and clear, and the song swelled until it was triumphant.

More and more of the Cloud Folk swept all around, holding onto the wing's edges, carrying it higher and ever higher, so high that the clouds below lost their bumps and seemed to flatten out instead like a woolen carpet.

Suddenly the wing was almost ripped out of the Cloud Folk's hands and they began to bob up and down with the straw wing.

"Who summons Naue?" a voice roared. "Who calls the hero of the skies? Who disturbs the mightiest of winds?"

"Windbags, more likely," Koko muttered to the others.

"Careful," Leech said, holding a warning finger up to his lips.

Unconcerned, Pele kicked her legs up and down like a girl on a swing. "I do, Naue. These are my friends." She motioned to Scirye and the others on the straw wing. "Take them to the top of the world. Oh, and tell them when they're at Nova Hafnia, eh?"

"I, Naue, the greatest of the air rivers that sweep around the world, hear and obey, goddess," boomed the wind.

Despite all his skill, the chief was having trouble maintaining his balance as his platform bucked underneath his feet. But he fought to stay near them so he could give some last-minute instructions. "When you decide to leave Naue, don't try to fight your way out of him. Angle the straw wing downward gradually as you would cross a swift current."

Bayang took her place by the wing's control loop, holding it like a pair of reins. "Thank you. At worst, I'll manage to carry everyone the rest of the way on my back."

The chief shook his head. "I wonder if you'll be thanking us at journey's end. But the goddess asked us to help you, and we have obeyed."

And then he was dropping away from them with the rest of his people, moving diagonally across the great currents as they continued to sing.

Naue swept them away so swiftly that the Cloud Folk dwindled into mere white specks above the gray clouds, and Naue's boisterous, confident song replaced the Cloud Folk's lovely tune.

"I am Naue," he sang. "In races, I am the swiftest. In wrestling, I am the strongest. I know the secrets of the stars. The sun and moon are my friends. I am the chosen of the goddess. She trusts only me to carry her precious friends. I bear them like treasure, like gold, like jewels."

And as the sun warmed Scirye's sides, she felt as irresistible as the wind sweeping them northward. Neither Roland nor his dragon would escape them the next time.

Afterword

At the time that I began writing this novel, I had no idea that Afghanistan was planning to send its treasures, including many precious Kushan artifacts, on tour. Nor did I realize that they would be exhibited at the Asian Art Museum in San Francisco. It was one of those odd coincidences that happen every now and then.

My thanks to my editor, Susan Chang, who suggested a novel on the mummies of the Silk Road. Some of these mummies, dating from as far back as 800 B.C., looked like Caucasians with red hair, and had cloth woven with a technique that was characteristic of the Celts of Europe. In 2007 National Geographic sponsored DNA testing that discovered they were of mixed ancestry.

Some historians think that the mummies belong to a tribal confederation known as the Yueh-Chih, who occupied part of what are now the modern Chinese provinces of Kansu and Sinkiang. Many also believe that the Yueh-Chih spoke an Indo-European language called Tocharian, which I've used as the model for Scirye's Old Tongue.

Enemies eventually forced the Yueh-Chih upon a long trek that looped around the mountains. During the migration, one group came to dominate the other tribes and created the Kushan dynasties. As they expanded their territory, they took over the lands that had belonged to the Greek kings (descendants of Alexander the Great's generals).

They left behind the amazing Gandharan statues—Western historians emphasize the classical Greek style of the sculptors and conveniently forget who commissioned the works of art in the first place. But I think the Kushans' real talent was in ruling the many disparate peoples who made up their empire.

Recent excavations of burials in the Russian steppes have found women warriors who belonged to the group of people known as the Sarmatians. I've based Lady Tabiti and the Pippalanta on them.

Next, a word on seaplanes. Before World War II, seaplanes were the most economical aircraft because they could land on any calm body of water instead of expensive concrete runways at an airport. However, multiple airports and runways were built for the war effort and they were then turned over to civilian use in peacetime. Seaplanes then fell out of fashion. Treasure Island in San Francisco Bay really was built to house a seaplane port for Pan America. During 1939 and 1940, it also hosted a world's fair. When Japan attacked Pearl Harbor, the U.S. Navy took over the area and converted it to a military base.

I should also say something about the evolution of Roland's island, Houlani. I've been fascinated by volcanoes and their creation ever since I saw a documentary on Surtsey in a college class. This was a volcanic island that suddenly rose off the coast of Iceland in 1963.

I should add that Leech is based on Lee No Cha and his pagoda-carrying father, whose story appears as part of the *Feng-Shen-Yen-I.*

Also, for readers who know of the Greek moon goddess, Selene, the Kushans depicted the moon deity as male and called him Salene.

Finally, a word of thanks to the staff of the Pacific Grove Library, who were so helpful in obtaining books and materials.

———

If you're curious about some of these topics, here are a few of the books I consulted for my research:

Douglas Q. Adams, *A Dictionary of Tocharian B* (Amsterdam: Rodolpi Bv, 1999).

Elizabeth Wayland Barber, *The Mummies of Ürümchi* (New York: W. W. Norton, 1999).

Craig G. R. Benjamin, *The Yuezhi* (Turnhout, Belgium: Brepolis Publications, 2007).

Robert Decker and Barbara Decker, *Volcanoes* (New York: W. H. Freeman, 2006).

Nathaniel B. Emerson, *Pele and Hiiaka* (1915; Rep. Rutland, Vermont: Charles E. Tuttle, 1978).

Sturla Fridriksson, *Surtsey: Evolution of Life on a Volcanic Island* (New York: John Wiley & Sons, 1975).

Fredrik Hiebert and Pierre Cambon, editors, *Afghanistan: Hidden Treasures from the National Museum, Kabul* (Washington, D.C.: National Geographic, 2008). (Note: This is the official catalog for the exhibition of art during its American visit.)

J. P. Mallory and Victor Mair, *The Tarim Mummies* (New York: London: Thames & Hudson, 2000).

Buddha Rashmi Mani, *The Kushan Civilization* (Delhi, India: B. R. Publishing, 1987).

Réunion des Musées Nationaux, *Afghanistan: les Tresors Retrouvés* (Paris: Musée Guimet, 2007). (Note: This is the catalog from an earlier exhibit in France. It has some different photos and essays than the American version.)

John M. Rosenfeld, *The Dynastic Arts of the Kushans* (Berkeley: University of California Press, 1967).

William D. Westervelt, *Hawaiian Legends of Volcanoes* (1916; Rep. Rutland, Vermont: Charles E. Tuttle, 1963).

Read on for a

sneak peek at

City of Ice,

Book 2

of the City Trilogy

Scirye woke to the storm howling as its airy claws tried to tear at the igloo, but then she heard stranger, more ominous noises nearby.

Whuff-whuff. Click-clack-click.

Barely managing to raise her eyelids, which felt as heavy as iron, Scirye saw a stranger dressed in a jacket and trousers of shaggy, dirty fur standing in the middle of the igloo. The jacket's hood had been pulled over the intruder's face, hiding it in shadow.

Around the intruder's waist was a belt woven from leather strings, and dangling from the belt on thongs were all sorts of beads, crude stone carvings, and shells. They bounced against the intruder's leg with a *click-clack* sound as he stuffed something into a huge brown leather sack.

At first, Scirye thought the intruder was stealing their supplies, but the unopened baskets and crates were exactly where they had stacked them. Her eyes swung back to the bag, and she glimpsed Bayang's green scaled tail protruding out of the mouth of the sack like a drooping scaly branch.

Grasping the tail in the gloved right hand, the intruder began to cram it into the sack. In horror, Scirye watched the sides of the bag ripple like the muscles of a jaw swallowing a large mouthful, and the sack swelled larger as it accommodated the dragon.

She tried to shout out a warning, but her vocal cords were as paralyzed as her body and no sound came out.

With a grunt, the intruder thrust an arm inside the bag, jamming the last bit of the dragon into the interior. But then the intruder seemed to become stuck. No matter how the intruder tugged and jerked, the bag now gripped the arm and would not let go.

Kles was a familiar weight in her arms, but from the corner of her eyes, Scirye searched for her other friends. There were no signs of them, though—only their sleeping furs scattered carelessly about.

Scirye had no idea how the bag could have contained all of them, and yet the girl was sure that it had somehow. The invader wasn't after their supplies. It was after them!

Slowly the intruder turned around to face Scirye, giving a little jump when it saw her last victim was awake. Then, dragging the bag along, the thief shuffled toward her in short, gliding steps. The fur trousers went *whuff-whuff* as the legs rubbed against one another while the belt rattled a *click-clack* counterpoint.

Scirye fought to move her arms and her legs, but they felt like stone. All she could do was lie there helplessly, watching as the thief loomed over her like a greasy, furry shadow. The thief stunk of sweat and rancid fat and a smell that Scirye knew all too well now: the odor of blood.

Propping the bag against a leg, the thief stretched out a gloved hand—not for Scirye, but for Kles. Fear for her friend gave Scirye extra strength. Finally, she found her voice. "Kles, wake up!" she screamed.

The little griffin did not stir. Only his buzzing snore told her that he was still alive.

Within the hood, the thief's eyes blazed angrily.

It hates me, the girl thought. "What did I ever do to you?" Scirye demanded.

The eyes narrowed to slits, and the fire behind them blazed hotter and fiercer.

I think it hates me just for being alive, Scirye decided. *It hates everyone.* It was that hatred that fed the fire behind the eyes. A hatred so deep and mindless that it had consumed everything inside the creature, leaving only those sickly green flames.

The thief's right hand touched another charm and a monotone muttering came from within the hood.

And suddenly Scirye felt like crying, though no tears came to her paralyzed eyes. Her friends were gone or dead. Scirye had never felt more alone in her whole life. What chance did she have? She was as small and insignificant and helpless as a bug on a glacier.

Then Scirye heard something. She was still half drowsy with sleep so she could not be sure if it was part of the nightmare or if she really heard a woman speak urgently in Kushan.

"*Yashe! Yashe!*" Honor! Honor!

Her sister and mother had shouted that as they fought Badik the dragon, and generations of Pippalanta had cried the same thing as they had charged into battle.

Scirye felt as if her mind had been locked inside a dark room and now someone had thrown open a window so that the light could stream inside again.

"The hag's cast a spell upon you," the voice continued, this time in English, "so all you feel is despair."

This was no time to wallow in self-pity or use it as an excuse to do nothing. Scirye was the last defender. It was up to her.

"*Yashe, yashe,*" she yelled as she surged from the ground, anger lending her extra strength and speed. Her hand reached for her knife but it was gone from her belt. From the corner of her eye, she saw it on top of the pile of weapons that the hag had taken from them while they were unconscious.

The girl's mind raced desperately through the lessons that her sister, Nishke, had taught her about hand-to-hand combat, but they'd only had time to cover some basics of self-defense.

Scirye swung her right fist, but the hag had whirled around, seizing the mouth of the bag in both hands and whipping it up so that the open mouth hung open, ready to receive Scirye's blow. All the hag needed to do was let the sack get a hold of Scirye's hand, and the girl would follow her friends inside.

The girl just managed to pull her punch in time and regain her balance before the hag thrust the bag out again, trying to trap the girl. Side-stepping, Scirye jabbed with her left fist, hoping to whack the side of the hag's head. But the hag pivoted, holding the open bag between them like a shadowy shield. The sack's insides looked as large as a cavern and Scirye thought she heard faint shouts from within the darkness.

Scirye feinted and the hag plunged forward, again trying to capture her hand, but Scirye darted back. They circled about the igloo, Scirye trying to find an opening for a strike and the hag trying to snare her with the bag. They looked almost as if they were dancing to the *whuff-whuff* of the hag's pants and the *click-clack* of her belt. Outside, the storm still raged and the winds shrieked.

Scirye's breath rose in cold streamers about her head, fists raised, eyes narrowed as she hunted desperately for an opening.

She had been so intent on watching the hag that she had not kept an eye on the tangled furs on the floor. Suddenly she stumbled over a pile. To her horror, she fell backward.

Screeching in triumph, the hag raised the sack like a leathery cloud about to engulf her.

Reader's Guide

ABOUT THIS GUIDE

The information, activities, and discussion questions that follow are intended to enhance your reading of *City of Fire*. Please feel free to adapt these materials to suit your needs and interests.

WRITING AND RESEARCH ACTIVITIES

I. Alternate Cities

A. You are a tourist visiting the fantastical versions of San Francisco or Honolulu depicted in *City of Fire*. On one side of a 4" × 6" (or larger) index card, write a postcard to your family at home describing your experience. Decorate the reverse side of the card with a drawing of something discussed in your note.

B. Go to the library or online to research San Francisco Bay's Treasure Island, the source of its name, its construction, its role in the 1939–1940 International Exposition, and/or its use as a seaplane terminal for Pan Am airlines and the U.S. Navy. Organize your research into a detailed outline. With friends or classmates, discuss how your discoveries about the real history of Treasure Island affect your reading of *City of Fire* and your understanding of the alternate reality the author has created.

C. In the character of one of Roland's servants, prepare a report on the building of his scientific-magical island, Houlani, including details on the mansion and its magical protections. Draw a map of the island construction site or use PowerPoint or other presentation software to develop your report. Make your presentation to friends or classmates.

II. Honor and Identity

A. Scirye's Kushan upbringing gives her a strong sense of honor, or Tumarg, which guides her actions. In the character of Scirye, role-play a telephone conversation with your mother, or write a letter to the Kushan Embassy in San Francisco, in which you explain why Tumarg dictates that you must continue your journey.

B. While the novel is told primarily from the viewpoints of Scirye and Bayang, Kles, with his strong sense of Kushan manners, provides entertaining commentary. Rewrite a chapter or scene from Kles's point of view, either in the first person (speaking in the "I" form as Kles) or the third person (describing what Kles thinks, says, and does during the scenes). Share your rewritten chapter with friends or classmates.

C. Throughout the novel, Bayang struggles with her true identity and with her changing relationships with her companions. Write a short chapter in which Bayang discusses her troubles with Scirye or Pele and asks for advice.

D. Leech begins the novel unaware of his true identity, yet he feels an indescribable connection to flight. Think of an experience, activity, or object that brings you happiness. Write a 3–5 page fictional story in which you discover that this is a clue to your true identity or something that will happen in your future.

III. Mythology and Magic

A. Go to the library or online to learn more about the Kushan Empire, dragons, salamanders, characters from Hawaiian mythology (Pele, Kampuaa, Menehune, kupua) and Norse mythology (Muspelheim, trolls), or other magical creatures from the novel. Make an informative page for each element you research, including illustrations, research facts, references for further study, and notes about how this character or idea is used in the novel. Bind your pages into a notebook to create a *Research Guide to* City of Fire, complete with cover illustration.

B. On a sheet of graph paper, chart the journey of Scirye and her friends through the sky, land, and sea. Note whether sky, land, or sea is the setting in each chapter, and which characters seem most powerful, worried, or helpful in that setting. Does this exercise help you understand the story in a different way? If you were a mythical creature, would you prefer to be most powerful on the land, in the sea, or in the sky? Take a class vote to see which setting most students choose.

C. Transpose a magical episode from the story into graphic novel form. Illustrate 4–6 storyboard squares showing the group's first pursuit of Badik, Pele creating the protective flower charms, an encounter with the Menehune, or another scene. Incorporate dialogue from the novel in speech bubbles. If desired, create a second storyboard sequence depicting what you imagine will happen to the friends as they begin their journey on the wing.

DISCUSSION QUESTIONS

1. What brings Bayang to San Francisco in the opening chapter of *City of Fire*? How does she feel about her mission? What has brought Scirye and her family to this place? How does Sciyre feel about her morning at the Hearn Museum? How has Leech come to be at the museum?

2. What is the importance of the Jade Lady statue? What is the history of the archer's ring the statue wears? How does Scirye misbehave as she and Kles are observing the statue? How does Scirye's admission of her error to Prince Etre show both her spirit and her sense of right and wrong?

3. What role does Lady Sudarshane give to Scirye when the museum attack heats up in chapter 5? How does Leech behave? Why doesn't Bayang kill her prey at this moment? Why does she join the battle? How does the battle change the destinies of Scirye, Bayang, and Leech?

4. How would you define Tumarg? How is Scirye's decision to punish the dragon, Badik, Tumarg? Compare this decision to Bayang's struggle with her relationship to Leech and her hatred of Badik. Find other examples of Tumarg and similarly honorable choices and actions throughout the novel.

5. As the group arrives on Treasure Island, what events make Scirye suspect that all of her companions harbor secrets? What secret identity is held by the peddler woman? How does Pele lift the veil from everyone's secrets? How does this change the relationship between Scirye, Bayang, Leech, and Koko?

6. Compare and contrast the carpet on which the friends begin their journey with the "wing" that they board at the close of the novel. How do images of flight enrich the story and its themes? What other magical and nonmagical vehicles play important roles in the novel?

7. Pele calls Koko "bad-bad" and, later, "maybe-maybe." What is she saying about his character by using these terms? Have you ever encountered a "maybe-maybe" individual in your own life? Did you give this person a chance to prove himself or herself to be a friend? Does thinking of an individual's potential to be a friend as "maybe-maybe" seem like a good idea? Why or why not?

8. At the close of chapter 2, Kles refers to the Kushan goddess as "mighty Nanaia, loving Nanaia, deadly Nanaia." What other characters' names from the novel do you think could be substituted for "Nanaia" and for what reasons?

9. How did Roland create the island of Houlani and what does this reveal about his character? What does Roland steal from Pele? Why does Roland want the Kushan ring? What do you think is the greatest conflict within the novel?

10. What happens when Bayang and Badik finally meet? How does their confrontation mirror the larger battle between Roland and the others? How is the destructive battle in Roland's mansion reflected in the elements?

11. Are Scirye's, Bayang's, and Leech's reasons for continuing their pursuit of Roland and Badik at the end of the novel the same as their reasons for beginning the journey? What has changed for and between these individuals? If you could give Scirye, Bayang, or another character one piece of advice as the novel ends, what would you tell them and why?

12. In chapter 28, Pele tells Scirye, "I know who I am.... That's my power.... If you don't know who you are, you're really nothing." What does she mean? Cite examples to show how this is a central idea of the novel.

13. In the alternate San Francisco and Hawaii of the novel, realistic Treasure Island is countered by the imaginary Houlani, and characters from Hawaiian and Norse mythology are joined by creatures with names from the author's imagination. What other contrasts between real and alternate stand out as you read the story? How does this mixture of real and imagined impact your understanding of the novel and its themes?

14. Is *City of Fire* best described as a story about honor, friendship, or understanding one's own identity? Explain your answer.

15. At the end of *City of Fire*, with Scirye's encouragement, Bayang and Leech agree to friendship despite generations of history as enemies. How long should a person, group, or nation seek retribution for past wrongs? Are there places in our own lives, and world, where Bayang and Leech's model of friendship might be worth considering?